D0908552

Praise for Melanie Dickerson

"Christian fiction fans will relish Dickerson's eloquent story."

—School Library Journal on The Orphan's Wish

"*The Goose Girl*, a little retold fairy tale, sparkles in Dickerson's hands, with endearing characters and a charming setting that will appeal to teens and adults alike."

—RT Book Reviews, 4½ stars, TOP PICK! on The Noble Servant

"Dickerson is a masterful storyteller with a carefully crafted plot, richly drawn characters, and a detailed setting. The reader is easily pulled into the story. Does everything end happily ever after? Read it and see! Recommended for young adults and adults who are young at heart."

—Christian Library Journal on The Noble Servant

"[The Silent Songbird] will have you jumping out of your seat with anticipation at times. Moderate to fast-paced, you will not want this book to end. Recommended for all, especially lovers of historical romance."

—RT Book Reviews, 4 stars

"A terrific YA crossover medieval romance from the author of *The Golden Braid*."

—Library Journal on The Silent Songbird

"When it comes to happily-ever-afters, Melanie Dickerson is the undisputed queen of fairy-tale romance, and all I can say is—long live the queen! From start to finish *The Beautiful Pretender* is yet another brilliant gem in her crown, spinning a medieval love story that will steal you away—heart, soul, and sleep!"

—Julie Lessman, award-winning author of the Daughters of Boston, Winds of Change, and Heart of San Francisco series

"I couldn't stop reading! Melanie has done what so many other historical novelists have tried and failed: she's created a heroine that is at once both smart and self-assured without seeming modern. A woman so fixed in her time and place that she is able to speak to ours as well."

—SIRI MITCHELL, AUTHOR OF FLIRTATION WALK AND CHATEAU OF ECHOES, ON THE BEAUTIFUL PRETENDER

"Dickerson breathes life into the age-old story of Rapunzel, blending it seamlessly with the other YA novels she has written in this time and place . . . The character development is solid, and she captures religious medieval life splendidly."

—BOOKLIST ON THE GOLDEN BRAID

"Readers who love getting lost in a fairy-tale romance will cheer for Rapunzel's courage as she rises above her overwhelming past. The surprising way Dickerson weaves threads of this enchanting companion novel with those of her other Hagenheim stories is simply delightful. Her fans will love it."

—JILL WILLIAMSON, CHRISTY AWARD–WINNING AUTHOR OF THE BLOOD OF KINGS TRILOGY AND THE KINSMAN CHRONICLES, ON THE GOLDEN BRAID

"Readers will find themselves supporting the romance between the sweet yet determined Odette and the insecure but hardworking Jorgen from the beginning. Dickerson spins a retelling of Robin Hood with emotionally compelling characters, offering hope that love may indeed conquer all as they unite in a shared desire to serve both the Lord and those in need."

—RT BOOK REVIEWS, 4½ STARS, ON THE HUNTRESS OF THORNBECK FOREST

"Melanie Dickerson does it again! Full of danger, intrigue, and romance, this beautifully crafted story will transport you to another place and time."

—SARAH E. LADD, AUTHOR OF THE CURIOSITY KEEPER AND THE WHISPERS ON THE MOORS SERIES, ON THE HUNTRESS OF THORNBECK FOREST

THE
WARRIOR
MAIDEN

Other Books by Melanie Dickerson

A Medieval Fairy Tale Series

The Huntress of Thornbeck Forest

The Beautiful Pretender

The Noble Servant

Young Adult Fairy Tale Romance Series

The Healer's Apprentice

The Merchant's Daughter

The Fairest Beauty

The Captive Maiden

The Princess Spy

The Golden Braid

The Silent Songbird

The Orphan's Wish

Regency Spies of London Series

A Spy's Devotion

A Viscount's Proposal

A Dangerous Engagement

THE
WARRIOR
MAIDEN

MELANIE
DICKERSON

THOMAS NELSON
Since 1798

The Warrior Maiden

Published in Nashville, Tennessee, by Thomas Nelson. Thomas Nelson is a registered trademark of HarperCollins Christian Publishing, Inc.

Thomas Nelson titles may be purchased in bulk for educational, business, fund-raising, or sales promotional use. For information, please email SpecialMarkets@ ThomasNelson.com.

Scripture quotations are taken from the King James Version and from the Holy Bible, New International Version®, NIV®. Copyright © 1973, 1978, 1984, 2011 by Biblica, Inc. ® Used by permission of Zondervan. All rights reserved worldwide. www.zondervan. com. The "NIV" and "New International Version" are trademarks registered in the United States Patent and Trademark Office by Biblica, Inc.®

Publisher's Note: This novel is a work of fiction. Names, characters, places, and incidents are either products of the author's imagination or used fictitiously. All characters are fictional, and any similarity to people living or dead is purely coincidental.

Library of Congress Cataloging-in-Publication Data

Names: Dickerson, Melanie, author.
Title: The warrior maiden / Melanie Dickerson.
Description: Nashville, Tennessee : Thomas Nelson, [2019]
Identifiers: LCCN 2018041182 | ISBN 9780718074777 (hardback)
Classification: LCC PS3604.I2253 W37 2019 | DDC 813/.6--dc23 LC record available at https://lccn.loc.gov/2018041182

Printed in the United States of America
19 20 21 22 23 LSC 5 4 3 2 1

CHAPTER 1

Galloping her horse past the big oak tree, Mulan pulled the bowstring taut. She aimed at the knothole with one eye closed and sent the arrow flying toward the target. It struck the tree but missed the knothole.

"Don't shoot behind you!" Andrei flailed his skinny arms. "Keep the target in front of you."

Shooting from a moving horse was much more difficult than when standing still, but she was improving. At least she'd escaped, for the moment, the cooking and cleaning chores. And practicing war skills kept her from facing the uncertain future—and her mother's grief.

Her stomach churned.

"You put yourself at a disadvantage if you have to shoot behind you." Andrei was only twelve years old, which was six years younger than Mulan, but he'd accompanied her father on his last two military campaigns as his attendant. "Shoot in front of you, before you reach the target."

As an orphan, Andrei would only accept food from Mulan and her mother if he worked for it. Mulan enjoyed his company, as he liked the same things she did—horses and archery. She learned war skills from him. He'd even taught her a bit about sword fighting, although she wasn't very good at that.

Mulan wheeled her horse around. Aksoma was sluggish and awkward at turning, unaccustomed as she was to war games. Perhaps Mulan should be training on her father's horse.

She dismounted and walked toward the tree. As she retrieved her arrow, placing it in the quiver strapped to her waist, she spotted a man in soldier's garb riding up the lane toward her home.

She glanced at Andrei. He bit his lip, unease lining his face.

Mulan dropped the longbow where she stood and raced up the hill.

At the back of the house, she could see straight through the back doorway to the front. Her mother stood in the threshold and greeted the soldier.

Mulan and Andrei stepped inside and hid behind Mother's painted wooden chest. Mulan slid her gaze to the curtain covering her parents' bedchamber door, concealing what was inside even as she concealed herself from the man at the front door.

"Greetings," the soldier answered. "Is Mikolai at home?"

Mulan held her breath at the mention of her father.

"He's not here now. Do you have a message for him?"

The soldier's expression never altered. "Is he likely to return soon?"

"No." Mother hid one arm behind her back, as if she didn't know what to do with it.

"Then tell him Butautas requires his service. He is to report to Vilkaviškis to join the army in fighting the Teutonic Knights who have besieged his ally's castle in Poland."

"His ally?"

"Duke Konrad of Zachev."

Mother inclined her head in a nod. "Very well."

"His service is required."

"You said that already."

Mulan ducked her head out of sight, but she imagined the soldier giving Mother a sullen look.

"I shall return three days hence so Mikolai and I can travel together."

"In truth, Mikolai has been unwell. He may not be well enough when you return."

"Three days is all I can give him. See that he is ready, or else this property is forfeit to Butautas."

"Of course."

Mulan's stomach twisted. A wave of cold came over her now that she was still. The hose and long shirt, cinched at the waist—men's clothing that she wore when she rode her horse and practiced shooting—didn't keep her as warm as her layers of skirts. And her long black hair was tied at the back of her neck, allowing a breath of cool air to send a chill across her shoulders.

A few moments later, a horse snuffled and hooves sounded on the path, plodding away from their long, one-level stone-and-timber house.

Mulan and Andrei emerged from their hiding place. Mother met Mulan's gaze, then walked past them. She pushed open the chamber door and sighed as she stared in at the body they still had to prepare for burial. "Mikolai could not have chosen a worse time to die."

Evening had fallen and Mulan was helping Mother clean the kitchen when someone called out, "*Ponia* Feodosia!"

Mulan ran to the front door. Her friend Agafia was trotting up the lane, breathing hard.

"Jankun is badly wounded."

"*Motina!*" Mulan called over her shoulder.

Mother came as fast as her bad hip would allow. "What is it?"

"Jankun . . . needs your . . . healing salve," Agafia huffed out, bending forward slightly, gulping air.

Mother grabbed a flask, closed the door behind her, and joined them on the lane. "Jankun has returned home?"

Agafia spoke quickly about her oldest brother as they walked, her face stoic and pinched. "His friends brought him home a few minutes ago. It took them a week to make the trip from Poland."

"How bad is he?"

Agafia stared at her feet. "The priest gave him the last rites."

"What happened?" Mulan spoke in a hushed voice as they made their way to the main road splitting the village in half, with homes and fields on either side of the rutted dirt path.

"He was captured by the Teutonic Knights. They tortured him, and when they felt he had told them everything he knew about the troops' position and plans, they left him to die. Some of the other Lithuanian and Polish soldiers found him."

They soon arrived at the small home Agafia shared with her family. Mulan steeled herself to see the worst.

Jankun was stretched out on a bed, unmoving. Swollen and bloody and bruised, his face was unrecognizable, though she had known him all her life. One of his eyes seemed to be missing, only a black hole remaining. Agafia had been her closest friend, and Jankun had been almost like a brother, once even defending her against the other boys in the village who taunted her because she looked different.

Jankun's mother was unwrapping bloody bandages on his legs.

Her eyes were big and round, her mouth agape. She stepped back to let Mulan's mother approach his bedside.

While Mother attended the young man, Agafia and Mulan went to sit in the corner of the room. Three young men from the village who had also gone to fight stood nearby. They must have brought him home.

Everyone silently watched as Mother held out the flask. She and Jankun's mother used their fingers to smear on the foul-smelling salve.

Tears streamed down Agafia's face. Mulan placed a hand on her shoulder. The only sound was the quiet crackle of the cook fire.

Mulan caught the eye of one of the young men. "What's the news of the battle?" she whispered. "Are we winning?"

He glanced at the door and moved in that direction. Mulan followed. When they were outside in the dim light of sunset, he said, "Our army retreated and is hoping for German reinforcements." He shook his head. "The captain fears the Teutonic Knights may continue conquering Polish territory and expand here next. They're brutal, stealing people's food, killing farmers and peasants if they tried to resist. And when they take prisoners, instead of trying to exchange them or putting them in prisons, they torture them."

His eyes took on a vacant look. "It's a miracle Jankun isn't dead. And they say when their grand master, Rusdorf, comes with more knights, there will be no stopping him."

The name Rusdorf was familiar. Her father and Andrei had told her stories about his fierceness on the battlefield, as well as his grudges toward certain people and his hatred for women.

"We will defeat him." Why had she said that? But she didn't want to take it back.

The young man's lip curled as he peered down at her. "Rusdorf wants land, castles, power. Thousands of trained fighters do his bidding, and his men are either hired mercenaries with no conscience or think they're taking other people's land in the name of God. How can our smaller army defeat them?" He turned and went back into the house.

Mulan's heart sank. How indeed?

But a strange yearning stirred inside her. She wanted to fight against cruelty and injustice. The threat might be coming to her small Lithuanian village. She had to protect herself, her mother, and her people.

For now, though, the fight was far away. She could almost see that foreign land of Poland, the fields and forests that had become battlegrounds, where innocent people were starving and being killed by the invading force. She longed to help them, to defeat the enemy so they never came to endanger her own people.

But how was that possible? A woman, eighteen years old, was expected to marry, to have children, to cook and clean and sew, not fight.

Marriage was the only way Mulan could take care of her mother.

She hastened to clean the crumbs of her breakfast roll off the table, avoiding her mother's gaze.

"Algirdas is healthy and strong, does not drink too much wine, and you'll never starve with him as your husband."

Mulan understood why her mother wanted her to marry Algirdas. But he smelled of his profession—bloody meat. He was not as old as her other prospects, and he was wealthy enough to take care of her and her mother when Butautas cast them out of their home. Except . . . she had always dreamed of leaving her village and seeing other places, doing something important.

But dreams could not keep her or her mother dry, safe, and fed.

"Algirdas is a hard worker," Mother said. "Try not to judge him until you've spent some time with him." She limped to the cupboard where a small barrel of spiced beer was stored.

Mulan placed the bread on the table, along with a knife and some butter. She took the cup of spiced beer from her mother's hand and carried it to the table, then ran back as Mother filled the other cup from the barrel's spout.

"There's no need to hurry." Mother got that look on her face—pursed lips, brows drawn together.

"Yes, Mother. I shall walk as slowly and gracefully as a swimming swan when Algirdas comes calling."

"Hmm." Mother still wore that worried look.

Mulan said a quick prayer and then saw the pigs wandering into the front entryway of the house.

"Shoo!" She bounded toward them and swatted the air with her hands. But the pigs were not as eager to leave as she was to get them out. As she pushed the sow's shoulder, one of the piglets darted between Mulan legs. She tried to step over it, but her foot caught on its portly body. She pitched forward and landed on her hands and knees on the stone floor.

Mulan jumped up and looked down at her pale blue kirtle. Her heart thudded at the mud stains marring the beautiful fine linen fabric of her best dress. Her wide headband had fallen askew, and she pushed it up.

A heavy sigh sounded behind her. Mulan turned to see her mother standing there, hands braced on her hips.

"It's not so bad. I don't think he'll even notice." Mulan snatched up a cleaning cloth. "Perhaps I can wipe most of it off."

Her stomach churned at the memory that sprang to mind of

her father yelling at her. She must have been only about six or seven years old, and her mother had been teaching her to make *cepelinai*. She was carrying the bowl of curd with which to fill the potato dumplings and spilled the creamy cheese all over the floor.

"Clumsy! Wasteful!" her father yelled. *"Can you do nothing without spilling?"*

His words still stung, even though twelve years had passed. Was it true? Was she so clumsy she could do nothing?

Mother seized the broom and used it to guide the pigs out the door while Mulan rubbed furiously at her dress with the wet cloth. But her rubbing did little to get rid of the stains. She didn't have another gown nearly so fine. Her next best one had a stain from spilling soup on it, and another had a hole burned in it from when she'd stoked the fire a little too vigorously and a hot ember flew out. She did have the green gown that was so tight she could barely breathe in it. "Should I go change?"

"No time. I see him coming up the path." Mother gestured toward the door. "You go greet him."

Mulan threw the cleaning cloth behind the cupboard, adjusted the embroidered belt that encircled her waist, and hurried to the door. *Move slowly. Take a deep breath.*

She jerked open the door.

Algirdas wore a plain gray shirt that laced up in the front and was open at the throat. His hair was slicked back with some sort of grease, and he carried a bulging hemp-cloth bag.

"Greetings." Mulan forced a smile.

He nodded and held up the bag. "Two fresh hares for your larder."

"My mother and I thank you." Mulan took the bag from his hand. "Please come in."

His gaze flickered over her dress, pausing a moment on the stains. Then he stepped inside.

So he saw the stains on my dress. Men didn't care about such things, did they? Perhaps she could impress him with something else.

Algirdas sat at the small table where Mother, who was all smiles, had directed him.

"Feodosia, it is good to see you looking well," Algirdas said, but his words were stilted, as if he'd practiced them. "And how is Mikolai?"

"Mikolai has not been feeling well." Mother stared down at the table while she spoke, something she did when she was not being forthcoming. "But we want to hear about you, Algirdas. All is well with your mother, I trust?"

"Thank you, yes. Mother complains of a pain in her shoulder, but she is otherwise well, and business is good."

Mulan sat beside Mother, across from Algirdas, and he stared at her face. No one spoke. What did one say to a butcher? Ask him about his favorite cuts of meat?

"Your sister just had a baby, is that not true?" Mother asked.

"Yes, her fourth. Mother only had two survive beyond infancy, but she is very pleased that all of my sister's babies have lived."

"Children are a gift from the Lord." Mother said the words cheerfully enough, but then an almost imperceptible grimace flickered over her face.

"Mulan is from the Orient, is she not?" Algirdas was still studying her face. "I think I've heard a story about Mikolai finding her as a small child after a battle and bringing her to you. Is that right?"

"Yes." Mother looked down at the table again.

"Why did you never give her a Lithuanian name? *Mulan* doesn't sound Lithuanian."

"The first time I saw her, I asked her what her name was. She said 'Mulan.' And Mikolai said, 'If the child knows her name, then we'll not be changing it.' So Mulan has always been her name." Mother smiled.

Queasiness flipped Mulan's stomach. Was her Oriental appearance—black hair, slightly darker skin, and almond-shaped eyes—unpleasant to Algirdas? Certain boys in the village had taunted her, calling her "Mongol," and even some women looked askance at her, as if they disapproved of her. But Mother always told her she was beautiful, and even her father when asked had grunted and said, "You are not an ugly girl."

But when Mulan was around twelve years old, she discovered that the story her mother had told her about being found as a child by her father after a battle had been false. She heard her parents arguing, and the next morning she asked her mother about it.

"Truth is, your mother was a woman Mikolai met when he was fighting east of here, a woman from the Orient. And when she died, she left a child—you—about three years old. Your father brought you to me, knowing how much I longed for a child."

Mulan and her mother had agreed not to tell anyone else the truth. Let them believe she'd been a foundling, the result of war.

Algirdas eyed the tankard of spiced beer nearest him. Mother looked at Mulan, raised her brows, then looked at the cup.

Mulan extended her hand and plastered on a smile. "Please, have some of Mother's delicious spiced beer."

"Mulan helped me make it," Mother was quick to point out.

They all picked up the cups in front of them and took a drink. Mother glanced at her, then at the bread on the table.

"Have some bread." Mulan stood and reached for the knife. "I shall slice it for us." Holding the loaf of bread in one hand and the knife in the other, she sawed through the bread. As she encountered the tough bottom crust of the loaf, she sawed extra hard. She broke through, and her elbow bumped into her cup and it tipped over. Beer splashed onto the floor and her feet—and Algirdas's too.

"Oh, I'm so sorry." Mulan ran to get a cleaning cloth. She came hastening back, and when she had almost reached where Algirdas was sitting, her foot touched the puddle of beer and shot out from under her.

She flailed her arms, trying to grab anything that might keep her from falling. Algirdas reached out, and she grabbed for his arm but missed. She hit the floor on her back.

"Are you all right?" Algirdas stood over her.

She blinked up at him. He reached toward her. She took his hand and pulled herself up.

"That was not as graceful as a swimming swan." She tried to laugh, but her face was warming. How could she make a fool of herself with Algirdas there to speak about marriage? And her dress was certainly ruined now, covered in spiced beer.

Algirdas was staring at her. In the meantime her mother must have finished slicing the bread because a slice lay on the table in front of each of them. Her mother was wiping the floor with the cloth Mulan had retrieved.

"Eat some bread and butter," Mother urged in her cheerful voice. "We will have some *šaltibarščiai* soon."

Mulan released an inward groan, wishing Algirdas wouldn't stay for dinner. But she didn't have the luxury of wanting him to leave. Her mother would have nowhere to go if Mulan didn't marry someone who would take them both in. They only had two days before they'd be forced to tell Butautas's guardsman that her father was dead and there was no one to take his place.

Mulan did her best to stand primly and properly as her mother finished cleaning up the spilled beer. But as soon as Mulan sat on the wooden bench, she felt how soaked her gown was. "Excuse me. I shall return in a moment."

Once she was behind the curtain separating her sleeping chamber from the rest of the house, she grabbed the soaked hem and yanked it over her head. *How could I have embarrassed myself so soon?*

She kicked the soiled gown into a corner, then shed the rest of her garments and added them to the pile. Her body reeked of spiced beer, so she grabbed a cloth from the basin of water and wiped herself down. She donned her second-best gown and took a deep breath. She was ready, but she pressed her hands to her head. *Do I have to do this?*

She said a wordless prayer and walked back out.

"A pig will bleed all over," Algirdas said to Mother, "but the secret is to wait overnight, letting it drain, before cutting it up."

"There is Mulan. Dear one, can you spoon up the soup for us?"

Mulan walked over to the pot with the cold beet soup and ladled hearty portions into three wooden bowls. She brought the bowls over to the table one by one. *Please don't let me spill it.* Algirdas was staring at her but averted his gaze when she met his eyes.

Mother asked Algirdas to say a prayer over the food.

"You are Christians, then?" The butcher glanced from Mother to Mulan.

"We are. My family converted when I was a young girl."

They all bowed their heads, and Algirdas said a rote prayer of thanks and dedication in the name of Jesus. Then they began to eat.

Mulan's mind kept drifting to Algirdas. What kind of husband would he be? Would he be kind to her and her mother? He owned a large house—a little larger than this one—a short walk from his butcher shop. He was not handsome, but she'd always thought that didn't matter if the man was kind. She would probably get used to the gamy smells of the butcher shop and not even notice them, especially if she felt he loved her. After all, she didn't mind the way horses smelled. She adored Aksoma even when, after galloping through the pasture, her mare stank of sweat and dung.

"Mulan?" Her mother was staring at her. "Algirdas just asked if you'd like to get married seven days hence."

"Uh . . . in seven days?" She gaped first at Mother, then at Algirdas. His expression was noncommittal, as if he was not sure he even wanted her assent.

She noted a mole on the side of his cheek, a black hair growing out of it. "I . . . y-yes." She could always change her answer later, could she not?

Algirdas grunted. "You'll have to listen when I speak to you and cook and clean and mend my mother's and my clothes."

A giggle bubbled up into her throat. Was this how he treated her before he even married her? Listing her duties, as if he were hiring a servant? The urge to laugh vanished, and her insides sank toward the floor. Was she to be treated even worse than her father treated Mother?

But she nodded, hoping to hasten his departure.

He slurped another bite of soup, then scraped the wooden bowl with his wooden spoon.

"Would you like some more?" The ridiculous urge to laugh came over her again. She cleared her throat.

His nondescript blue-green eyes met hers. Her stomach twisted.

"You may come to visit me at the shop tomorrow if you wish."

He stood up and nodded at her mother. "I thank you." Then he nodded at Mulan—no, he was looking her up and down before his gaze came to rest on her face. "I bid you a good day."

Mulan watched him turn and saunter toward the door. Mother nudged her arm, and she hurried after him.

"Good day." She stood by the threshold as he made his way down the path from the house. He didn't turn around to acknowledge her.

A heaviness settled on her shoulders. How could she marry this man? But how could she allow her mother to be homeless? As soon as Butautas's soldier returned in two days, he'd discover her father was dead and he'd force them out of the house she and her mother had lived in for sixteen years.

An idea, more muddy than clear, wiggled its way into her thoughts, as if it had been waiting for the right moment.

Mulan's fingertips tingled. Mother would never agree to it.

But perhaps Mulan could convince her it was a better way out of their predicament than marrying Algirdas. Because she'd rather do anything, she suddenly realized, than marry that man. And she could appeal to her mother's religious zeal by reminding her of the prophecies.

Mulan filled her lungs with air, then let the deep breath out slowly. Could she do this? Hadn't she been preparing most of her life? She couldn't stop the smile that spread over her face.

But if she failed, her mother would have nowhere to go, and Mulan could never show her face in Mindius again.

CHAPTER 2

Wolfgang's heart beat faster as he and his brother Steffan strode through the castle to meet their father in the library. Would he finally get to do what he'd been training for his whole life?

Father stood by the window, a shaft of late-day sun streaming into the room. Steffan, who was older by a year and a half, was silent, so Wolfgang stepped forward.

"Father. Gerhard said you wanted to speak with us."

Father turned to look at them, and Wolfgang had never noticed before how deep the wrinkles around Father's eyes were.

"I do." Father spoke a bit about the weather, about how it would be getting warmer soon with the onset of summer. Then Father's sober, almost severe expression returned.

"Wolfgang. Steffan. You've both been training with my knights since you were young boys."

"But because you wouldn't send us to train in another lord's castle, we may never be knighted." Steffan spat the words out, his eyelids drooping low over his blue eyes.

"We've been over this before. Your mother had suffered the loss of your sister, and when the accident happened involving you two and the shepherd's little boy . . . I thought it best to keep you both at home. I feared you were not mature enough." Father's gruff voice hardened. "I'm sorry you can't seem to understand or forgive that. Even though, at twenty-two years, you are well old enough."

Steffan glared at the wall behind Father.

"Father, do you have some news for us?" Wolfgang pointed at the missive his father held.

"*Ja.*" He moved closer to them. "The Teutonic Knights have been burning fields and killing innocent people in Poland, trying to take over the region controlled by a longtime ally of Hagenheim: Duke Konrad of Zachev. I'm dispatching a group of knights and soldiers to help defend his castle and his people. The Teutonic Knights are gathering an even bigger force to—"

Steffan stepped in front of Father. "Shouldn't we be helping the Teutonic Knights instead?" He folded his arms across his chest. "After all, they represent God and the Church and are our German brothers, and what do we truly know of this Polish Konrad?"

Father seemed to study Steffan. He spoke in a low, deliberate tone. "You know how I feel about the Teutonic Knights. They may have begun with hearts to do good, but for more than a hundred years, they've used their affiliation with the Church as an excuse to oppress and dominate, to take land that rightfully belongs to others. And they could set their sights on German lands next if someone doesn't stop them."

"They claim they are Christianizing the pagans in Livonia and Lithuania and—"

"Those countries are now officially Christian. You know this." Father's jaw flexed and his lips pressed in a hard line. "If you wish to travel with the rest of my men, you will ready yourselves. They leave tomorrow morning for Poland."

"Yes, Father." Wolfgang nodded.

Steffan smirked. "Will Mother allow it?"

Wolfgang's shoulders tensed, and he felt the urge to take a step back, to distance himself from Father's anger—and from the object of it.

Father's gaze never left Steffan's. Finally he spoke. "Son, I don't know where your anger and rebellion come from, but if you're unable to control it, your attitude may land you in more trouble than my title and fortune can extricate you from."

Steffan's cheeks grew red. Wolfgang held his breath, waiting to see how his brother would react.

"I love both of you, and your mother and I'll be praying for your wisdom and safety in battle."

As usual, Wolfgang found himself wishing he could do something to help make peace between Steffan and their father.

Steffan's chest rose and fell with rapid breaths. Then, without speaking, he turned on his heel and left the room.

Wolfgang met his father's eye. "I shall watch over him the best I can."

Father heaved a sigh. "He's not your responsibility, son. But I would be grateful to God to have you both come back to us alive and well." He clapped his hand on Wolfgang's shoulder.

Wolfgang bowed his head, and his father prayed over him. "God in heaven, Your power knows no bounds and Your love for Your children is endless. Bless my son Wolfgang and bring glory to Your great name through him. Let him be mighty in battle, gracious in defeat, and humble in obedience to Your decrees. Protect him and protect Steffan, and forge in them the character and nature of Jesus. I pray this in the name of Jesus the Son. Amen."

Wolfgang and his father made the sign of the cross over their chests and then embraced, perhaps for the last time for a very long while.

When Wolfgang left the library, Steffan was waiting for him. "I'm going to join the Teutonic Knights."

"Did you not hear what Father said?"

"Unlike you, I don't wholeheartedly swallow everything Father says. Besides"—Steffan's lip curled—"I want glory and honor in battle. What glory is there in defending the castle of some foreign ally? How am I to rise in power and status that way? With the Teutonic Knights I can become a marshal, a commander, or even the grand master and be declared a grand prince by the pope." Steffan smiled. "Why would I give up that ambition to obey the man who thwarted the dream we've had since we were small boys, to be true knights of the realm?"

"Steffan, you know Father cares about us. Besides, we could be knighted by Duke Konrad if we impress him with our valor and skill in battle."

Steffan speared him with a cold glare. "Believe what you want, but after we leave Hagenheim, no one will be able to stop me from joining the Teutonic Knights."

Wolfgang's chest felt hollow as he watched his brother stride away. Would he be forced to fight his brother on the battlefield?

Mulan strode down the dirt street searching for Andrei. She only had one day before Butautas's guardsman returned, so she moved with haste toward the makeshift shack at the edge of their village. When she drew near the trees that surrounded it, she heard a noise behind her.

"If it isn't the Hun girl."

Mulan froze, then made a slow turn. Dilgunos stood there, a rock the size of her fist in his hand. He tossed the rock up, then caught it, while two boys stood beside him.

Her stomach sank but she lifted her head, placed a hand on her hip, and focused her eyes on his. "I am not a Hun."

"Then what are you?"

The boys on either side of him laughed.

"My father is Mikolai the Lithuanian and my mother is Feodosia the Lithuanian, so that makes me Lithuanian."

"That's not what I hear."

"Your hearing is faulty." Her heart beat hard and stole her breath, but she had to pretend to be confident. Although they were all younger than she was, they were larger.

"I think it's your lineage that's faulty." Dilgunos was glaring now, his smile gone.

She didn't have time for this. "Go away unless there's something you want."

"No one tells us to go away," one of Dilgunos's friends said.

"A little too high and mighty for a girl." The overgrown boy glanced to one friend, then the other. "What do you think? Shall we show the Mongol girl not to talk to us that way?"

A frisson of fear snaked through Mulan's middle. She glanced around, but no one seemed to be on the street, no one she could call on to help her. Algirdas's butcher shop was not far away, but perhaps she could rid herself of the boys on her own without becoming beholden to the man.

She caught sight of Andrei. Unfortunately, he was too far down the street to get to her before the boys.

To her right was the rock outcropping. She ran toward it, climbed up about the space of her own height, but above that, the face of it was nearly straight up with few crevices or footholds. But she kept going. It was as if her desperation enabled her to see the holds she needed. She scurried up the rock face while the boys yelled insults at her from below.

She was nearly to the top when her hand slipped, then her foot. With only one toehold keeping her from plunging to the ground, she reached frantically and clutched the tiniest crack with the tips of her fingers. The boys laughed and taunted.

If I fall, God, let me fall right on their heads.

The rough rock surface scraped her fingertips, but she held on and managed to pull her body up and find the next hand- and toeholds. She finally reached the top and scrambled over the edge.

Mulan lay on her stomach, her breath heaving in gasps. She closed her eyes to whisper, "Thank You, God." That was terrifying, but she was alive.

The boys' taunts had ceased. Were they running around the side of the rocks to catch her? She peeked over the side and looked down. The boys were nowhere to be seen, but Andrei was standing below.

Her friend motioned with his hand. "Come down," he called in a loud whisper. "They're coming for you."

Andrei had accompanied her father to battle, but he was younger and much smaller than the band of bully boys who taunted her.

There was no time to go around the sloping side of the large rock. She'd have to go back down the way she'd come up.

She lowered her feet off the edge of the rock and finally found a toehold. It was actually a bit harder going down than coming up since she couldn't see as well where to place her feet. But finally she slid the last few feet and landed on the ground beside Andrei.

"Let's go hide." He ran and she followed him. They raced around the side of the blacksmith's shop and sank into the tall grass.

They were silent as Mulan waited for her breathing to slow. Andrei's face was streaked with dirt and his shirt was torn in more than one place. When he came home with Father after a battle, he would sleep in his own makeshift abode just outside the village.

"Your fingers are bleeding." Andrei took the cork out of his flask he kept tethered to his belt. He took her hand and poured water over the tips of her fingers.

"That's all right. I am well." Mulan let the water drip on the ground. "I was coming to find you, to ask you some questions."

"Me?"

"You have been with Mikolai when he fought the Teutonic Knights. Will you teach me how to behave like a soldier?"

"Why would you want to know that?" Andrei's sandy-brown brows drew together.

"I want to take Mikolai's place."

Andrei frowned at her. "You are talking nonsense."

"Now that Mikolai is dead, Mother will have to forfeit her house to Butautas since Father didn't have a son who could fight in his stead. As soon as he discovers Father is dead, Butautas will throw Mother out and give her house to someone else. Mother found me a husband—Algirdas the butcher—but I cannot marry him. So I must fight in Father's stead."

Andrei raised his brows. "You want to go and fight the Teutonic Knights?" He shook his head. "You'll never survive."

"I'm glad to hear your confidence in me."

"How could you fool people into believing you are a man? Your hair comes all the way to your waist."

"I'll cut my hair."

"You also have other . . . things that might be difficult to hide." Andrei's cheeks turned red.

"My *things* are not large, so they won't be that difficult to hide."

"Also, you may be good at archery, but you're small and you're just not as strong as a man. What will happen if the truth is discovered?"

Mulan's heart sank. These were the fearful thoughts that had been darting through her own head. But something rose inside her. Courage?

More likely desperation.

"I can do it. I just need a little help and information from you. Father was a seasoned soldier, but I can . . . well, I can pretend to be his son, ready to learn to be a seasoned soldier."

"That's not how it works. They will expect you to already know what you're doing, to be able to fight with a sword. They will assume you've been training all your life to take your father's place."

"I have been training at archery all my life, and I'm a very good rider. Besides, don't they need longbowmen even more than knights and swordsmen? What is the worst thing that could happen?"

"They could discover you are a woman, send you home in disgrace, and take your mother's house anyway. Or do worse things to you. You don't know how crude some of these men are. Besides, it's against Church law for a woman to wear men's garments and pretend to be a man."

Being excommunicated was the worst thing that could happen to anyone. But wasn't she an exception to that law because of the prophecies made by the priest and the friar?

"And who knows how the other soldiers will react when they find out you've fooled them. The last time I went with Mikolai, there was one man who couldn't fight, and during a training exercise, he started crying. The knight in charge ran him through with his sword. He simply wiped off his blade and said, 'There's no crying in war.'"

Mulan pushed back a strand of hair. "Then I'll be sure not to cry."

Wolfgang and the other soldiers and knights from Hagenheim had almost reached the Polish border. Tonight they would bed down on the Margrave of Thornbeck's land, as he was an ally of Wolfgang's father.

All afternoon Steffan had ridden his horse like a madman, galloping far ahead, then coming back looking amused. Steffan didn't like to talk about anything serious, but Wolfgang was determined to force him to talk tonight.

Wolfgang watched where Steffan placed his blanket. He laid his right beside it and then went to make certain his horse was brushed down and fed. When he returned, Steffan was laughing and drinking wine with two other men. *Ach*, but he was not willing to wait halfway into the night until Steffan was done drinking.

Wolfgang strode up to him and tapped him on the shoulder. "Brother, I need to talk to you."

Steffan turned and looked at him, as did the men with him. "But I don't need to talk to you."

The other men raised their brows and waited.

Wolfgang expelled a breath. "Excuse us, men." He took Steffan by the arm and led him away a few steps.

Steffan snatched his arm away. "What do you want?" Wine sloshed out of his cup and onto Steffan's hand.

"I want to know what is wrong with you."

"Nothing is wrong with me."

"You know how you are when you drink too much wine—you do foolish things."

"You're not my father."

"You have been angry and unreasonable since you were eight years old, when that boy—"

"Shut your mouth." Steffan grabbed Wolfgang's neck, digging his thumb into his throat.

Wolfgang took hold of Steffan's wrist and pried his fingers off, then shoved him.

Steffan shot him a venomous look and stalked away.

Perhaps that had not been the best way to get his brother to listen to him. Wolfgang groaned. He went to his bedding and lay down. Aware that several men had witnessed the unfortunate exchange between Steffan and him, he laid his arm over his eyes.

His brother had drifted further and further away from Wolfgang and his family over the last few years. Truthfully, though he and Steffan had spent so much time together as boys, they hadn't had a real conversation about what had happened in a long time.

Steffan refused to talk about it, refused to talk about anything that made him uncomfortable. He held in every thought and every emotion—except anger—and had only accepted Wolfgang's company if he went along with Steffan's less-than-noble antics, like teasing their sisters or playing some prank on an unsuspecting person.

When Wolfgang had started passing more time with his father and older brother Valten and stopped going along with Steffan's foolish impulses, their relationship deteriorated quickly.

Wolfgang had felt so guilty since that terrible day when everything changed and the world no longer seemed like a safe or joyful place. His initial thought was that they should tell their father exactly what they had done, but Steffan had been furious, had even threatened him with violence if he ever told anyone. And since Wolfgang had always looked up to Steffan as older and wiser and stronger, he never told.

But instead of fading from his mind, the secret seemed to grow bigger. He no longer had any doubt that the secret was eating at Steffan, too, making him do the foolish things he did. And yet . . . what had the secret done to Wolfgang? He felt the same shame as Steffan, but he had not become angry, nor had he rebelled against Father as Steffan had done. Had he gone the opposite direction?

Steffan often accused him of never having his own opinion, of always believing whatever Father said. Was Steffan right? Was Wolfgang so afraid of disappointing his parents that he could not be his own man? Was he afraid to disagree? But he had proved himself a capable soldier, had he not? He was no weakling, and was it not wise to listen to his father?

He let out a deep sigh. Neither of them had escaped the effects of what had happened. But it seemed too late now to tell anyone about it. After all, it was so long ago, and there was nothing anyone could do to make it right. But he also didn't want his brother hurting himself and everyone who loved him.

Wolfgang would wait until Steffan came to sleep, and then he would try to talk to him again. Steffan seemed determined to defect to the enemy, and Wolfgang had to stop him.

A while later, most of the other soldiers had bedded down. Finally Steffan arrived. But he grabbed his blanket off the ground and started rolling it up.

"Where are you going?" Wolfgang sprang up to stand before Steffan.

"Away." Steffan wouldn't look at him.

Wolfgang's stomach churned. "Away where?"

Steffan turned a crooked grin on him. "I'm joining the German Order of Teutonic Knights."

Wolfgang's voice vibrated as he said, "Are you willing to fight against your friends from Hagenheim? Your own brother?"

"The Teutonic Knights are our German brothers, knights who have consecrated themselves to God and the Church. They are just as convinced that they're doing right as you are. Who's to say who's right and who's wrong?" He shrugged.

"That's only an excuse to go your own way, to rebel against Father."

Steffan blew out a noisy breath. "As if I still care what Father thinks. I am my own man now. Unlike you."

"Listen. We can still be knighted. If we distinguish ourselves in battle, Duke Konrad might knight us and grant us land."

"Duke Konrad! Who is he compared to the Teutonic Knights? I can join them and not have to beg for some foreign duke's favor."

A heavy stone pressed against Wolfgang's chest. "No matter what I say, you won't listen because your heart is hardened to reason."

"Face the truth, Wolfgang. From now on we're no longer brothers. We are enemies." With that Steffan snapped around and stalked toward the horses, leaving the ground next to Wolfgang's bedding as empty as if he'd never been there.

The heat deserted Wolfgang and was replaced with a cold, heavy feeling. Should he go after him? What good would it do? Steffan would not listen.

Wolfgang closed his eyes. *O God, I don't know what else I can do. But You can do anything. Please help him come to his senses.*

CHAPTER 3

"What have you done to your hair?"

Mulan paused in her packing and glanced up at her mother. A pang twisted her stomach.

Her eyes wide, Mother gasped again as she reached out and touched the short ends.

Mulan took up the leather string and tied it around her hair, making a short tail, the way her father sometimes wore his.

"It's too dangerous." Mother's voice was hushed, and when she lifted her hands to cover her mouth, they were trembling. Then she grabbed Mulan's arm. "You cannot do this. I won't let you."

"It's all right, Mother. I'm taking Andrei with me. He'll know how to help me stay safe."

"He's only a boy! A mere child! He cannot help you."

"He knows what is required of a soldier and how I should conduct myself. He can also help me prepare." Mulan continued placing her father's clothing into her bag.

"Those clothes will not fit you."

"I can alter them. I've already altered some of them."

"Mulan. Don't do this. Algirdas . . ."

Mulan opened her mouth. What could she say? If she said, "I just can't marry that man," it wouldn't actually be true. It wasn't that she *couldn't* marry him, but that she'd rather take her chances as a soldier. After all, she'd always been terrible at cooking and humbling herself to men—even her own father. She wanted to be loved, not used, and it seemed unlikely that any man would want a wife like her. She'd rather be outside making pets out of the new piglets, practicing with her bow by shooting wild birds, or taking long walks with her mare, Aksoma. And no one was better at climbing trees and rocks than she was.

"I don't want to wed Algirdas. Besides, there are the prophecies. Don't forget those."

They'd rarely ever spoken of them, but she knew her mother had not forgotten.

"That's the only reason I can bear to let you do this, believing that perhaps it is God's will. Perhaps it was His plan all along."

If only Mulan had applied herself to learning swordplay. She'd asked Mikolai to teach her, but he refused.

"Butautas's messenger will be here any moment." She closed the cloth bag and hefted it to her shoulder. "I love you, Mother. I always will. I'll pray for God to keep you safe and well."

Tears welled in Mother's eyes, and one spilled over onto her cheek.

Mulan rushed out of the house, her gut sinking at having to leave her mother, especially when she was crying. Andrei met her coming down the lane from the stable with his own pack on his back, but his face was the opposite of Mother's.

"I already saddled Mikolai's horse for you. He's spirited, loves to run, but is reasonably obedient and calm in battle. I packed up your father's weapons and quilted gambeson. It will be a little big on you, but too big is better than too small."

They went to the stable where Boldheart stood just outside,

dancing around skittishly. Did he know his master was dead? He eyed Mulan with equal parts suspicion and disdain.

She could not cower. She must show this big black gelding who his new master was.

She took hold of his bridle. "Hold still now, Boldheart. I'll be riding you and I don't want any problems from you." Standing on the mounting rock, she held on to the saddle and sprang up into it.

Mulan smiled as she sat up straight. The horse must realize she wouldn't let him get away with disobeying her. But then she noticed Andrei standing on the other side, holding the bridle, his other hand on the horse's shoulder.

"Andrei, you can saddle my mare for yourself."

"Already done." He smiled up at her before retreating into the stable and bringing out Mulan's short, stocky Konik with her silvery-gray, blue-dun coat. Aksoma had belonged to Mulan since they were both very young. But a soldier would be expected to ride a taller, stronger warhorse.

It was strange to ride the big horse, and even stranger to see Andrei on Aksoma. She said a quick, silent prayer that God would keep her beloved horse safe on this adventure they were embarking on.

Mulan led the way, urging Boldheart into a trot. But he was not very cooperative, pulling on the reins, turning his head to look back at her, obviously questioning her authority to tell him where to go. He stopped altogether and began to eat the grass at the edge of the lane between the house and the road ahead. By the time she forced him to move forward again, Butautas's messenger was riding toward them.

The moment of truth. Or, rather, untruth.

Mulan suddenly wished she had rubbed some dirt on her face to disguise the fact that she had no beard, no stubble of any kind emerging from her chin or upper lip. She did her best to make her expression stern and . . . masculine?

The man seemed confused as he approached them. "Andrei I recognize, but who are you?"

"I am Mikolai's son." She did her best to deepen her voice. Fortunately, her voice was already rather deep for a woman's.

"I didn't know Mikolai had a son."

"He fathered me out of wedlock . . . while fighting in a foreign land." At least that part was true. "Feodosia took me in as her own." She should probably try to speak as little as possible, as her father did.

"Where is Mikolai?"

"I'm taking his place."

"Why?"

"He got sick."

"Sick?"

"Mikolai is dead. I shall fight in his stead."

"Do you have experience in battle?"

"No battles you would have heard of."

He frowned.

"But I'm a fighter, a warrior after my father."

"That is true," Andrei said, opening his eyes wide. "He is quite the warrior."

"And I'm eager to battle these fiendish usurpers who are besieging Zachev Castle. Shall we go?"

Unmoving, the messenger kept staring at her.

Mulan's hands trembled, wanting to cover her face.

"How old are you?"

"Eighteen years." Perhaps she should have said she was younger. Would he believe an eighteen-year-old boy had no hair on his face?

"What is your name?"

"Mikolai, named after my father."

"You don't look like Mikolai." His eyes narrowed to slits.

"Do you look exactly like your father?" *No, don't antagonize him.* "I resemble my mother. She was from Asia."

He frowned again. "We have a lot of riding to do before we get to Vilkaviškis. Let us go."

Andrei looked relieved and even smiled. Mulan wasn't sure if she should feel relieved—or terrified.

Three days later, Mulan and Andrei arrived in Vilkaviškis. Zachev Castle was only a half-day's ride away, but the allies would meet here and plan their attack on the besieging Teutonic Knights.

There were so many men and not a single woman. They all stood around talking and scratching themselves. The waiting was making the men restless. So when someone announced an archery contest, the men all shouted and hastened to fetch their bows and arrows.

Mulan wanted nothing more than to fade into the background out of everyone's notice, but she should probably mimic what the men were doing, so she went to retrieve her bow and arrows.

Someone had set up targets on some trees at the edge of the clearing. The men all lined up to shoot. One caught her eye. He was particularly handsome, with wide shoulders and a thick chest, and he had the proud but easy bearing of a knight. His hair was medium brown, thick, not too long, and slightly wavy. He had a strong chin. He was also taller than the fellows around him. But would he be any good at archery?

The men shot their first arrows. Four or five were clustered together in front of each target, which was at least fifty paces away. The tall, handsome one shot an arrow that struck the very middle of the target. The other four men with him did not do as well, although they all managed to hit the target.

Another group of men were motioned forward. The winner in each group was allowed to compete again. And once again, the tall, handsome man hit the middle of the target while the others came close but did not strike the center.

Andrei suddenly appeared at her side.

"Who is that man there?" She cast a nod in the man's direction.

"He is the son of the Duke of Hagenheim."

"A knight, then?"

He shook his head. "He has not been knighted, but he trained with his father's soldiers. I believe they said his name is Wolfgang."

"Should I shoot?" she said quietly to Andrei. "Perhaps no one will notice that I haven't taken a turn."

A few men who had been defeated already looked around, calling for men to come and shoot at the targets. One pointed at Mulan. "You there. Come forth." He motioned with his hand.

Mulan stood paralyzed. Finally Andrei nudged her forward and she took a step. She had little choice but to join the first group—the one with the Duke of Hagenheim's son.

She stepped up to the spot. The man nodded at her. She nodded back, trying not to stare at him. Would she even be able to strike the target? Her knees were trembling and this contest seemed meaningless. Shouldn't they save their arrows for the real battle?

She took a deep breath as two other men stepped forward. Once again, the duke's son took the first shot. And once again, his arrow struck the middle of the target.

The next man advanced and his arrow struck a hand's length from the center, and the third man's arrow struck the space between those two. Now there was no one left but Mulan. The three men turned their eyes on her.

Mulan already had the arrow nocked to the bowstring. She pulled it back and aimed carefully, willing her hand not to shake, resting her thumb against her cheek. Finally she let go.

The arrow flew through the air, a bit too high. But because they were so far from the target, it arced and struck the center, pushing Wolfgang's arrow sideways.

Mulan's heart skipped a beat. Gasps rippled through the crowd, followed by a hush.

The duke's son turned to her. "Very good." He even gave her a tiny smile.

"Oh, it was just a lucky shot. I'm not that skilled at archery." Why did she say that?

His smile vanished and he raised his brows at her.

The other groups shot their arrows, while Mulan's insides quaked. All she had wanted was to blend in and be unnoticed. She'd only hoped to hit the target somewhere, not the middle. How could she—?

"I am Wolfgang."

The man had moved closer. Mulan faced him. "I am Mu- Mikolai. Mikolai of Lithuania."

He was a whole head taller than she was. Standing this close, would he realize she was a girl? Would he recognize that the darker skin on her jawline and chin was mud instead of facial hair?

"Well, Mikolai of Lithuania, it looks as though all the winners have been determined in the other groups, but the judges are asking us to shoot again."

Another man spoke up, looking straight at her. "Best two out of three shots."

"You first," Wolfgang said.

A boy had pulled the arrows out of the target and was running back toward them. He handed her the arrow she'd shot.

She could feel people watching her. *All I have to do is shoot two more times, as long as Wolfgang wins both shots. That should be easy.*

"I'll bet on the short Lithuanian!" someone shouted.

"It would be amusing to see him defeat the Duke of Hagenheim's son." Laughter broke out.

Mulan couldn't help but glance at Wolfgang. His jaw twitched, but he kept his gaze straight ahead.

Her hand shook as she nocked an arrow to the string. Should she deliberately miss the center of the target so he'd think her first shot had been lucky? But something inside her rebelled and wanted to win, to show that she actually was good with a bow. Besides, if she didn't try, her arrow might miss the target altogether, and everyone would laugh at her.

Mulan raised the bow and arrow and aimed at the target. The arrow flew toward it and stuck fast just a finger width off-center.

Without hesitating Wolfgang stepped up, took aim, and struck the very center of the target.

The crowd let out a few "aahs" and "oohs" of appreciation.

Mulan took out another arrow. *Time to get this over with.* But she fumbled and dropped the arrow on the ground. She hastened to pick it up, glad her hand wasn't shaking visibly.

"Come on, boy! Show the German how it's done!"

Mulan's stomach sank. The back of Wolfgang's neck was red. No great love existed between the Poles and the Germans, but they should not goad him. After all, German or not, he was obviously willing to risk his life for them.

She tried to clear her thoughts and concentrate on her task. She nocked the arrow, lifted the bow to her cheek, one eye closed, and let out the breath she was holding. Pulling the bowstring back even more, as hard as she could, she released the arrow.

It sailed toward the target, moving straight and sure through the air—and struck so close to Wolfgang's arrow that it must have loosened the arrowhead from the wood, because a moment later, Wolfgang's arrow fell to the ground while hers was still protruding from the center.

"Oh, I'm sorry!" The words popped out and she immediately covered her mouth with her hand.

An equal number of cheers and guffaws erupted from the crowd.

Mulan lost her breath, unable to take her eyes off the way her arrow had knocked his clean off the target. She had always shown skill with a bow and arrow, but even she was surprised. And she should not have apologized. After all, she was a soldier, Wolfgang was a soldier, and they were competing as equals in a contest.

Wolfgang stood stock-still, staring at the target, his face a mask of stone. He wouldn't even look at her.

After the arrows were removed from the target, Wolfgang grabbed another and stepped up to the mark. He aimed for a longer time than before, and the arrow again struck the very center of the target.

Good. He would win, and she would make sure of it. She would deliberately miss the target altogether. Her vanity and pride had drawn too much attention to herself, and it was time to remedy that.

She took her third and final arrow, in a hurry to put an end to this spectacle. She pinched the arrow's end and lifted the bow, setting the nock against the string. She started pulling the arrow back, but she lost her grip on the bow. In her fumbling she released the arrow. It flew toward Wolfgang. She screamed.

Wolfgang dodged to the side as the arrow passed only a handsbreadth from his head.

"Forgive me! I didn't intend to—"

"Are you trying to kill me, boy?" He leaned toward her, his hands fisted at his sides.

Mulan took a step back, wishing she could transform into smoke and disappear. People all around them were shouting and laughing. Wolfgang's face was crimson and his eyes seemed to flash lightning at her.

"I didn't mean to." But her voice was drowned out by the people around them. Some appeared angry and others laughed.

Wolfgang glared at her. "Make haste and shoot your last arrow."

At least that's what she thought he said. He seemed to be switching back and forth between the Polish language, which she understood, thanks to Andrei teaching her what he knew and some lessons from the village priest, and the German language, which she did not know.

She reached for another arrow, blowing out a breath to steady herself, keeping her body and her arrow pointed toward the target. She lifted her bow and tried to aim, but she just closed her eyes and shot.

The arrow went to the right of the target, missing it entirely. Wolfgang was declared the winner, but some of the men were still laughing at him, describing to each other the look on his face when her arrow almost struck him in the face.

Wolfgang glared as she slunk away.

Andrei met her with a tentative smile. "You nearly defeated him."

"I nearly killed him is what I did." Mulan covered her face with her hand. "I wonder what the penalty is for shooting out the eye of a duke's son?"

"Why are you worrying? He still has both eyes."

"At least it's over."

Andrei went to collect her arrows while Mulan hurried to the tent Andrei had set up for them. She crawled under her blanket, covering her head. "God, please let me be invisible."

CHAPTER 4

"Tomorrow we leave here and march to Zachev Castle."
Wolfgang's page brought him his arrows from the final
archery match.

Wolfgang was still clenching his teeth from his encounter
with the skinny Lithuanian, Mikolai. Which might explain why,
in the final round of the archery contest, the older Polish soldier
had defeated him with three near-perfect shots, while Wolfgang
had been way off the center mark.

But it was Mikolai who'd made a mockery of him, knocking
his arrow off the target, then nearly shooting him—pretending
it was accidental—then missing the target entirely. He couldn't
decide if the boy was intentionally trying to make a fool of him or
if he was truly incompetent. Neither boded well for their upcoming battle.

"But first they're proposing a sword-fighting competition with
practice swords."

Good. Wolfgang was even better at sword fighting than he
was at archery.

When he emerged from his tent with his practice sword, he
looked around for the young Lithuanian. But before he could pick
him out of the men milling about, one of the Hagenheim soldiers,
Dieter, came and challenged him.

They both fought hard. Dieter was younger than Wolfgang and not as strong, as he had a smaller build, but he was tough. Wolfgang was starting to sweat when he managed to pin Dieter's sword to his chest. A judge ruled Wolfgang the winner.

He again searched for Mikolai. A soldier walked by with a bloody nose, and another was holding his arm and wincing. Though they were fighting with blunted practice swords, there was still the possibility of serious injury.

Another would-be opponent came and challenged him to fight. Wolfgang fought four or five opponents—he lost count—and defeated them all. Then he finally spotted Mikolai talking to an even younger boy in the entryway of what he assumed was his tent.

He could still hear the other soldiers laughing at him when Mikolai's arrow nearly sliced through his ear. The way everyone had gasped when the beardless little Lithuanian's arrow knocked Wolfgang's arrow to the ground. But perhaps what rankled the most was how he had then missed the target entirely, letting Wolfgang win instead of allowing him to earn it.

Also, soldiers didn't say they had just made a lucky shot when they bested another soldier. And they certainly didn't apologize! Inside they might boast and smirk, but they would behave honorably by complimenting their opponent.

Wolfgang walked with all haste straight through the crowd. When he finally reached Mikolai, he clapped him on the shoulder, hard. "Mikolai, I challenge you."

The boy clutched his throat as if in fear. But only for a moment. He stood up straight and squared his shoulders. "I'll get my sword."

He sounded sad, but no matter. He was about to receive instruction on sword fighting—and be sorry he had humiliated a man double his size.

Mikolai emerged from the tent and plodded forward. He took his fighting stance as they waited for a judge. Soon one came and gave them the signal to begin.

Wolfgang landed a hard blow on Mikolai's blunted practice sword, then another and another. The Lithuanian was much less skilled at sword fighting, so Wolfgang held back, not wishing the match to be over too soon, keeping Mikolai on the defensive as he struck blow after blow.

The young Lithuanian blocked Wolfgang's strikes, but he was barely moving fast enough. Anyone else might have already struck him in the head, but Wolfgang made sure he gave this upstart a workout. Sweat was making Mikolai's face shiny, and he stumbled backward. Wolfgang increased the power behind his blows until he had the boy backed up against a tree at the edge of the clearing.

Time to speed things up.

Wolfgang struck fast and furiously until Mikolai was holding his sword still, unable to parry.

Not wishing to break his arm, Wolfgang struck the boy on the side with the broad side of his wooden blade.

Mikolai didn't make a sound as he bent over to protect his side. His knees buckled under him but, leaning heavily against the tree, he managed to stay upright.

The judge declared Wolfgang the winner.

Victory was sweet as Mikolai straightened, then bowed his head in the customary way.

"Very good match," Mikolai said, his voice raspy, as if he could barely breathe.

Wolfgang only nodded. He probably should tell the boy that he would be slain if he fought like that in an actual battle. Hopefully the captain of their company would recognize how unprepared he was and assign him some other task.

Mikolai walked stiffly toward his tent. His servant was staring at Wolfgang with lowered brows and narrowed eyes. It was only bruised ribs. He deserved it, too, especially if he couldn't fight any better than that. But an emotion—one he was all too familiar with—stabbed Wolfgang's chest.

Perhaps he shouldn't have gotten so angry and taken it out on the boy. He hoped he hadn't hurt him too badly.

Mulan moaned as she lay down on her pallet. It was her own fault for not staying hidden inside her tent.

Her shoulders and arm ached from fending off Wolfgang's blows, but it was her side that hurt the worst. At least he didn't draw blood.

"No more contests." Andrei shook his finger at her, worry in his eyes.

His sandy-brown hair was too long, hanging over one side of his face. She would have to remember to cut it when she wasn't in so much pain.

"You should not have fought that man. He's angry with you for what happened with the archery contest. And yet . . . how dare he come and find you to challenge you? Can he not see that he's twice as big as you? He's a coward for not challenging someone his own size."

"He's not a coward." Pain stabbed her as she tried to move herself into a more comfortable position. She lay as still as possible. "He's a good soldier and was rightfully angry. I shouldn't have apologized for besting him. Besides that, I nearly killed him with my carelessness."

"I still don't like him." Andrei's usually mild expression was twisted into a scowl. "He didn't have to beat you so badly. Arrogant show-off."

"He could have done far worse and no one would have thought the worse of him."

"Why are you defending him? I would think you'd be angry."

"I'm not defending him." Mulan tried to shrug but pain racked her side.

"No doubt he'd be sorry if he knew you were a woman."

"But he will never know." Mulan stared hard at Andrei. "You are *not* to tell him or anyone else. Do you hear me?"

"Do you think I'm a fool? I know not to tell anyone." He folded his skinny arms in front of his chest. "You would disgrace your father's good name and bring disaster on your mother. Not to mention what the less chivalrous among them might do. But I would defend you." Andrei was not looking her in the eye.

Her heart expanded at his sincere words. "You would make a noble knight, Andrei."

"I will never be allowed to be a knight." He picked at the grass, pulling it up by the roots. "I have no wealth or sponsor."

He was right, except . . . "With God, nothing is impossible." She'd heard her priest say that, more than once.

Andrei glanced up at her, hope flickering in his eyes. Then he turned his face to the ground again and shrugged.

"If it's what you really want, don't give up on it." Mulan couldn't bear to see him this way.

Andrei suddenly stood and grabbed some flasks. "I'm going to refill our water." He disappeared through the tent flap.

She sighed. He was such a brave boy.

Her poor mother. She must be so worried. If only there was a way to get word to her that she was well. But her mother wasn't much for worrying, truth be told, and she would likely assume Mulan was well as long as she heard nothing. Because as soon as it was known that Mulan was a woman—if or when she was killed—Butautas's men would be sure and inform her. And throw her out of her house.

The next morning Wolfgang was readying his horse for the ride to their battle a half day away. He glanced around. Groups of men talked among themselves as they worked to get ready to move out. But he hadn't seen Mikolai since he defeated him in the sword-fighting contest. Had he hurt him more than he'd intended to? He might have broken a rib, which would affect how hard he could fight in the upcoming battle.

A sharp pain stabbed his own side at the thought. Steffan would scoff at his compassion.

The day before, Wolfgang had continued to take challengers until he was nearly exhausted. No sooner had he gone inside his tent to rest than a new contest was announced: horsemanship. He had wondered if they would have a jousting competition.

Wolfgang might not be as good at jousting as Valten, who had competed all over the Continent, but Wolfgang had practiced as much or more than most knights his age. He and Steffan had both been very good jousters. Steffan was slightly better than he was, and his brother never let him forget it.

However, they announced there would be no tilting with lances. It was too dangerous on the eve before battle.

Gerke finished packing Wolfgang's saddlebag and loading the extra horse with their supplies.

Two of his father's knights from Hagenheim, who had been talking with Wolfgang since before Stéffan left their group, were nearby checking their horses' legs and hooves. They called out to Wolfgang.

"That little fellow certainly gave you some trouble in the archery contest yesterday."

"Nothing I couldn't handle."

"True," the dark one said, "and then I saw how you destroyed him in the sword fighting later. I haven't seen him since. You really taught him a lesson he won't forget."

"Yeah, you had him limping like an old man." The blond one raised his brows. "I wonder if he'll even be able to ride today. Perhaps you should not have beaten up on a child like him, someone so much smaller than you."

"Is that how you speak about your fellow soldiers?"

The voice made them turn to see who was behind them. There stood Mikolai.

"This man did not injure me, I am no child, and I will have no problem riding my horse. He fought me in a fair fight and won." The Lithuanian turned and hoisted himself into the saddle of his steed. "I shall see you at the battle." Then he rode away.

A few moments passed before one of them spoke.

"He's a feisty one."

"For a smooth-faced boy."

A couple of men grunted. Respect for Mikolai's spirit overcame some of Wolfgang's resentment toward him for exposing him to ridicule. "*A man has to stay humble,*" his father often said, "*and that's why it is good to meet someone who can defeat you.*"

Mulan enjoyed telling those soldiers that she was not injured. But then she had to force herself not to groan in pain as she threw herself up on her horse. Not an easy feat. Her side was still quite sore, as were her arms and shoulders. But it could have been worse. The duke's son was obviously holding back. He could have ended the match much sooner with worse injuries to herself.

And he couldn't have known he was fighting a woman.

Andrei rode beside her. A few men had tried to talk to her. She learned their names but kept them at a distance. She couldn't afford to risk anyone getting too close and finding out her secret.

When they were nearly to Zachev Castle, their company was met by a man on horseback bearing Konrad's colors, which were blue and gold.

"The Teutonic Knights have breached the first wall and are breaking through the gatehouse door with a battering ram! You must make haste or you will be too late to stop them."

Wolfgang and his friends were at the front of the group, and Mulan was behind them. Wolfgang asked, "What is the fastest way to the castle?"

"It's just beyond this mountain." The messenger pointed behind him. The nearly sheer face of rock met their eyes.

"We can't go that way," one man said.

Wolfgang spoke up. "The mountain's too steep and wide. The road is the only way."

They all turned toward the road they'd been traveling, which led to the right, circling around the rocky cliff face.

They were discussing how long it would take along the road. Wolfgang shouted, "Let us be off!"

Mulan's quiver of arrows was already strapped to her back. She slung her bow over her shoulder and slid out of the saddle. Andrei urgently whispered something behind her, but she ignored him.

She focused on the rock face, already seeing her first hand- and footholds.

A few people shouted behind her as she started to climb. Whenever she looked up for her next handhold, she found it. Just as when she climbed to get away from the bullies in her village, soon she had reached the top. But when she tried to pull herself up over the ledge, the pain in her shoulders and arms and side throbbed and stabbed her. But if she allowed herself to think too much about the pain, she'd end up falling to the ground.

She mustered all her strength. With a growl she held on, her feet scrabbling over the rock face to find footholds for her toes. She pushed and pulled herself up over the ledge.

Lying across the top of the flat, shelflike rock, she looked down. The men below were staring up at her. A few started climbing, while the rest kicked their horses into a gallop and charged down the road.

Mulan got up and ran, following a vague trail, around rocks and small bushes and grass, going up the mountain. At some points she had to use her hands to help her up, but this trail was much less steep than the first part of the climb.

Soon she could hear voices behind her. Some of the men must have joined her in going up and over the mountain on foot. Would they reach the castle in time to stop the invaders from breaking through the gate?

Mulan's heart pounded. She thought of all the people—villagers, women and children—who had taken refuge in the castle. Would the enemy kill them? How many of the defending soldiers would die if they did not get there in time?

She pushed herself to climb faster. As she reached a particularly steep part of the trail, she latched on to a tuft of grass to help pull herself up. Then she grabbed a tiny bush, then a rock. The rock came loose, and she nearly lost her balance and fell backward.

Mulan lay against the side of the mountain in the dirt, panting. Her breaths came fast, drying her throat. The pain in her arms and shoulders had subsided, but the soreness in her ribs had increased, stabbing her with every breath.

She rested a few moments, then glanced behind her. She caught a glimpse of the men climbing below her. Wolfgang was in the lead.

Mulan's strength surged as she continued climbing. Finally the mountain leveled off some, and then she was descending on the other side in full view of a large castle.

Zachev Castle's towers were round, some capped by roofs that rose to a point in the middle, while others were square and ringed with crenellations, behind which the archers could take aim. The rhythmic thundering of the battering ram assailed her ears, but the ominous sound gave her hope that she and her fellow soldiers were not too late.

The gatehouse came into view. The heavily armored Teutonic Knights gathered behind the battering ram, waiting for them to break through the heavy door. From there they were only a short distance to the castle.

A few bodies lay scattered on the ground wearing Duke Konrad's colors, but other than those poor souls, no one else was in sight. Were the remainder of Duke Konrad's knights and soldiers inside the castle, waiting to mount a counterattack once the enemy had breached their doors?

Mulan continued down the side of the hill wondering when the Teutonic Knights would catch sight of her running toward them.

A noise made her turn her head. Wolfgang was not far behind, an intense look in his eyes.

Mulan pressed on, moving a bit more carefully now so she wouldn't lose control and go careening down the steep hill. She had her eye on a boulder. *God, help me reach it before anyone spots me.*

Her body flinched with every thunderous blow of the battering ram. How much longer could the entrance to the castle hold?

Mulan slid the last few feet to the big boulder. She grabbed her bow and nocked an arrow to the string while glancing over her shoulder.

Five or six men were descending the mountain, still exposed and in full view. Wolfgang led them, and he was already holding his bow and reaching for an arrow. His eye met hers and he nodded.

Mulan turned back and took aim at one of the men on the giant wooden instrument of destruction. He wasn't wearing armor— obviously not a Teutonic Knight but one of their hired mercenaries.

Her stomach clenched and she hesitated. *He wouldn't hesitate to kill you, Mulan.* She aimed at the soldier's shoulder and let the arrow fly.

She drew another arrow and took aim, seeing that her first arrow had found its mark. The man let go of the battering ram and clutched at the arrow sticking out of his shoulder. Several of his fellow soldiers on the battering ram looked up, searching for the source of the attack.

Mulan took aim at another soldier who hadn't yet let go of the battering ram. Just as she let her arrow fly, she heard the telltale *whoosh* of Wolfgang's arrow flying past her. Then he slid in beside her. The other men who had been behind him also joined them, shooting arrows and ducking behind the rock. The space was just big enough for them all.

The sudden volley of arrows caused the men to drop the battering ram and grab their weapons. A few answering arrows flew past their boulder. But it was clear they weren't sure exactly where the attack was coming from.

"When they start battering the door again," Wolfgang whispered, "we'll shoot again. Get ready."

All was quiet. The men were crowded around her, tense and smelling of sweat and fear. *God, if I have to kill someone in battle, give me the courage to do it.* Already she sensed if she thought about the man whose shoulder she'd wounded with her arrow, she would get sick. So she pushed him out of her mind. *This is war. I have to be strong.*

A thought struck her. Were the Teutonic Knights and their men creeping up the hill toward them? Wolfgang must have had the same thought because he raised his head above the rock to assess. He ducked back down as arrows flew past their hiding place.

"Are they coming?" someone whispered.

"No, but they're watching."

They all stayed still, waiting. Wolfgang's shoulder was pressed against hers. He also had his bow in his hands, an arrow at the ready. The only sound was the harsh, heavy breathing of the men near her, which was gradually slowing after their hike over the mountain.

Suddenly, the pounding of the battering ram started up again. Once, twice. Mulan and Wolfgang stood at the same moment.

Mulan barely took the time to take aim before releasing her arrow. Then they both ducked behind the boulder again as arrows flew over their heads. She turned to see that Wolfgang was uninjured. The other men were in various stages of shooting their arrows as well.

Mulan quickly nocked another arrow. She stood just long enough to aim and shoot.

Angry shouts mixed with cries of pain below them. But the sound of the battering ram had ceased again. Then someone behind her groaned. An arrow was sticking out of the upper arm of one of their men. Mulan spun around and nocked another arrow.

Wolfgang placed a hand on her arm. "Wait."

They all froze in place and listened. Everything was quiet below. Too quiet. After a few more moments, Wolfgang raised his head above the boulder, then ducked back down. "They're coming," he whispered. "Knights with swords, with archers out front."

It was inevitable that they would counterattack. They would have to fight them face-to-face now, hand to hand. Would their small group be slaughtered?

The battering ram started up again. She thought she heard the huge wooden door crack. Soon it would be splintered. Their efforts would have been in vain.

Had Mulan led Wolfgang and the others to their deaths?

CHAPTER 5

Wolfgang could feel the blood pulsing through this arms and legs, galvanizing him. The knights were charging up the hill, preceded by archers who would pick them off as soon as they showed themselves, leaving the knights to slay the rest with the sword.

Teutonic Knights fought to the death.

The pounding of horses' hooves drifted to his ears, gradually growing louder. Urgent shouts, horses thundering into the area below. Mikolai turned hope-filled eyes toward him. The men behind him exclaimed in half whispers, then louder cheers. His ears welcomed the clang of steel on steel.

Wolfgang raised his head over the top of the rock. The approaching soldiers ran back down to join the battle below.

Wolfgang sprang up, along with his fellow men-at-arms, and loosed a volley of arrows, felling a few of the enemy as they headed downhill. Some of them turned and shot at them, but Wolfgang took cover behind the boulder.

Soldiers in Konrad's colors emerged from the trees not far away and ran toward the melee with war cries and swords raised.

Wolfgang didn't have his sword, and neither did the others, as they were still strapped to their horses. They'd all grabbed their bows following Mikolai's example, which had been a good thing. But now that the battle was well engaged . . .

"The swords!" Wolfgang shot another arrow, then ran down the hill to find his attendant and his horse.

Mikolai was just in front of him, moving surprisingly fast. He reached his horse and stash of weapons the same moment Wolfgang reached his. After his bravery in scaling the mountain and stopping the Teutonic Knights from battering in the door, would Mikolai now be slain because of his poor sword-fighting skills? There seemed little doubt. But Wolfgang had to let the Lithuanian fend for himself. This was a battle, after all.

Wolfgang drew his sword and was instantly confronted by a Teutonic Knight wearing a white surcoat with a plain black cross emblazoned across the front. He roared his battle cry and slashed at Wolfgang with his broadsword.

Wolfgang fought back and was horrified to find that when confronted with fighting for his life, he actually fought rather clumsily, his sword heavy, his arm sluggish. But he continued to strike, and the big Teutonic Knight stumbled backward. Wolfgang knocked the knight's sword out of his hand as he fell flat on his back.

Wolfgang wrenched the knight's helmet from his head and pressed the point of his sword to the man's throat. "Surrender to me! Or I shall kill you where you lie."

The knight's teeth were clenched as he bared them to Wolfgang. He would not have given Wolfgang the same courtesy, as Teutonic Knights were well known for not taking prisoners, and when they did, they sometimes slaughtered them while they were helpless and unarmed.

Through clenched teeth, he said, "I yield."

Gerke, Wolfgang's attendant, leapt on the man and bound his hands together before he could try to stand.

Wolfgang moved to challenge his next opponent. But all the knights and their men were already fighting others.

Then he noticed Mikolai struggling to hold his ground as a Teutonic Knight slammed his sword blade against his and then shoved. Mikolai stumbled back while keeping his blade engaged. But his knees were slowly buckling under the weight of the much larger knight.

Wolfgang charged at him.

Mulan stumbled back, barely able to keep her sword blade pressed against the enemy's. The man leaned all his weight on his sword, bending her backward. She couldn't hold him much longer. Mother, standing in the door of the house, flitted across her mind. *I'm so sorry, Mother.*

The soldier lifted his weight off his sword and turned to the side, blocking a blade that slammed into his. Wolfgang engaged the enemy knight. The knight turned fully away from Mulan. But before she could catch her breath, another enemy soldier attacked her.

Mulan parried his strikes a few times, then leapt to the side to miss a blow altogether. That seemed to work well, as the soldier lost his footing and she was able to thrust her sword point under his arm and down, toward his ribs.

He roared, baring his teeth and striking a massive blow. Mulan nearly dropped her sword as it vibrated in her hand. But suddenly her first opponent was leaning against the body of her new one.

Wolfgang forced the knight, with several hard blows in quick succession, to press his back against the side of the soldier engaging her. Soon Wolfgang managed to get in a blow that struck both men's swords. He was fighting them both. How long could he keep that up?

Mulan fell to the ground on her hands and knees and pressed herself against the back of the enemy soldiers' legs. They both fell over her, landing flat on their backs in a heap of clanging metal.

Mulan sprang up as Andrei and Gerke fell on the two downed soldiers and bound their hands.

Wolfgang already looked as though he was searching for his next opponent when a bugle sounded on the other side of the melee.

The Teutonic Knights struck a few more blows, then retreated.

Wolfgang started running, and since Mulan was unsure what to do, she followed suit. Wolfgang and their fellow soldiers pursued the Teutonic Knights and their men across the green grassy area to the wall they'd broken through. They leapt onto the stones and scrambled over the brick and mortar they'd torn down. The moat was just beyond the wall, and they crossed it on the makeshift bridge of felled trees they must have placed there.

Wolfgang and the others halted. One of their fellow soldiers set fire to the wood bridge.

As the smoke billowed, the captain of the guard clapped Wolfgang on the shoulder. "Good fighting," he grunted.

"How many did we lose?" Wolfgang's jaw twitched as he fastened his gaze on the captain.

"Not sure. One, at least."

Mulan felt slightly numb. A man, one of the men she'd met and conversed with perhaps, had lost his life near her. And it could very well have been her—if Wolfgang had not intervened.

But she was a soldier. She must think like one. At the very least, she'd have to push any thoughts of pity, fear, or squeamishness aside and think them later.

Wolfgang was staring down at her. "Good thinking, tripping those men like that."

His brown eyes were soft, sending a warmth all through her middle—but only for a moment. His jaw stiffened as he gave her a crooked frown.

"And good work not getting killed in your first battle."

"What are you talking about?" Another man came up behind them and slapped Mulan on the shoulder. "This man saved your life."

"Weren't you supposed to be fighting, not watching us like a little girl at a miracle play?" Wolfgang scowled at the man.

The man bristled. "I had just dispatched my man. Left him gurgling on his last breath."

Mulan's head felt light, and her vision went a little dark. She breathed in and out, focusing on a tree in the distance. *Pretty tree . . . It would be prettier in the spring, no doubt . . .*

"Your first battle?" The man leaned over to peer into her face. "Good work!" He laughed and slammed his big hand into her back—a friendly pat, though it nearly sent her to her knees.

Mulan straightened, focusing her mind on Wolfgang's chest— very broad—and the new man's face—very pockmarked—and the grass—very green. But they couldn't keep away the memory, the feel of her blade entering under the soldier's arm where the breast- plate ended, the slicing of his flesh as the sharp blade penetrated his mail shirt.

Tree. Wolfgang's chest. The man's pockmarks. Andrei.

Andrei. Thank goodness Andrei was here. He was gazing at

her with a look of half caution, half fear. He seemed about to speak, but Wolfgang took a step toward her.

"Thank you. You did . . . help. With those two."

"Well, you saved me a moment before that, or I would be dead myself."

"All in a day's fighting." Wolfgang's face cracked into a smile.

Her heart tripped over itself at his masculine chin and jawline. *So handsome.*

He reached his hand toward her. She wasn't quite sure what he wanted. She held out her own hand and he clasped her arm. She mimicked the action and clasped his. Then he let go and took a step back.

"It's always a good fight when we rout the Teutonic Knights and send them retreating," the man said, first facing Mulan, then turning to Wolfgang. "And I wasn't talking about how he saved you. What about the way he climbed that mountain face when no one else even considered it? He scaled that wall like a tree squirrel and saved the castle. They were just about to break through the door when he led us all in firing the arrows that stopped them. Very brave." He nodded.

Several other soldiers had gathered while he was talking and they raised a cheer. "Mikolai the Lithuanian!"

Andrei's eyes were glowing. Mulan wasn't sure where to look. In her gruffest voice, she mumbled, "We all fought bravely."

But the next thing she knew, two burly men were lifting her up. They sat her on their shoulders and carried her toward the castle gatehouse where the horses were waiting.

Her heart was thumping hard. *O God, don't let me fall.* The ground was a long way down.

How could they make a hero out of her when she'd nearly

died? Would have died if not for Wolfgang. He was the hero. He knew how to fight with a sword, was brave and noble, leaping to her aid when he didn't even like her.

How he would hate her if he knew her secret.

The soldiers continued to cheer and laugh like men who had consumed too much strong drink. They all seemed to want to touch her. Some of them grasped her leg and shouted, while others were tall enough to slap her on the back. What an awkward place to be! But her fear was somewhat assuaged by the fact that they all thought she was a man.

When they placed her feet back on the ground, Captain Bogdan was calling and waving to her. Wolfgang stood beside the captain.

"Mikolai, Duke Konrad wishes to meet you and Wolfgang. We are expected at the castle now."

One of the duke's guards stood by waiting. Should she prepare her hair? She glanced down at her garments. Shirt and leather gambeson soiled with dirt and blood. Hose and shoes covered in dust, and everything baggy and hanging awkwardly. Her face would be covered in dust and dirt as well, her hair scraggly and grimy, half out of the leather thong holding it, but at least she couldn't be mistaken for a woman.

Still, as she walked with Wolfgang and Captain Bogdan, following Duke Konrad's guard, she wished she could wear a pretty dress, have her hair washed and arranged with flowers, before meeting her first nobleman—a duke, no less. But then again . . . she was meeting him as a warrior, a soldier who had fought well and helped save him and his castle and his people.

She lifted her chin and prayed she would not do anything embarrassing, like stumble over a pig and fall into a puddle on the floor.

The entrance hall of the castle was beautiful, with intricate, variegated designs worked into the floor and walls using colored stone. Huge fixtures loaded with candles hung from the ceiling as she and Wolfgang were ushered into the castle's Great Hall. The duke's colors and coat of arms hung on the wall in the form of banners and flags alongside shields and swords and battle-axes. Carved wooden panels graced the wall at one end of the long room. There, on a raised dais, a gray-haired man sat on a throne-like chair, dressed in armor.

He motioned them forward. The guard bowed and went to stand by the door, while Wolfgang and Mulan accompanied the captain to a few paces in front of the duke. Captain Bogdan and Wolfgang knelt and bowed. Mulan did the same, watching Wolfgang out of the corner of her eye for her cues.

"Captain Bogdan, I have heard the stories of the exploits of these two soldiers. And now I wish to know their names."

"Your Grace, allow me to present Wolfgang Gerstenberg, son of Duke Wilhelm of Hagenheim. And this is Mikolai, son of Mikolai, the Lithuanian, faithful soldier of liege lord Butautas."

Wolfgang remained on one knee, bowing before the duke in his polished armor.

"Rise."

The duke was probably thirty years older than she was, but she liked his face. Wrinkles radiated from the corners of his eyes, and he had not shaved in a couple of days, with gray whiskers showing on his chin and jaw.

"Thank you for coming to our aid, for your bravery." His voice was solemn. "Wolfgang, I knew your father and grandfather. The Dukes of Hagenheim have been our friends and allies these fifty years. I met with your grandfather on three different occasions, and he was a good friend of my father's. And I have met with Wilhelm on two occasions, and he impressed me very much with his integrity and piety. Your father is a good man." The duke studied him for a moment, tilting his head just slightly. "You look like him, I think."

Wolfgang bowed. "I am grateful you remember my father. He is a good man."

"And you, Mikolai. I believe I actually met your father as well, once when we were fighting with Butautas's men near the Lithuanian border. I remember him as a very strong, hard-fighting soldier. Rusdorf, who is the grand master of the German Order of Knights now, was only a commander then, but Paul von Rusdorf had a particular dislike for your father."

"My father?"

"Yes. It was his healing salve that he said his wife made for him. Rusdorf and his men were fighting, they said, to convert the heathen Lithuanians to Christ, but it was only a pretext to get revenge on their leader, King Vytautas, and take over the land. Rusdorf had injured many of our soldiers, but they were able to fight again soon afterward, and he found himself facing the same men he had wounded, sometimes only one day later.

"When he demanded what sort of pagan magic they were using to heal the men, someone told him, 'It is the healing salve of Mikolai the Lithuanian.' Rusdorf was furious, and he promised to reward any man who was able to capture Mikolai. But no one did. I'm sure you have heard this story."

"My father's attendant, Andrei, told me of it." Though Mulan had always considered her mother to be the hero of that story. Which might be why she'd never heard her father tell it. He never complimented her mother.

But Andrei said the Teutonic Knight was even more furious when he discovered the salve was created by a woman healer. He was known for saying that women were the devil's favorite instrument for doing evil and working pagan magic.

"Is your father among your company?"

"No, Your Grace. He died and was buried two weeks gone. A sickness."

"I am sure he would be proud of you."

Her mother's despondent face came to mind, standing before her father's grave, and tears sprang without warning to Mulan's eyes. She could not be seen crying! Men did not cry. Her heart thumped hard and she took a deep breath.

"It is good to meet God after having been a faithful soldier in this life. I am grateful for faithful soldiers such as yourself, your father, and Wolfgang here."

Mulan did her best to concentrate on the duke's words and dismiss the sad memory. Where did those tears come from anyway? She'd told herself she would not mourn her father's death, and indeed, she didn't weep for him, even when her mother did. But thankfully, her fear and awe of the duke in front of her helped her forget what had made the tears threaten, and the salt drops soon dried up.

CHAPTER 6

S teffan should have been fighting alongside him. They'd talked many times as boys about the battles they would one day fight together, attacking and defending castles, rescuing fair maidens in distress, making their own names famous. But Wolfgang was no longer sure what he wanted, and making his own name famous seemed foolish now. He suddenly wanted a nobler goal than that.

The duke was talking to Mikolai about his father. Wolfgang's heart went out to the boy, whose voice hitched when he spoke of his father having died only two weeks before. Thankfully, the duke didn't seem to notice, or at least he didn't call attention to it.

"You must stay for a small feast tonight, to celebrate today's victory. Perhaps soon we will drive the Teutonic Knights and their mercenary soldiers from our Polish homeland forever, and then we shall have a celebration the like of which has never been seen. Now we must be glad for even the smallest victory, to keep up the men's spirits, as many of my best men have fallen."

"You are very gracious to include us. And may God so will that your enemies be driven from Poland forever."

"I thank you." He nodded solemnly. "You may bathe now and prepare yourself for the feast. I have arranged for my servants to give you whatever you need." Duke Konrad motioned with his hand, and a guard stepped forward and escorted them out and down the corridor.

A bath would be quite a blessing after being in battle and away from home for so long, sleeping every night on the ground. But when he glanced over at Mikolai, his face had gone pale.

As they walked he whispered, "Are you well?"

Mikolai stared at him a moment. "Of course. Yes. Perfectly well."

But he still looked as if he had just been told he was going to the executioner instead of to a bathing room.

Mulan's stomach turned flips at the thought of taking a bath. Would she be allowed to bathe in private? She knew these wealthy people often bathed together, and certainly always had their servants attending to them even in their baths.

This was not how she'd wanted to end her soldiering.

They entered a small room that contained a hearth and two wooden tubs large enough for a man to sit in and stretch his legs part of the way out. Two servants, both female, were pouring water into the tubs. They looked up, curtsied slightly, then scurried out of the room, leaving drying cloths hanging beside the tubs and two sets of clean clothing.

Glancing desperately around the room, Mulan spotted a tall, freestanding screen fitted with a large tapestry. Could she somehow hide behind that screen while she disrobed? Her cheeks heated.

"Why don't you go ahead and bathe?" Wolfgang was taking off his leather gambeson. "I need to visit the garderobe. And I think I'll see if I can procure some food from the kitchen."

"But I thought we were invited to a feast?"

"Yes, but it will be an hour or two at least— Oh, here's a servant."

An older woman came in the open door and curtsied. She spoke and Mulan strained her ears, but she couldn't make out what the woman was saying. It must have been a Polish dialect or accent that she wasn't familiar with.

Wolfgang answered her. "Can you show me the way to the garderobe? And then could you be so kind as to fetch us a bit of bread and butter?" He smiled at her as if she were a woman of dignity and honor.

The woman began chattering, smiling, and nodding. Wolfgang started to follow her.

"Wait."

Wolfgang and the servant turned to look at her.

"I don't understand," Mulan said under her breath.

"Don't understand?"

"What she said. What is she saying?"

"Oh, she asked if there was anything we would be needing. Now she's taking me to the garderobe."

"Well, could you tell her I don't need anything and please not to come back until after I've had my bath?"

Wolfgang smiled slightly and nodded. "If you wish."

Mulan breathed a sigh as they left the room, the woman chattering away, but she lurched toward the screen and dragged it across the floor until it completely shielded one of the tubs. She snatched up half the drying cloths and the smaller set of clothing and tossed them on the floor by the tub. Then, huddling behind the tapestry, she threw off her clothes and jumped into the tub.

The water was almost too warm. Would she be scalded? But as she eased herself down, her skin grew used to the heat. She sat on the bottom, which was covered with waxed leather to keep the water from seeping through the cracks, and leaned back.

The water came up to her neck, and she was able to tuck her knees under the water. She closed her eyes, soaking in the heated bath.

If only she could take her time and enjoy it.

Her eyes popped open and she caught sight of the hunk of soap on the floor beside her. She used it to scrub herself, every moment fearing someone would enter the room and find her there. Should she take the time to wash her hair? It seemed worth the risk, and Wolfgang was kind enough not to come around the screen if she asked him not to. He would think she was a shy boy unwilling to be seen by the woman servant, matronly as she appeared. Hopefully he wouldn't suspect the real reason behind her modesty.

She dunked her head underneath the water and rubbed her scalp with the soap. She moved fast and dunked her head again, using her fingertips to massage all the soap out. As soon as she finished, she stood, let the water roll off her, grabbed a drying cloth, and wiped her body. She wrapped another cloth around her hair, stepped out, and snatched up the clothes that had been supplied to her.

They were so small! The hose and shirt would fit much more snugly than the ones she had been wearing, and her thick, heavy gambeson was too soiled to wear to a feast. She eyed the other set of clothes, obviously meant for Wolfgang, longing to take them instead. But it would be embarrassing when Wolfgang returned and all he had to don were the garments that were too small for him. He would demand she swap with him.

No, she couldn't do that.

So she pulled on the tight hose, her damp fingers shaking. Then she drew the shirt over her head. She tugged on the bottom. It barely covered hers. She'd have to be careful not to raise her arms. Someone would surely notice she was curvier than a man would be. At least she was not well-endowed on top, and the shirt was loose enough not to show anything. Still, she'd be nervous about the shirt getting drawn tight across her chest.

Lord, help me.

She took a deep breath and looked down at herself. With any luck, no one would notice she was in any way womanly.

But her hair! She'd nearly forgotten. Rubbing it vigorously with the drying cloth, she searched for her leather hair string. Her hair was short, but Andrei had said, "You have to keep your hair tied back."

"Why?" she asked.

"Trust me. You look too much like a girl when it's not."

Her face was also clean now. Anyone could see, if they peered closely enough, that she had no whiskers on her face. None. At all.

Her hands began to shake again when she didn't see the leather thong anywhere. She squeezed her eyes shut. Where had she taken it off? Or had it fallen out somewhere?

She went over to where her dirty clothes lay on the floor, snatched them up one by one, and shook them. Then she saw it lying on the colorful tile floor.

She huffed a sigh of relief and picked it up.

"Finished already?"

Mulan let out a squeak and spun around. Wolfgang stood staring at her with wide eyes.

Wolfgang halted in midstride. Had he walked in on a woman? No, it was just Mikolai, but with his wet hair hanging down by his cheeks . . . Wolfgang would never want the boy to know he had mistaken him for a girl. He'd probably challenge him to a fight of some sort, and Wolfgang didn't want to have to defeat him again.

But why had Mikolai cried out? Was he so afraid of someone walking in on him? Strange, strange boy.

"Oh, you just startled me. I was . . ." Mikolai cleared his throat. "I was just searching for my hair tie." He held it up. "Found it." He quickly snatched his hair back.

"Well, I can hardly wait for my bath. It's been too long since I've had a proper one." Wolfgang pulled his shirt over his head and tossed it on the floor. He started to take off his hose, and Mikolai scurried away as if he was trying to hide behind the screen.

"The servant is bringing us some dried fruit, bread, and cheese. Will you meet her at the door?"

"Oh, yes."

Why did the lad seem so nervous? And why was he hiding behind that screen?

Wolfgang stepped into the tub and sank into the water. It was still quite warm thankfully. He closed his eyes. Nothing would stop him from enjoying this bath. He felt his muscles relax, all the tension of the battle melting away . . . the ugly resentment of watching Mikolai scale that rock face when Wolfgang didn't even think it was possible . . . of seeing Mikolai reap the glory of victory, being carried on the other soldiers' shoulders. It all seeped out of him as he remembered how Mikolai had saved his life, how the lad had been so brave, in spite of his lack of brute strength and skill with the sword. Respect had welled up inside him at the heart the boy had displayed.

Wolfgang had even felt a bit guilty for how he'd treated him. But the fact that he had also saved Mikolai, at least once, during the heat of battle . . . He felt a kinship with the boy, a bond that was somehow similar to his bond with Steffan.

Steffan. He took a deep breath and let it out, trying to release the tension that suddenly formed a knot in the middle of his back.

His water would be getting cold soon, so he emptied his mind and just focused on how good it felt to be soaking in a tub of warmth.

A knock sounded at the door. Was that a groan he heard?

Mikolai shuffled out from behind the screen and went to the door, pulling at his new clothing. He didn't look quite so small and childlike wearing garments that weren't drooping and hanging off of him, but he seemed ill at ease.

"Bring some food over here," Wolfgang called over his shoulder.

Silence. Finally he heard quiet footsteps padding up behind him.

"Do you want to wait until you get out?"

"Just give me a handful of something." Wolfgang held out a hand, his eyes still closed. Finally he felt something being pressed into his palm. He opened his eyes, but Mikolai was still behind him. He shoveled the handful of raisins and nuts into his mouth, then held his hand out again. "Got any cheese?"

Wolfgang swiveled his head around to see why Mikolai was so quiet. The boy's eyes were closed, as if he were in pain!

"Mikolai?" He turned his body and looked up at him.

The boy's eyes flew open. He held his gaze as steadily as one of those hypnotized snakes in the Holy Lands, as if terrified to turn away.

"What's the matter?"

"Nothing. Here's some cheese." He placed the cheese in his hand and stared down at the floor.

He didn't tell the boy he was being strange, for he must know it himself. Wolfgang watched him a minute longer, then took a bite of the cheese and sat back in his bath.

"Will you not eat any of the food?"

Mikolai shuffled away. "Of course. I am." The last two words were muffled by food. At least he was not too addled to eat.

The water was already starting to cool, so he sank in over his head and proceeded to wash his hair and body with the soap. Finally, when the water was too cold to be relaxing, he stood in the tub and groaned at having to leave his comfortable position. Water sluiced off of him. When he'd dried himself, he donned the clean clothes that had been provided.

"It feels good to take a bath, huh, Mikolai?"

"It does." His voice came from behind the screen.

"Mikolai, were you injured somehow and just don't want to tell anyone?"

"No, I'm not injured. Why would you say that?"

"You are behaving strangely."

A pause, then, "I'm sitting down, resting and . . . contemplating."

"Are you feeling bad about your first real battle? Is that what's amiss?" His father had told him about the effects of battle, nervousness and guilt and such, especially after a soldier's first.

"I do feel a bit strange, about killing and injuring other men."

"I feel that way too." He was trying not to think about it, so why had he brought it up? But there was something Father used to say . . .

"It's important not to ignore it—the harsh ugliness of killing, that is."

"What do you mean?"

"My father says a soldier can become hardened to battle and to killing other human beings. Or . . . they can feel so guilty they can't stop thinking about it. They can't forgive themselves, and they don't believe God forgives them."

"Oh yes. I've heard of knights who go on pilgrimages to try to receive forgiveness of their sins, or who think they need to perform some feat or quest to have their guilt absolved."

"Exactly."

"Truthfully, I'm not thinking I'm in danger of either of those things."

"Good. Have you eaten all the food I went to so much trouble to acquire for us?"

"So much trouble? All you did was ask a servant to fetch it for you."

"Yes, but I asked her, didn't I?"

Mikolai laughed, a rather musical sound. One eye appeared around the edge of the tapestry screen, then he came toward Wolfgang carrying the food tray. They shared the rest of the food, and Wolfgang realized Mikolai was not behaving in the odd, nervous way he had before. They talked and laughed until a servant came to fetch them for the feast.

At the banquet in the same large hall where they had met Duke Konrad, the duke introduced them to the crowd. One of the duke's own soldiers who had fought in the battle explained their brave acts—embellishing and exaggerating them a bit, Wolfgang thought. When he glanced at Mikolai, he was grimacing, too, also embarrassed. But everyone around them cheered and made so much noise, it seemed impractical to correct him. So they accepted the praise as graciously and modestly as possible.

The food was delicious. As barren and oppressed as the area had been due to the recent raids from the Teutonic Knights, Wolfgang was in awe of such sustenance—pheasant, eel, pork, eggs, and several fruits that were stewed and spiced and poured over the meat. He'd not had a meal this good since he left Hagenheim. But he could hardly enjoy it, wondering what their fellow soldiers were eating back in camp.

CHAPTER 7

Wolfgang and Mikolai arrived back at the field where the men would be sleeping that night. The few small fires burning around them, along with the full moon, illuminated Mikolai's face as they walked toward their respective tents. He looked as if he wanted to say something. Wolfgang nodded at him and he stopped.

"Do you know what is next for us?"

Wolfgang fixed his eyes on him. He had disliked the boy, but that was only because of his clumsiness during the archery contest. Since then he'd shown bravery and resourcefulness. He was not the most skilled soldier, but his courage had made up for it. And he was younger, probably only seventeen or eighteen, and Wolfgang felt a certain protectiveness toward him.

And yet, at the same time, an uneasiness, almost a suspicion toward the boy, nagged at him.

"It seems we were able to rout the enemy because most of their men were out gathering supplies from the peasants in the countryside. They were unaware of our presence and thought they could attack the castle without the bulk of their troops."

Mikolai nodded thoughtfully.

"For now, we are waiting to see how and where they attack next."

Mikolai grunted, as if trying to appear more manly. He had such a baby face.

"Where did your father fight?"

"Many places. He owed fealty to his lord, Butautas, who was allied with Duke Konrad and most of the noblemen of Poland and Lithuania. He also did some fighting in the Kievan Rus."

"Is that where your mother was from?"

"It was thought she was Mongolian, but I don't remember her."

Perhaps that was rude of him to ask. Of course Mikolai wouldn't want to talk about something so personal. And perhaps painful as well, by the look on his face. His birth must have been illegitimate, but half the men here were born outside of wedlock, with fathers who were dukes or earls or margraves.

"You knew your father?"

"My father was rarely at home." Mikolai shrugged. "I didn't see him often, and he died two weeks ago."

"Two weeks is a short time. I'm very sorry."

Mikolai waved his hand. "Do not feel sorry. I didn't mourn him."

"You didn't mourn at all?"

Mikolai rubbed a hand down the side of his face.

There seemed to be no stubble at all on Mikolai's jaw and chin.

"I was sorry he was dead, of course, for my mother's sake." He was not looking Wolfgang in the eye.

"But I thought your mother was . . ."

"Dead. Yes, but the woman who raised me was Mikolai's wife, Feodosia. I have always called her Mother. She was a good mother to me. She had no other children."

Something about Mikolai's manner heightened Wolfgang's suspicion. Was the boy hiding something?

"I hope I don't sound as if I wish to dishonor my father. He was my father, after all."

"Of course. Understood."

"So, what is your reason for being here? Did your father send you to fight?"

"He was sending a small band of his knights and soldiers to fight for Konrad, and he gave my brother and me permission to join them."

"Your brother is here, too, then?"

"No, he did not . . . join us."

"And your father is a duke, I heard."

"Yes, the Duke of Hagenheim."

"German, is it not? Why did you not join with the German Teutonic Knights?" A tiny smile graced Mikolai's face as a brow quirked up.

"My father doesn't like the Teutonic Knights' practices. They oppress other people for their own gain, and my father does not—I do not—approve of that."

Mikolai was studying him with such calm interest, almost concern, in his eyes.

"My brother, who left Hagenheim with me, vanished from our group a few days ago. I only hope . . ." Wolfgang shook his head. "He doesn't listen to me anymore, if he ever did. We were such good friends as children, being close in age, but he has chosen a rebellious path."

"I'm sure that causes you pain. But prayer is powerful, as our priest says. What is his name? I shall pray for him."

"Steffan."

Mikolai seemed as if he might reach out and hug him, but then he took a step back and cleared his throat.

"I thank you for that. All will be well, no doubt." Wolfgang nodded. "Nothing is too hard for God, and He will surely hear the prayers my parents speak for Steffan. They are godly people." Next he'd be telling this boy his deepest secrets. It was almost as if Mikolai had put a spell on him. Was he some kind of spy for the Teutonic Knights?

Shouts came from the other side of the field. Wolfgang turned his head, his nose and throat suddenly stinging at the smell of smoke.

The shouts grew louder and the horses whinnied. A faint orange glow came from the direction of where the horses were tethered. Mikolai bolted toward them, and Wolfgang was right behind him.

Mulan raced to her tent.

Andrei was with the horses, untying Aksoma. Mulan seized Boldheart's bridle and untied him as fast as she could. *Stay calm, Mulan. Be strong and brave.* Her heart pounded. The Teutonic Knights had to be behind this. They would be setting the fire all the way around them to block them in and burn them and their horses alive. *God, save us.*

Andrei grabbed her bundle out of her hands and tied it to the saddle. Then he turned and took a step.

Mulan grasped him by the arm. "Where are you going?"

"To get the rest of our things, our tent—"

"No."

"Your father's sword!" He broke free from her grasp and ran like a rabbit, twisting his way through the crowd of men running all around, shouting.

Mulan gripped the reins of both horses. The sound of licking, consuming flames sent a tremor through her limbs. Her pounding heart stole her breath.

She couldn't leave Andrei.

She hurried after him, pulling the horses behind her. Aksoma's eyes were wide and wild. She wasn't trained as Boldheart was for chaos and danger and loud noises. Would Aksoma bolt? Mulan wrapped her reins around her wrist.

Men swarmed around her, impeding her progress across the field toward their tent, as the sky began to glow orange.

Andrei emerged from the tent with a big bundle, her father's sword hanging at an awkward angle. Mulan pulled it from his arms.

"Get on your horse!" Andrei flung himself, the bundle still in his arms, into Aksoma's saddle.

The flames were getting closer. A tree behind Andrei transformed into a giant torch as it suddenly burst into red-orange color.

Mulan struggled to scale Boldheart's great height without help, but how could she slow Andrei by making him get down to boost her into the saddle? *God, help me.*

She grasped the saddle horn with both hands, the sword handle wedged between her hand and the saddle. With her foot in the stirrup, she pushed and pulled with all her might.

Lying across the saddle on her belly, she nearly dropped the sword but held on as she used her other hand to push herself up to sitting.

Andrei urged Aksoma forward. She whinnied, reared up, and then bolted forward. Mulan followed after them on big black Boldheart.

The ring of fire was nearly complete, but horses and men were charging toward one tiny opening about as wide as one horse length. Men were beating at the flames on either side of it with blankets, but the flames seemed to grow bigger with their efforts and they soon stopped.

Suddenly horses screamed, and the shouts took on a sharper tone. Mulan watched as a rider was flung from his horse, an arrow sticking out of his chest. Another horse and rider both went down in a heap beside him, arrows protruding from their bodies.

The Teutonic Knights were picking them off as they rode through the opening in the fire ring.

"Andrei! Stop!" Mulan screamed at him. How could she bear it if he and Aksoma were killed?

Andrei hauled back on the reins, stopping Aksoma short, and looked back at her.

"Where is my bow?" she yelled.

Andrei dug through the bundle that lay across the saddle in front of him and pulled out her longbow and quiver. She grabbed them and nocked an arrow. She searched through the flames. There stood Wolfgang, just on the other side of the flames, shooting one arrow after another into the darkness where the Teutonic Knights were launching arrows at their riders.

Mulan strained her eyes toward where he was shooting, but because of the bright flames, she could see nothing past the light of the fire. She shot a few arrows in that direction anyway. She had to cross these flames, to get to the other side and help Wolfgang, because where he had positioned himself he was almost certain to be shot.

Other men were reining in their horses as they saw their fellow soldiers go down. They milled about, fury and confusion on their faces.

She glanced around, then motioned for Andrei to follow her

as she turned Boldheart hard to the right, following alongside the flames, searching for a place where the fire was not so high. There was one spot, and she headed toward it. But just before she crossed, some movement caught her eye. A Teutonic soldier aimed an arrow at Andrei.

"Andrei, get down!" Mulan screamed.

He ducked his head. The arrow hummed past Mulan's ear as she nocked an arrow to her own bow and sent it in the archer's direction. Unable to tell if her arrow found its mark, Mulan turned her horse back toward the way they had come.

The big black gelding bounded forward. She glanced back to make sure Andrei and Aksoma were following. If they didn't escape from the ring of fire, the smoke could kill them. It was already so thick she could hardly breathe, her throat burning.

She had to get back to Wolfgang. But first she had to make sure Andrei and Aksoma escaped the smoke. She turned and waited for them to catch up to her.

Aksoma's eyes were glowing white in the firelight. She kept raising her head and pulling back against the reins, pulling up short. "No, Aksoma. Trust us." But her horse reared, her front legs lifting off the ground. Then she danced sideways.

Mulan leapt off Boldheart's back. She pulled him along behind her, took off her hood from around her neck, and draped it over Aksoma's head, covering her eyes. She tied it in place.

She tried to get back into Boldheart's saddle, but her arms were too weak. She fell back to the ground. "God, give me strength." She grasped the pommel tighter and used her leg muscles to push as hard as she could. Scrambling the last bit, she found herself sitting high atop her horse.

She motioned Andrei forward, and pushing Boldheart into a

gallop, she aimed him straight toward the fire. He leapt at the last moment, and they burst through the line of flames.

She pulled on the reins, stopping him. An arrow sailed past her and stuck in the ground thirty paces away. She took note of the angle and direction from which it came and, almost without thought, nocked an arrow to her bow and spotted the archer aiming at her. She shot. The arrow struck him in the arm. He cried out and dropped his bow.

She turned around to see Aksoma, with Andrei on her back, gallop through the fire. She only hoped her hooves would be tough enough to withstand the heat. She'd check for burns and injuries later.

Now that they were on the outside of the ring of fire, she sent Boldheart galloping toward where she'd last seen Wolfgang. He was kneeling behind the body of a fallen horse and shooting one arrow after another—as if he didn't have an arrow's shaft protruding from his shoulder.

Her stomach churned at the sight. She leaned close to Boldheart's neck and urged him forward.

Wolfgang again caught sight of, out of the corner of his eye, the shaft of an arrow sticking out of his shoulder. The sharp, aching pain was distracting, but it wouldn't kill him, not in the next hour, anyway. So he reached for another arrow, nocked it, and shot. He had to keep up the pressure on the archers or they would kill every rider who came through the gap in the fire.

The pounding of a horse's hooves broke into his thoughts. Mikolai pulled his big gelding to a halt behind him. A moment later, he was kneeling beside Wolfgang with his longbow in his hands and a quiver of arrows.

Men and horses were still pouring through the gap. A few others had positioned themselves farther away from the gap to shoot back at the Teutonic Knights and their men, but Mikolai was the only one brave enough to join him so close to the gap.

Mikolai shot at a reckless pace, exposing himself more often than not. Any moment he might be fatally shot.

Wolfgang shot another arrow and started to think that no one was shooting back. Had they left? He stared hard at the rocky outcropping from whence the arrows had come. Mikolai was still shooting, so he set his hand on his arm.

Mikolai paused and stared at Wolfgang's shoulder, which was starting to seize up as the muscles convulsed around the foreign object.

They both waited and listened. The only sound was the crackling of the fire and the occasional sound of another horse and rider escaping through the gap, probably unaware of the enemy lying in wait nearby. But now Wolfgang was fairly certain they had withdrawn, as no more arrows came.

He sat back and gasped, the pain in his shoulder taking his breath away. He squeezed his eyes shut. *Don't pass out.* He took in a breath and let it out. Then another.

"Are you all right?" Mikolai's eyes were wide as they stared at his shoulder.

"*Ach, ja.* I'll live, whether I want to or not." He didn't want to sound weak. "Only a shoulder wound." But his vision was not terribly clear. If he fell over, he hoped he'd fall on the other side and not on the arrow.

"Someone should see to that. Can I fetch a healer for you?"

"We don't travel with a healer. If you could break off the point and pull it out, I'd be grateful. And hand me some bandages from my saddlebag." He pointed to the bag that lay beside him on the ground.

Mikolai's mouth fell open.

"Or you can go get someone else to do it."

People were beginning to examine the men who lay on the ground, ascertaining who was seriously injured and who was dead.

Mikolai stood and hoisted his bag. He eventually pulled out a roll of bandages. His poor mother had prayed over those bandages, hoping he'd never have to use them.

Andrei ran toward them.

"Are Aksoma and Boldheart well?" Mikolai's voice sounded quite feminine. Could it be? Surely not. Something about him reminded Wolfgang of his sisters.

Ridiculous. What woman would pretend to be a soldier?

Mikolai turned back to Wolfgang and, without warning, grabbed the arrow sticking out of his back and broke it.

Searing pain shot through his body, radiating from his left shoulder. He cried out, then fell over onto his right side. If only he could lose his senses, but no. He heard Andrei say, "Let me do it." Then the arrow shaft was ripped out from the front.

Were a thousand splinters tearing through his flesh in that moment? Surely it only seemed that way. He gritted his teeth to keep from crying out again, coughing and grinding his teeth instead.

Someone was pressing hard against the front and back of the wound. He closed his eyes again. *It's only a shoulder wound.* Wolfgang forced himself to sit up. He leaned his back against the dead horse he'd been taking shelter behind. While Mikolai pressed the bandages to his wounds, Andrei tied them in place.

Sweat beaded on Wolfgang's face, and the cool night breeze sent a chill down his spine. Mikolai's grim face was near to his, so near he could see the smoothness of his cheeks. Either he was much younger than he claimed or . . . Well, he must be very young.

Thinking about Mikolai and Andrei, trying to remember everything he knew about them, helped distract Wolfgang from the pain.

"Should we get some moss to stanch the blood flow?" Mikolai said to Andrei, this time in a gruffer voice. Was it his imagination that Mikolai was forcing the gruffness?

"I think he'll be fine." Andrei shook his head. "It's not bleeding that much."

Even at twelve, Andrei had a more masculine look about his brows and mouth than Mikolai.

It was unkind and unjust of him to think such things about his fellow soldier. Mikolai had proven himself a worthy fighter, had been wildly brave more than once. Surely no woman would be so brave in battle. Women were squeamish and skittish. Few women could break off an arrow shaft sticking out of a man's body as Mikolai had.

How disrespectful of Wolfgang to speculate about him this way.

Mikolai had proven himself a friend. After all that they had been through already, Wolfgang now trusted him almost as much as any other soldier he had met.

He steeled himself against the pain that movement would cause and made an effort to stand. Mikolai immediately grabbed Wolfgang's right arm, then placed himself under it, serving as a crutch.

Wolfgang leaned on Mikolai and took a step as Gerke ran over to him, pulling his horse behind him. "I was afraid you were killed!"

"I am far from killed." He kept moving toward his horse, and when he reached it, Mikolai backed away and let Gerke help him into the saddle.

Mikolai looked as if he wanted to say something but then pressed his lips together and gave him a quick nod.

The back of Wolfgang's neck prickled, but the pain in his shoulder soon drove away all thoughts beyond the agony in his body.

CHAPTER 8

Mulan stared down at the sticky red blood drying on her hands and shuddered. As she walked back to Andrei, who was holding their horses, she couldn't help remembering Wolfgang's face contorting, the guttural sounds of pain coming from his throat.

She had to do as he asked and break the arrow sticking out the back of his shoulder, so she'd turned around and done it without warning him first, before she had time to really think about what she was doing. But when she tried to prepare herself to pull out the arrow . . . Thankfully Andrei was there so she didn't have to.

Her knees wobbled when she thought about it.

But it was over. Wolfgang would live, God willing.

She examined Aksoma's legs and hooves the best she could in the waning light. Men were beating at the fire with blankets, and most of it appeared to be extinguished. Both horses had come through the ordeal seemingly unscathed.

A body was carried past her. But as sad and horrific as the sight of the bloodied face was, the image she saw when she closed her eyes was the pain on Wolfgang's face as she broke off the arrow that impaled his body.

Wolfgang groaned as he turned over on the hard ground, waking himself up. The medicinal herbs the town healer had given him were burned up in the fire, along with his tent and blankets. Gerke had only been able to save his clothes and weapons. And now he'd trade all his clothing—well, most of it—for something to ease the pain in his shoulder.

But he shouldn't complain. So many men had worse injuries. And at least he wasn't dead.

The light of dawn was beginning to illuminate the scene around him. His fellow soldiers were bedding down among the trees now, where there was less grass and dry brush to burn. Some had escaped with their tents, but many, like him, were sleeping without any shelter.

"Wolfgang? Is that you?" someone called out in a whisper.

He rolled over, groaning again. Mikolai crouched beside him.

"I brought something that will hasten the healing of your wounds." Mikolai held out a leather pouch. "It's a paste my mother makes. But it works, I can assure you, and will certainly not harm you in any way."

Wolfgang took it from his hand and sniffed. "It smells foul." Like garlic and old cheese.

"My mother used it on a boy in our village whose leg had turned putrid with disease after a broken bone punched through the skin. After several applications of this, his leg healed and mended as good as new. She always used it on my father's cuts and injuries. Even if the injuries were many days old, this always cured them."

"You don't have to convince me. I'll try anything."

Mikolai glanced around. Wolfgang turned to look for Gerke, but the boy must have gone to relieve himself. His place was vacant.

Wolfgang sat up and pulled his shirt up and over his head, then wrapped it around his middle to keep warm. Mikolai squatted beside him. His eyes were wide but focused on the bandage, and he started unrolling the cloth.

Mikolai dipped his small hand in the foul-smelling ointment and smeared it into the bloody hole in his shoulder. Wolfgang clenched his teeth to keep from crying out and embarrassing himself.

Mikolai moved to the back, and Wolfgang leaned forward as he smeared the cold green mess into the hole in the back of his shoulder. Then he cut the bloody end of the bandage off and wrapped the rest over his shoulder and under his arm to keep it in place. The entire time Mikolai was quiet, his eyes wide, darting nervously past his shoulder but never looking him in the eye.

And again, Wolfgang couldn't help noticing that Mikolai had a very smooth, young-looking face. He seemed to be deliberately smearing dirt on his face to disguise the fact that he had no beard at all.

"Here. I'll give this to you." Mikolai thrust the leather pouch at him. "Put it on thrice a day."

Wolfgang nodded. "I thank you."

Mikolai averted his gaze. He stood and hurried away.

A strange lad. But it was kind of him to bring Wolfgang his wound remedy.

Mulan bent and entered her leather tent through the small opening.

"Where have you been?" Andrei folded his arms in front of his chest. "Did you just take your mother's curative to that Wolfgang?"

Mulan stared back at him. "What do you mean? He is wounded, so yes, I took some to him." Mulan pretended to search for something in her bag.

"What will you do if *you* get wounded?"

Mulan kept her back to him and pretended not to hear.

"Mulan"—he lowered his voice—"what *will* you do if you get wounded?" Then he lowered his voice even more to a low whisper. "You must not let them take off your clothes."

"Do you think I'm daft?" Mulan spun around and pinned him with a glare. "I would never—" She huffed and turned away, rubbing a hand through her cropped-off hair.

She shouldn't get angry at Andrei, but he'd pointed out her biggest fear.

When they'd had to take baths at Duke Konrad's castle, she narrowly escaped seeing far more than she wished of Wolfgang. She'd had to keep her eyes carefully averted. But when Wolfgang had taken off his linen shirt and bared his chest so she could rub Mother's salve on his wound, once again she'd had to avert her eyes. He was the most handsome man she'd ever been around, and it was difficult to stop thinking about that fact—and about how he made her feel. Thankfully, he had no idea. But if she'd been the one to take an arrow to the shoulder . . .

"And what if," Andrei went on, "you are so badly wounded that you lose your senses?"

"You won't let anyone take my clothes off."

"What if I'm not there?"

"I just have to not get injured." Mulan gave her young friend a smile. One of them had to pretend not to worry.

"And as for this Wolfgang, you need to stay away from him. What will he do when he discovers you're a woman? As much as you seek him out—"

"I do not seek him out. What do you speak of? And how will he ever discover I'm a woman? He sees me as a soldier. Have I not proven myself?"

Andrei's skinny shoulders rose with a deep breath, then sank as he blew it out. "You need to be careful around him. I've seen something on his face when he looks at you. He is suspicious."

"Andrei, I never thought of you fretting like an old woman." She tried to laugh, but he just glared at her and shook his head.

She could tell he was angry with her when he didn't speak to her for a while as she sat mending some torn hose and he cleaned and polished her sword.

"You want to marry him, don't you?" Andrei finally broke the silence.

"What? Who?"

"Wolfgang. You wish you could marry him."

"That's a foolish thing to say." Some emotion she didn't want to name forced a hard edge into her voice. "And I'm no fool. His father is a duke. He would never think about a poor Lithuanian, the illegitimate daughter of a soldier." But the truth of that statement made her bite her lip. *Remember that, when you're thinking how handsome he is and how kind and noble he seems.*

Shouts sounded from outside their tent. Mulan threw down her mending and hastened to see what it was.

Wolfgang shrugged off the pain in his shoulder, which already felt somewhat better, probably due to Mikolai's salve.

He pulled on his quilted gambeson, readying to take his turn to scout out the area around the castle, when he heard shouting.

He grabbed his sword. Gerke strapped it to his back. Wolfgang took his longbow and quiver of arrows and ran toward the commotion.

"Teutonic Knights are burning the fields and houses of the villagers." A soot-covered soldier hurried toward a horse, mounted, and galloped away.

Captain Bogdan strode toward him. "Wolfgang!" He glanced around and pointed at Mikolai, motioning him forward with his hand. "Go to the river road and follow it until you see where they've been burning. Climb one of the trees, hide, and strike the Teutonic Knights when they start coming this way."

Wolfgang locked eyes with Mikolai. They both ran toward the road.

Wolfgang dodged around the tents, leaping over bushes and bedrolls. When he glanced over his shoulder, Mikolai was close behind. He didn't have his sword, but his longbow and quiver were fastened to his back.

He smelled smoke, bringing back the memories of the night before. He pressed on, and soon the only sound was of his and Mikolai's footsteps tramping through the brush alongside the road that followed the river. The pain in his shoulder shot down his arm and up his neck like little bolts of lightning, but he refused to give it heed.

They trotted along until they reached a field that was charred and still smoking. A pile of blackened wood and debris sent white smoke snaking up. Near it, a woman was holding a small child and weeping. The child clung tighter to the woman's arms. His eyes were wide and hollow as they tracked Wolfgang and Mikolai over his mother's shoulder.

"Hello there," Wolfgang called out softly. "What has happened here?"

The woman turned around and shifted the child to her hip.

"What has happened?" She stared at him with her mouth agape, her face red and tear streaked. "The Teutonic Knights and their evil soldiers have stolen our food and burned everything. Was it not enough that they killed my husband and my oldest son? Can no one stop them? Is the devil so powerful in this land? It matters not who rules because there is naught left for me."

"Duke Konrad will welcome you and your child inside Zachev Castle's walls. There are provisions and protection there."

She spat on the ground. "And who will protect me from the protectors, now that I have no husband?"

The angry tears in her eyes and the ragged tone in her voice sent a tremor through his gut. His mind raced to think of something he might do. But how could he help them?

Mikolai reached into his leather bag and drew out two bread rolls. He held them out, and the child took one in each little soot-covered hand.

Wolfgang stepped closer to the woman and waited for her to look him in the eye. "When you go to the castle, tell them Wolfgang Gerstenberg and Mikolai of Lithuania are your protectors. If anyone lays a hand on you or your child, they'll answer to us."

She stared back at him, then lowered her eyes.

Wolfgang dug in his bag and handed her a small round of cheese.

"I thank you," she said softly.

"What's your name?"

"Jacyna, widow of Oleszko."

"I shall come to the castle if I can and check on you and the child."

"And so shall I," Mikolai added.

The woman nodded.

CHAPTER 9

A heaviness settled on Wolfgang as he and Mikolai walked away, heading for the forest. He couldn't help muttering, "We have to stop these invaders before they kill even more innocent people."

His mother's face flashed across his mind's eye. She would be overcome with compassion if she could see the way these people were oppressed by the Teutonic Knights and their soldiers.

Women were much kinder creatures than men. They stayed at home, loving their husbands and children, taking care of orphans—at least, his mother did. She made sure they not only had enough food and a bed to sleep in, but that they also felt loved. And his four sisters were the same. They would never conceive of fighting and warring and killing people to get what they wanted.

But that wasn't true of all women. Some women were evil, such as his aunt Gothel, who had to remain locked away under guard, and the evil Ermengard, who had tortured his brother Gabe's wife, Sophie, and tried to kill her when she was a child.

And it was hard to accept what Steffan had done—defending the Teutonic Knights. He might have even done what he'd said he would do—joined up with them.

What was to become of his brother?

"We will stop them." Mikolai broke into his murky thoughts.

"Who? Oh, yes."

"I have heard that we will be greatly outnumbered when the Teutonic Knights' reinforcements arrive."

"I have heard that as well. But perhaps we have reinforcements coming too."

"Either way, I believe God will fight on our side." Mikolai's tone and expression showed quiet sincerity.

Perhaps Wolfgang could learn from a faith like his.

They entered a stand of trees that were relatively unscathed from the fire. They walked for a while longer, until they could see another open space ahead.

"I think this is where Captain Bogdan meant for us to hide." Wolfgang searched the limbs overhead. "If we can climb one of these trees, we can lie in wait for soldiers, should they pass this way to attack again."

Mikolai secured his longbow by looping his arm through it and hanging it on his shoulder, then started up the nearest beech tree, his hands and feet darting from one limb to the next.

Wolfgang gazed up at him.

"Aren't you coming up?" Mikolai grinned.

"Easy for you. You scampered up that tree as if your father were a tree squirrel."

Mikolai's grin grew wider.

Wolfgang was much bigger and heavier. But he couldn't let Mikolai laugh at him either. So he grabbed a limb and hoisted himself up, finding a foothold in the crook between the trunk and two branches. It took him much longer, especially hampered as he was by his injured shoulder, but finally he was as high as Mikolai. He settled himself as best he could on a branch and leaned back against the trunk.

"Not bad." Mikolai looked as comfortable as if he were propped up on a feather bed. "I've heard bears can climb trees. If my father was a squirrel, yours must have been a bear."

"Very amusing." After the climb, his shoulder was burning like coals of fire. He pressed on it through his gambeson and shirt, hoping it wasn't bleeding again.

"Is your shoulder paining you?"

"Not too much." Maybe some conversation would take his mind off the pain. "What made you wish to become a soldier like your father?"

The boy chewed his lip, as if he didn't know how to answer.

"You've obviously had a lot of practice with a longbow. You were trained to be a soldier like you father, *tak*?"

"Ah, well . . . yes. But my archery skills also come from the fact that I've been providing for my mother's table since I was a child—birds and badgers and small animals. I even shot a wild boar that was about to attack my horse. Also . . . I didn't want to stay in my little village my whole life. I wanted to see other lands. But mostly I wanted to provide for my mother. That's why I became a soldier."

"And your mother is alone now? Did she not mind you going away to fight?"

Mikolai's mouth twisted and he was looking down at his hands, over into the trees, anywhere but at him.

"I only ask because my mother didn't want me to come here and fight, but my father convinced her that sons want to be active, not staying at home."

"I imagine my mother felt the same, but she would have lost her house, would have had nowhere to live if I had not come to fight for our lord. But I'm sure she would have liked to have me close. She wished me to wed but . . . I wanted adventure, and to hear what other priests could teach me about God."

"That's what you wanted?"

"I always wanted to learn how to read, to read the Holy Writ for myself, but . . . I was poor, my father a simple soldier in his liege lord's service. And besides that, no one in my village knew how to read except the priest." Mikolai shrugged. "It was impossible."

"'With God all things are possible.' That's in the Holy Writ."

"Have you read the Scriptures?"

"Of course. I even have a portion I carry with me."

"Isn't that blasphemy? To separate one part from the whole and carry it around with you?" Mikolai's eyes were wide, and he may have turned a bit pale.

"Who gave you that idea?" Wolfgang reached inside his shirt and pulled out the First Epistle of Saint John. "I can read aloud while we wait."

"I would like that." The lad blinked rapidly. He would not cry, would he?

Wolfgang read for a while, then came to the part that said, "'Anyone who claims to be in the light but hates a brother or sister is still in the darkness. Anyone who loves their brother and sister lives in the light, and there is nothing in them to make them stumble. But anyone who hates a brother or sister is in the darkness and walks around in the darkness. They do not know where they are going, because the darkness has blinded them.'"

"Stop." Mikolai's brows were low as a wrinkle formed between his eyes. "What does that mean? Is 'brother or sister' everyone? Or only other believers? And shouldn't we ask a priest?"

"I may not know as much as a priest, but I think it means anyone in your life, any person you know. If you hate people, especially fellow believers, then you've been blinded by darkness, the darkness of the devil."

"Wouldn't some people say the Teutonic Knights are our brothers? They are believers and claim to be the righteous defenders of Christ."

"But just look at their deeds of darkness, attacking people who have no quarrel with them because they want their land and their castles. That is not righteous. Besides, this is war."

"Why would that make any difference?"

"God allowed His people to fight wars, even instructed them to do so. Sometimes war is necessary to right wrongs and defend the innocent." Wolfgang shrugged. "In truth, I don't think it's very clear, and there are different opinions about what it says. But that's what I believe."

Mikolai nodded, then sat frowning down at the paper in Wolfgang's hand. "But it is the Holy Writ, is it not? This is good. I have not heard these words before. You may read more if you wish." He raised his brows in a hopeful look.

"Someday I should teach you to read it—when we're not sitting in a tree."

"Me?"

"Of course. I could use the Bible to teach you. It's the only writing I brought with me."

Mikolai, rather than turning pale this time, seemed to be blushing.

Wolfgang started reading again. "'I am writing to you, dear children, because—'"

"Wait," Mikolai whispered, grabbing for his bow and an arrow.

Wolfgang reached for his own bow as a soldier wearing a white surcoat with the black cross appeared on the road below.

A very familiar-looking soldier.

Steffan.

Mikolai was pulling back the arrow, aiming it at Steffan.

Wolfgang grabbed Mikolai's arm. "Don't shoot," he said in a harsh whisper.

Mikolai lowered his bow.

Steffan looked up. Their eyes locked.

"What have you done?" Wolfgang heard the anguish in his voice even as he stuffed it down. How could he join when he knew he would be fighting his own brother? Hurting his parents, if they knew?

An angry sneer curled Steffan's lips. In the next moment he raised his bow and arrow and shot. Mikolai gasped and dropped his bow. He clutched his side and doubled over.

A red mist descended over Wolfgang's vision. He leapt from the tree.

Steffan's eyes went wide. He dropped his bow and was raising his hands when Wolfgang landed on top of him, sending them both to the ground.

Wolfgang wrapped his hands around Steffan's neck as a growl erupted from him. "You shot my friend! You fiend."

Steffan grabbed his wrists and pushed, but Wolfgang kept choking him. Steffan's face reddened as he pushed harder. Finally Wolfgang loosened his hold.

Steffan gasped for breath. "And now you try to kill me?"

"You are no brother to me," Wolfgang ground out through clenched teeth. "I shall take you back as my prisoner. At least we don't murder our prisoners the way the Teutonic Knights do."

"Before you take me prisoner, you should go save your *friend*. He's about to fall out of the tree."

Wolfgang imagined punching his brother's face. But he couldn't let Mikolai die. If he died, it would be Wolfgang's fault.

He used Steffan's shoulders to push himself up. Then he turned his back on him.

Just as Steffan had said, Mikolai was slowly tipping forward on the branch, wobbling, dangerously close to falling headfirst.

"Mikolai, I'm coming up to you." Wolfgang's heart pounded as he leapt onto the first branch and started climbing.

Mulan was falling. This was the end. She was about to die.

Something hard caught her around the waist, halting her fall. She was jostled and slung over someone's shoulder. Wolfgang. Then he started climbing down with her.

The sharp pain in her side made her draw a loud breath. *I have to stay awake.* What would happen if she lost her senses? She fought to keep her eyes open. But even with them wide open, darkness closed in on her.

They will find out my secret.

Not everyone in their troop of soldiers was as honorable as Wolfgang.

She felt herself being lowered to the ground onto her back.

Perhaps she wasn't badly injured. She took her hand off her side and held it up. Bright-red blood covered her palm.

Wolfgang's face hovered over her. "I'm so sorry. Please forgive me."

What was he saying? It made no sense.

"O God, please don't let it be bad." He took hold of the hem of her shirt and started to lift it.

"No." Mulan grabbed his wrist and held it as tight as she could.

She stared up at his face, but no matter how wide she opened her eyes, the edges continued to grow dark.

"Let me see." Wolfgang's voice was gruff and demanding. "I have to see how bad it is."

"Please." She stared up into his eyes. "Please, Wolfgang." Could she get away with not telling him?

"What is it? We have to stanch the bleeding." He was suddenly gone from her sight.

O God, please don't make me tell him.

Wolfgang returned with a roll of bandages. "Let me—"

"No! Please. It's not bad. Just . . . wrap it over my shirt."

"I'm not doing that. What's wrong with you?"

"Wolfgang, I'm not . . ."

"You *are* hurt bad."

"No, please listen. I need your help, please."

"What is it?" An impatient scowl contorted his face.

"Please don't let anyone care for my wounds."

"You don't make sense!"

"Wolfgang, I'm not a man. I'm a . . ."

Wolfgang's face paled and his mouth hung open. "You're a woman."

"I can help you wrap it. It will be all right." Her hand was shaking as she reached for the roll of bandages.

He snatched it away from her, his gaze moving from her face to the blood soaking her gray shirt. "You have to trust me. I won't . . . won't do anything to"—his throat bobbed as he swallowed—"to take advantage of you. I just need to see the wound."

Without another word, with the hand that still held to the end of her shirt, he eased it up on one side.

Mulan blinked, fighting to stay conscious.

W olfgang pulled the end of the shirt up, just enough to reveal the wound. He used one end of the bandage roll to wipe as much blood away as he could so he could see.

The arrow had gone straight through. It was low enough to have missed his—her—ribs and far enough over, hopefully, so that it missed the important internal organs like stomach, liver, and kidneys. But he was no physician. How would he know?

She was losing a lot of blood. Remembering what the healer Lena had taught him before he left Hagenheim, he took a second roll of bandages from his bag and pressed a roll firmly against both the entry wound in the front and the exit wound at her back.

Mikolai moaned, a soft sound that she quickly suppressed.

Mikolai. That wasn't *her* name.

"So, what is your name?"

She stared up at him. "My name is Mulan."

"Why? Why did you lie to us? Why would you come here and pretend to be a soldier? Are you a spy for the Teutonic Knights?" A pain went through his chest at the thought of her betraying him.

"No. Everything I said was true, except that I am no son, but my father's daughter. And if I didn't come in his place, my mother would have been thrown out of her house. She had nowhere to go."

He eased up on the pressure and she cried out, then bit her

lip. His heart squeezed with pity, as he had a good idea just how much it hurt.

He quickly wrapped the third roll of bandages around her middle, trying not to let his fingers brush her bare skin. As he did so his mind raced. What had he said to her when he thought she was a man? She had nearly beaten him at archery and then he'd sought her out for the sword-fighting competition— *Oh no.*

He had purposely beaten her, injuring her, though not seriously. *God, forgive me. I didn't know.*

He had let his stupid pride cause him to treat her harshly. And now, after all her bravery and fierce fighting, she was injured because he had told her not to shoot Steffan.

His brother was possibly betraying their whereabouts to the enemy at this very moment. Would his brother do that to him? He no longer knew his brother, and he certainly couldn't trust him.

"Can you walk?" He glanced up at her face as he tied the bandage in place. She was pale, but her eyes snapped open at his question.

"Yes, of course."

"Yes, of course," he muttered under his breath. She was bleeding and possibly badly injured, but of course she could walk.

He lifted her up by her arms. Since her right side was injured, he hung her left arm around his shoulders. But it was clear that wouldn't work. She was so much shorter than him. So he bent and lifted her in his arms. He started back toward their encampment at a fast walk.

"The Teutonic Knights could come through here any moment."

Now her voice sounded like a woman. Gone was the affected gruff, low voice. How had he not known? But he had been suspicious.

"You should leave me here and go back to camp. I can hide in the trees."

Wolfgang made a guttural sound low in his throat. "You'll do no such thing. I'm not leaving you." Even though she was small, his shoulder was already burning, but he wasn't about to put her down.

His mind was reeling with everything that had just happened. But he kept his eyes straight ahead, kept walking at as fast a pace as he could.

Two men Wolfgang recognized appeared on the road ahead. They hurried toward him, and one reached out to take Mikolai—or Mulan—from him.

She grabbed his arm in a surprisingly strong grip. "Take me to Andrei—only Andrei."

"Do not worry." He couldn't help frowning at her. "I'll take care of you."

His heart beat fast and strength surged through his limbs as he let someone else carry her for a while, but he stayed right beside her, making sure she could see him there.

Why did he care? He should be angry. She had betrayed him and tricked her fellow soldiers, endangering more lives than her own by disguising herself as a man and a soldier and coming here to fight among them.

But perhaps she had felt she had no choice. And she had proven herself a worthy warrior.

He peevishly bested her with the sword, purposely drawing out the fight and even risking her life. But she had borne it with perfect noble character.

He pushed all these thoughts from his mind and focused on getting her back to camp—and concealing the fact that she was a woman.

Mulan lay gasping for breath. A candle was still burning between Andrei and her, and the boy's heavy, even breathing reassured her that she had not awakened him.

The pain was so sharp at times, it took her breath. She couldn't spread her mother's healing salve on the wounds until they ceased bleeding. But perhaps they had stopped.

Slowly she unwrapped the bandages Wolfgang had put in place. He'd wrapped them quite snugly, but not too tight. When she got to the end, she carefully lifted the padding against the front wound, just above her hip bone.

Was that it? It looked so small.

She reached for the flask of her mother's salve. Wolfgang had tried to return the one she had given him, but she refused it, telling him she had more. Now she smeared on the bad-smelling concoction, first on the front, then on the back where the arrow had exited.

What would Wolfgang do now that he knew her secret? Would he demand she leave the troop and go back home? She could see that he was angry, and when he brought her back the salve, he'd looked at her so strangely, almost as if *he* had betrayed *her*. Had he already told the captain? The other soldiers?

Or perhaps he felt bad because it had been his brother who shot her. But that was daft. She would never hold him responsible for his brother's deeds. Then she remembered how he'd stopped her from shooting him, giving Steffan the chance to retaliate.

A fresh, sharp pain went through her side and she gasped. Lying back on her blanket, she breathed in and out, forcing away the groans that might wake up Andrei.

Poor boy. The look on his face when he'd seen her covered in blood and being carried into the tent made her stomach twist. She remembered how Wolfgang had stayed and talked with Andrei about her injury. When he left, she'd admitted to Andrei that he now knew her secret.

Andrei had rubbed a hand over his face. "Perhaps we should sneak away tonight and hope no one follows us."

"No, no. We cannot do that. We have no choice but to hope he will not tell anyone."

She was in too much pain at the time to worry much about it. But now . . . Truly, she didn't think her injury was serious. If Wolfgang could carry her with a fresh arrow wound to his shoulder, she should be able to fight again in a day or two. And if the Teutonic Knights' reinforcements arrived, they would need her.

She let herself relive Wolfgang carrying her and the looks of concern on his face—although at times she couldn't be certain if he was concerned or just angry, there were other times when she was sure compassion filled his eyes.

She relived the apology—"*I'm so sorry. Please forgive me.*" And then, "*O God, please don't let it be bad.*"

He did care about her at that moment, when he thought she was a man. But then he'd discovered the truth. He would never want to talk to her or fight by her side again. After all, it had only been a few days since he'd hated her and wanted to show off how much stronger and more skilled he was at sword fighting.

She sighed. Going over and over it in her mind wouldn't help. Besides, what did it matter how he felt about her? She was nothing to him. He was a duke's son. He'd go back to his family and his castle in the Holy Roman Empire, and she would go back to Lithuania, far away from him. And what would she do? Marry a butcher or baker or chandler and live in her little village for the rest of her life, concerned only with the daily chores of cooking and cleaning and raising her children. Some women seemed happy with that, but . . . it filled *her* with dread.

And she'd never see Wolfgang again.

But she would never forget him. And she liked to think that he'd never be able to forget the soldier he fought alongside who turned out to be a woman.

Wolfgang sat staring out at the trees from where he had broken his fast with some bread and cheese. Dieter, a friend and one of the other soldiers from Hagenheim, sat beside him.

"I'm sorry about Steffan."

Wolfgang nodded. "I just can't believe he would do this. And yet . . . he never wanted to do anything Father and Mother expected of him."

There was no use talking about it. Steffan had sworn him to secrecy many times about the event that had changed Wolfgang's brother when Steffan was only eight and Wolfgang was six. Steffan had grown defiant and angry, while Wolfgang had felt as if he should always try to atone for what had happened.

Once when they were around twelve and fourteen, Wolfgang had told his brother, "God forgives us. All we have to do is ask for forgiveness and He grants it."

Steffan sneered, then laughed. "Do you think I still care about that? It wasn't my fault anyway."

But Wolfgang remembered Steffan's expression when he'd found out the repercussions of their childish antics. The horror on his face was unforgettable. But he'd made Wolfgang promise not to tell Father, not to tell anyone, their part in the tragedy.

Wolfgang had been so terrified, he'd readily promised, not wanting his father, whom he loved and revered, to think he was bad. But his father had figured out most of it himself, and he'd told their mother. Poor Mother. She'd worried so much about them after that.

But they'd never told the whole story, and the secret had weighed heavy. He'd urged his brother several times to tell their father what had happened. And the last time, Steffan had called him names and vowed never to see him or his family again if Wolfgang told.

Not wishing to lose the brother who had been his constant companion throughout childhood, he had agreed.

And now . . . He hadn't known Mikolai—Mulan—for very long, but she occupied his thoughts even more than his brother. Wolfgang couldn't get her and her secret out of his head. Did he hate her? Was he angry at her for fooling him and pretending to be a man?

He was angry, but . . .

His stomach flipped as he remembered the last time he looked into her face. Her black hair had come loose from the leather tie that normally held it behind her neck. The hair framed her face and matched the long eyelashes he hadn't noticed before. Her lips were pink and full—also something he hadn't noticed before he knew she was a woman.

But he had to stop thinking about her that way.

Wolfgang rubbed his burning eyes. He'd hardly slept at all.

Gerke clapped him on the shoulder and he startled. He'd forgotten his page was there.

"Don't worry about Mikolai. Andrei says his wounds are not serious."

"He doesn't know that," Wolfgang grumbled.

Why did he say that? He should have shrugged and nodded to show he wasn't worried about "Mikolai."

As the only person besides Andrei who knew that Mikolai was a woman, he almost wished he could guard her tent and make sure nothing happened to her. Would she insist on staying with the other soldiers and fighting? Perhaps he could convince her to go home. Surely now she would see the necessity.

Mulan met the captain with as much confidence as she could muster, forcing her shoulders back and lifting her head high.

"Mikolai. I heard you were injured. Lost a lot of blood."

"I wouldn't say it was a lot of blood." Mulan's lips tipped up in a half smile. "I'm well enough to fight now."

"Wolfgang seems to think you aren't able, that your injuries could be internal and severe."

Mulan blew out a breath. So this was how it would be. "I don't believe my injury is any more serious than Wolfgang's shoulder wound. In fact, I'd say I'm in better shape to fight than he is."

"Is that so?"

She turned to see Wolfgang standing behind her, his brows lowered.

"Yes, that's so." She braced her hand on her hip, then realized how feminine that might look, so she removed it and spit on the ground, cocking one foot out at an angle. "You have to use your arm to shoot, but my wound is in my side." She shook her head. "It shall not interfere with my fighting."

"If Mikolai says he's able to fight, then I trust him." Captain Bogdan's brows were raised as he eyed Wolfgang.

Wolfgang scowled but said nothing.

"I'm glad you both are so willing to fight, but I need more scouts. The enemy is encamped not far away and we believe they intend to attack soon. If you could get close enough to eavesdrop and discover when they intend to attack, we could surprise them before they're ready."

Wolfgang's eyes narrowed as he stared past them.

The captain named the scouts he was sending on this mission. Then he described the place where the enemy encampment was, the hiding places around it, and the positions of their guards.

"They've already burned every field around here, killing many of Duke Konrad's tenants in the process. They've vowed to annihilate every one of Duke Konrad's men and allies. And the Teutonic Knights don't make vows lightly."

Wolfgang's gaze met hers. Intensity simmered in his eyes—concern, anger, or warning, she wasn't sure which—but he didn't want her going on this mission.

He had no choice. The captain had given an order, and Wolfgang couldn't argue.

CHAPTER 11

Wolfgang clenched and unclenched his fists as he strode toward the big beech tree at the edge of their encampment, his meeting place with Mulan. Then he saw her out of the corner of his eye approaching him.

"Shall we go?" She actually smiled.

"Are you so determined to die for Duke Konrad?" How dare she tell the captain that his injury was worse than hers. She should be afraid, should show some humility, since Wolfgang could easily end her foolish pretense by telling the captain.

She frowned at him. "I'm doing my job, like any other soldier. Any one of us could die, but I'm willing to take that risk."

"But you're not like any other soldier, are you?"

She stuck her finger in his face, pointing right at his nose. In a low voice she said, "You should stop talking now."

"This is not a game. This is life and death. And . . ." He pressed his lips together as tightly as he could.

"And what?"

"You . . . you shouldn't be here."

"Duke Konrad says I'm the most courageous soldier who's ever fought for him. And the captain has sent me on a mission, so I have every right to be here. I am a soldier. And if you don't want to accompany me, I'm certain the captain will find someone else to go." She tilted her chin up and stared with defiance into his eyes.

Wolfgang could threaten to tell her secret, but that seemed petty and childish. And it would only be a threat, because he would never do anything that would endanger her. Instead, he ran his hands through his hair. "Let's go."

Mulan made sure to walk beside Wolfgang instead of behind him. She couldn't let him think she considered herself anything less than his equal.

"What were you thinking about back there, when Captain Bogdan was talking to us?"

"What do you mean?" He didn't look at her.

"It seemed as if you were thinking of doing something the captain might not give his approval for."

"Next you'll be telling me you can see my thoughts using a bag of bat-wing bones your mother gave you."

"Don't say such a thing, even in jest." Mulan moved slightly in front of him, walking sideways, and stared him down. "That kind of talk will get my mother burned at the stake for practicing pagan magic. The priests in Lithuania don't allow anything that even hints of heresy. We were a pagan nation, you should know, until three or four decades ago."

"Forgive me." He looked her in the eye. "My father always employed at least one healer, but I know some rulers in the Holy Roman Empire occasionally accuse healers of witchcraft. Would your mother be in danger for her healing salve?"

"The priests have always allowed her that, after she explains every ingredient and that the recipe came partially from some monks at a monastery near our village. But she had a great-grandmother who was accused of practicing witchcraft and had to hide out in a cave. I don't know all the details about that . . ."

She let her voice trail off. She shouldn't be chattering away like a magpie. But now that Wolfgang knew she was a woman, she let her guard down. She no longer needed to make her voice low and gruff around him. But she probably should not lower her defenses. Anyone might be watching and listening in these woods while they were traversing the open road, with the dense trees and thick underbrush crowding alongside.

Now that she was walking beside Wolfgang again, she glanced at him from the corner of her eye. When their eyes met, he averted his gaze.

What did he think of her now that he knew she was a woman? Was he disgusted by her? Men didn't like strong women, after all. Or that was the impression she'd gotten from her father and some of the men in the village. But that had always made her feel defiant. She'd never cared about gaining the favor of any man. Even Algirdas.

Except, perhaps, she felt a bit more disposed to gaining *this* man's favor.

That thought sent a pang through her middle. *Very unwise, Mulan.*

"The truth is," Wolfgang said quietly, "I am hoping I might be able to find my brother and talk to him."

"What? That sounds foolish. He might shoot *you* this time."

"I'll capture him. He will be safer as our prisoner than he would be anywhere else." A pained look slid over his face. "I'm very sorry he wounded you. It was my fault."

"It's not your fault. This is a war, after all. Enemies shoot to kill."

"But . . . I stopped you from shooting him, which wasn't fair to you."

"You're right." She raised her brows and looked askance at him. "It wasn't fair. But I understand. And I forgive you."

He stopped, so she stopped too.

"Thank you. For not telling the captain about that."

"Of course."

The look in his eyes . . . so gentle, understanding, even tender. Her heart beat wildly inside her chest. She'd never known men like Wolfgang existed. He wasn't perfect by any means, but he also didn't treat her like a pack animal, a slave, or an object to be ignored.

The only tenderness she'd ever seen in her father was when he rubbed down his horse.

Perhaps that was why she never wanted to be married, never felt an attraction for a man.

Her stomach flipflopped as much as her heart at the thought. How would it feel if a man—this man—spoke to her in a kind and gentle voice, expressing his love while staring deeply into her eyes? Would he kiss her? If she were his wife, would he show affection to her, even hold her in his arms?

Mulan quickly looked away, her breaths quickening as she started walking again. Could he tell what she was thinking? Did he know what she was feeling? *Foolish, foolish girl.* He didn't know and he didn't care, not about her. *Tenderness, bah!* She was imagining it.

But they were friends again. For some reason that made her feel lighter, and she started singing, quietly under her breath. Then she halted the ballad that was rolling through her head. They were not that far from where the enemy was encamped.

"What's it like to have a brother?"

"I rather suspected Andrei was your brother."

"No, Andrei was my father's attendant. He accompanied him on his last two campaigns."

"And he knows your secret?"

"Yes."

Now Wolfgang was looking at her askance with raised eyebrows.

"He's just a boy, barely twelve. He was my friend back in our village. We both were harassed—he because he had no parents, and me because . . . well, I look like someone from the Far East lands." Her cheeks burned at bringing that to his attention.

"People can be cruel. I'm sorry, Mulan."

She had to turn away from the compassion in his face as sorrow threatened to constrict her throat. But, of course, he wouldn't understand. He was born to a life of privilege.

"You were about to tell me about your brothers." Mulan hoped he would talk so she could stop thinking about herself.

"I like my brothers, and we all got along, except for Steffan. He was always teasing someone, always annoying our sisters, playing pranks on people, and I admit, I went along with him, which I later regretted." He heaved a sigh. "I let him influence me more than I should have for far too long. But I realized several years ago, we all have a choice as to what kind of man we want to be." He glanced at her. "What kind of person."

"Of course."

"I could be angry and only care about myself, or I could be the sort of man my father was—kind and generous and determined to do right instead of wrong." He frowned. "Steffan could never seem to see Father as a good and noble person. He always wanted to rebel against every suggestion he made."

"Well, I'm glad you stopped letting him influence you. What changed your mind?"

"Some things happened. My father had to fight against an evil man who tried to take over Hagenheim—he did seize control for a while. Father and my older brother fought to save us, to rescue Mother and my sisters and Steffan and me. There was such a stark difference between evil and good, and I finally saw it then. Here was a man who didn't care who he hurt. He was selfish and wanted what he wanted, no matter what it cost other people. But it was my father, my brother Valten, my brother-in-law Gerek, and the other knights under my father who showed not only courage but also concern and compassion."

Wolfgang waved his hand. "I suppose it sounds obvious, but it was a revelation for me. And then there was my sister's husband, Aladdin. He never let anyone discourage him. And he loved Kirstyn and even sacrificed himself once, when they were children, to save her."

"Sacrificed himself?"

"He got between her and a bear. Nearly lost his leg, but he lived." Wolfgang's face was framed by the green leafy trees behind him as he rubbed the back of his neck.

"Not very many men survive a fight with a bear."

He nodded and smiled, which made her want to think of more things to say that would summon another smile.

"So with examples like that, how could I let Steffan continue to lead me down a bad path? I only wish I could have convinced him"—he stared past her again, his face falling—"to follow my lead for once."

Her heart squeezed at the pain in his voice and expression. "Perhaps you will. Perhaps it's not too late."

But his face lit up and he took a step toward her. "I'm so glad you think so, because I believe if I could just remind him of those things, he might change."

"But how will you find him among the enemy? How will you get close enough without getting captured yourself?" Her breathing quickened as she imagined him getting snatched by the heartless Teutonic Knights, tortured, and killed.

His jaw tightened and he didn't say anything. He knew the danger. "God will make a way."

It seemed a foolish thing to say, but the priest said that without faith it was impossible to please God. Perhaps God *would* make a way. However, it seemed unlikely Wolfgang could convince his brother now if he couldn't convince him before.

"If you think it's foolhardy and don't want to be a part of it, I understand. In fact . . ." Wolfgang rubbed his chin. "When we reach their camp, I want you to stay a safe distance away while I search for Steffan."

"Our orders are to find out the plans of the enemy, so we have to get close enough to hear what they're saying. We've already talked about this. Captain Bogdan trusts us both to be on this mission. I am a soldier just like you."

He narrowed his eyes at her. He didn't like it, but he had no choice.

"And while we are listening for information about their plans, we can keep an eye out for Steffan."

Andrei would tell her she was being daft. She mustn't think foolish thoughts about Wolfgang. But when she saw that smile and look of gratitude on his face . . . she wouldn't take back her words for anything.

Was he leading Mulan into danger? She wouldn't listen to reason. If he had to leave her to look for Steffan, he would do it to keep her safe.

Wolfgang and Mulan approached the encampment in broad daylight, crouching as they moved, glancing all around. When they were so close they could see glimpses of the tents between the bushes, a guard appeared ahead of them, leaning back against a tree, his bow and arrow in his hands as he scanned the forest in front of him.

Mulan saw him too. They stood still and watched. After several minutes, the guard pushed himself off the tree and walked away, constantly surveying the area.

When he was gone, they climbed a tree to get a better view.

Mulan moved a little slower this time, looking less like a squirrel as she gingerly progressed from branch to branch, wincing when she reached up with her right hand. Wolfgang climbed up behind her, trying to use his right arm instead of his left, but his shoulder was paining him as he went. Finally he reached the highest branch that would hold his weight and sat down, staring out at the enemy soldiers.

Almost immediately he spotted Steffan's tent, proudly displaying their family crest.

Mulan mouthed, *"Do you see him?"*

He shouldn't have told her what he was planning. She was so reckless with her own life. If only he could have convinced Captain Bogdan that she should stay at camp. Perhaps it would be best if he told the captain that she was a woman. He would send her away, and then at least she'd be safe—even though she and her mother would be forced to leave their home.

Wolfgang shook his head in answer to her question. They both turned their eyes back to the encampment.

MELANIE DICKERSON

Men moved about with purpose, as if readying for something. They watched until the air grew cooler, a soft breeze blowing. Clouds overhead made the afternoon seem like evening. He was exceedingly cramped on the tree limb. He tried to change his position, holding on so he wouldn't fall. Mulan rested against the trunk, appearing almost comfortable. She was staring out at the field in front of them, but her eyes were weary.

Suddenly she sat forward and pointed.

Steffan. He was headed toward the trees, probably searching for a place to relieve himself.

Wolfgang began climbing down, making sure no one was nearby. He moved as quietly as he could, then noticed Mulan was ahead of him.

"What are you doing?" he whispered.

"I'll help you, make sure no one slits your throat while you're talking to Steffan."

"No. You stay here."

But the tightly pursed lips told him she would not listen.

What kind of madness was this? A woman saying she would protect him? His pride refused to allow it, but how could he stop her?

Everything he'd ever been taught told him to protect her. But she was not a wilting flower. She had proven herself capable.

He nodded and said a silent prayer for their safety as he ran in the direction Steffan had gone.

CHAPTER 12

As Steffan strolled through the woods to clear his thoughts, he couldn't stop reliving the moment when he shot Wolfgang's friend and the look on his brother's face.

Steffan had always been the one who didn't fit in with his family. It used to seem as if Wolfgang was the only one who understood him, but now . . . even his little brother and former best friend was his enemy.

Wolfgang might have choked the life out of him had he not drawn his attention to the boy falling out of the tree.

What was this boy to Wolfgang? He had released Steffan to go save him. Had simply let Steffan go. That boy, surely a near stranger, meant more to Wolf than he did.

Now Wolfgang only cared about pleasing Father and being just like him—the hypocrite. But there had to be more to life than following after a man who'd cared more about his people, cared more about his older sons, and even cared more about his knights and his daughters' husbands than about Steffan and Wolfgang.

Why did Wolfgang not feel the same way? Why was he chasing after Father's impossible standards? Father didn't care about either of them or he would have sent them out to train as knights when they were boys so they could have achieved glory and success as men—even if it wasn't the kind of success Valten or Father had achieved. They had titles and wealth and power handed to them.

His little brother had always been prone to running and telling Father everything.

Not Steffan. He wasn't one of Father's servants, blindly obeying and bowing and groveling. And now Father would never accept him. There was no going back home now that he had defied the Duke of Hagenheim by joining with the Teutonic Knights, attacking his father's ally, Duke Konrad, and even fighting against his own brother.

So be it.

He'd always been alone, and he always would be.

Wolfgang had tried to tell Steffan that his anger with Father had to do with what happened when they were boys, but it had nothing to do with that. He should just forget about that and stop talking about it.

Steffan clenched his fists, resting his forehead against the tree in front of him. He imagined the tree was a person and hit it just hard enough to feel the pain in his knuckles.

A footstep sounded behind him. He spun around.

"I need to talk to you." Wolfgang and the boy Steffan had shot stood there.

Steffan pulled the knife in his belt out of its leather pouch, and the boy knocked it out of his hand.

Wolfgang grabbed him by the throat as the boy clutched his wrists and pinned them behind his back before he could stop them.

He fought like a madman, kicking out, heaving his body this way and that to get loose, but they slammed him on the ground face-first and leaned on his back.

They stuffed a cloth in his mouth. A crimson mist descended over his vision.

"Steffan, we don't want to hurt you."

How dare his little brother think he could best him? Steffan threw his head back, trying to butt Wolfgang like a mountain goat. He tried to flip himself over, but the weight on his back made it impossible. He tugged on his hands, but someone was wrapping rope around his wrists.

Even though it was Wolfgang, Steffan would kill him. Just as soon as he freed himself.

Wolfgang's heart beat fast. Why did his brother have to fight so hard? "I'm sorry, Steffan. I just want to talk to you."

Steffan was growling like a wild animal, his breath loud and raspy.

This was not going the way he had hoped. But they couldn't let the Teutonic Knights catch them, so Wolfgang and Mulan each took an arm and dragged Steffan farther away from the enemy encampment.

After several minutes, Mulan was growing pale.

"Let's stop here."

Steffan was still kicking and thrashing, his eyes full of dark threats.

"Steffan, I'm taking you prisoner. It's for your own good as well as mine since I know you will kill me if I release you now."

His face red, Steffan's glaring look confirmed it.

"Whatever happens, you will always be my brother." Wolfgang's stomach sank as it became clearer and clearer that this was a foolhardy thing to do, and he could see no good way out. If he took Steffan prisoner, he'd never forgive him. And the purpose of trying to reason with him would never succeed now. He read the same thoughts on Mulan's face.

She obviously needed to rest after dragging Steffan so far. Her wound wasn't nearly healed. She would never complain, though.

Wolfgang looked at Mulan and said softly, "I think we should let him go."

"Are you mad? He'll slit our throats."

He turned to Steffan. "You did shoot her and could have killed her—"

"Him!" Mulan speared him with a glare.

What had he done? "Of course. Him. Mikolai here, a soldier from Lithuania. You could have killed him."

Had Steffan noticed his mistake in calling Mulan "her" instead of "him"? His brother's eyes were fixed on Mulan now, studying her face, then looking her up and down.

Wolfgang felt sick. Would Wolfgang's mistake get her killed? And how would they keep Steffan prisoner? He was so angry, he would hurt himself trying to escape.

Wolfgang pressed a clammy hand to his forehead. A drop of sweat dribbled down his temple, and he wiped it with his hand.

Mulan touched his shoulder from behind. "What will we do? Your brother . . . ?"

"We cannot free him."

"We do have a few prisoners. We'll have to confine him with the others."

Wolfgang pushed the panicked thoughts from his head and nodded. "Let us depart before we are seen."

Mulan could see the regret on Wolfgang's ashen face and bowed shoulders. But there was nothing to do but walk back to their encampment with their new prisoner.

When they neared camp, Wolfgang stopped and took the gag from Steffan's mouth. "Are your troops planning to attack the castle again? Or are you waiting for reinforcements?"

Steffan would have been handsome if not for the sneer curling his lips. He had a similar build and look to his brother, but his hair was lighter and the way he walked and carried himself reminded her of the boys who harassed her in her home village.

She very much disliked those boys.

"Surely you don't expect me to tell you anything—you or your . . . *girl* friend." Steffan raised his brows, his mouth twisting into a smirk. "Tell me. Do you plan to wed her? Or is she more like a sister?" Steffan belted out a laugh.

Mulan's face burned, but she kept her gaze away from Wolfgang, lest his reaction further humiliate her.

"You talk nonsense, Steffan."

"Here you were, capturing me to find out my secrets, but instead I have found out yours." Steffan laughed again. "Your most courageous and skillful soldier is not a man at all, but this little, foreign-looking girl."

She finally chanced a glance at Wolfgang. His eyes were wide and his face seemed frozen. Was he horrified that his brother had thought he might wed her? Or horrified that he'd unwittingly revealed her secret?

Mulan couldn't think about that now. Instead, she did what she always did when her masculinity seemed to be in question. She grunted, leaned her head and shoulders back, and folded her arms in front of her chest.

Wolfgang gestured to her to follow him. Steffan sat on a large boulder, still grinning, while Wolfgang and Mulan walked several feet away.

He whispered, "We can't take him to be guarded along with the rest of the prisoners. He'll tell them your secret. And it's all my fault." Regret filled his expression. "Please forgive me."

"Perhaps you could keep him in your tent, away from everyone else."

"I have no tent. It burned."

"You could use my tent."

"I think you need your tent." He gave her a significant look. He was right.

"I don't suppose I could keep him gagged all the time."

"Probably not." This was indeed a problem.

Wolfgang walked back to his brother.

"Steffan, do you remember how Sir Gerek sought our sister, even when everyone else had given up on finding her?"

Steffan's face seemed made of stone. He didn't move or speak.

"Do you remember how much we admired him? How we wanted to be like him?"

"But there's no way we could be like him, could we? Unlike Sir Gerek, we were never sent to train as squires so we could become knights."

"What about Gabe? He was never a knight, but he fought for a woman's honor and freedom."

"And married an heiress. Ja, he was very wise."

"And Aladdin? He was not a knight or a duke's son. He was an orphan, but he never reacted to his position in life with anger, never rebelled against authority. He worked hard and was known by everyone as a person of integrity. And now he is wealthy and prosperous and—"

"Spare me the rest of the homily, brother, made even more ridiculous by the fact that you are neither a priest nor my elder."

"I'm only trying to make you understand that the path you have taken is not the honorable way to attain your goals. Fighting with a bunch of mercenaries instead of fighting for what's right—"

"Who are you to say what's right? I happen to think the Teutonic Knights are the righteous ones in this fight."

"How are they righteous? They attack innocent people because they desire their lands, burning and raiding—"

"Are you God? Before his master a servant stands or falls. Who are you to judge knights who have taken vows before God?"

Wolfgang turned away, closing his eyes and pressing a hand to his forehead.

Mulan wanted to tell him to give up on trying to reason with Steffan. He would not listen.

"So, who knows your friend is a woman?" Steffan smirked. "Your fellow soldiers?"

Wolfgang spun around to face him again. "Steffan, I am asking you . . . Please don't tell anyone."

"That Duke Konrad's hero is a female?"

"It would cause a lot of harm to befall her."

"And what will you do for me if I agree?"

Wolfgang's jaw twitched.

"Will you untie my hands? Will you set me free? Because I'm not accustomed to being treated like a common thief, even if I am the despised one of the family."

"Will you promise not to tell anyone our secret?"

"*Our* secret?" He huffed out a laugh, grinning and sneering at the same time. "Have you betrothed yourself to her? Or perhaps you are not interested in marriage to her. Perhaps there is another, less noble reason you are protecting her."

"How dare you." Wolfgang shoved Steffan against a tree. They glared at each other. He looked like he wanted to punch his brother, but it would not be a fair fight with Steffan's hands still tied. Wolfgang took his hands off him and stepped back. He took a breath and said softly, "Is protection of women not part of the Teutonic Knights' vows?"

"Is it a woman's duty now to go off to war, fighting against men? I don't understand your intention. Or hers."

"You are determined to make a jest of the most serious of subjects. I'm asking you, as your closest brother, to please not say anything about this to anyone. And it would give me both peace and pleasure if you would leave the Teutonic Knights and join our side of the fight, to fight alongside me and my friends."

"Your requests are noted. And now I shall make a request of my own." He leaned forward. "Release me and allow me to go back to *my* friends."

"I cannot release you. I'm sorry."

"You are not sorry." Steffan narrowed his blue eyes to slits. "But you will be."

CHAPTER 13

The sinking feeling in Wolfgang's gut remained after he and Mulan led Steffan into camp and installed him with the other prisoners.

The late-morning sun warmed the air as he and Mulan made their way back out to fulfill their spying mission. Walking through the forest toward the enemy encampment, he told himself that Steffan wouldn't be treated badly. Steffan would get plenty of food and he'd be safe from danger. That was the best gift he could give his mother, wasn't it? But the sick feeling only grew worse as he remembered his brother's cold, bitter glare and the sneer when he called Mulan his *girl* friend.

They went to the same tree and climbed it again to watch the enemy camp. But when he glanced at Mulan, her face was pale and her eyelids drooped.

"We should go back. You have not recovered enough from your wound to be climbing trees."

"No, no, I just need to rest a few moments."

"Mulan, I'm sorry. I'll make it up to you. I shall have my father do something for you, give you money or give your mother a place to live so you don't have to fight."

"Money for what?"

"For you being injured."

"This is battle. Soldiers get shot. I am not seriously injured and will be perfectly well in a few days. For now, I'm fully able to sit in this tree and spy on any enemy soldiers who happen by. I wish you would stop feeling responsible for me."

"I am responsible. If I had not stopped you, he wouldn't have seen you there and wouldn't have shot you."

"I've never known anyone so eager to accept blame and guilt." She frowned.

"I don't take the blame for things I'm not responsible for." But even as he said the words, he knew she was right.

Why did he do that? Did he think God would see him punishing himself by feeling guilty and then grant him atonement based on the extent of his feelings? How daft.

But he was concerned about her and she'd distracted him from pursuing the subject. "Your wound's not bleeding again, is it?"

She didn't say anything.

"Pull up your shirt and let me see."

"My mother warned me about men like you." The jest was as weak as her voice.

Wolfgang maneuvered up and over the branch between them, until he was sitting next to her in the tree.

"What do you think you're doing?" Mulan held up her hands in a defensive gesture.

"Then *you* check to see if it's bleeding."

She speared him with a steely gaze, then looked down and lifted her rough woolen tunic and the linen shirt under it. A big spot of bright-red blood stained the front of the bandage.

"That's not good."

"You worry like an old woman."

But there was an edge of worry in her own tone.

"I think I just need to rest. And it won't help to climb back down and walk all the way back to camp." She closed her eyes and leaned her head back against the tree.

He watched her face. *God, don't let my mistake and Steffan's reckless rebellion cause another human being to die. Especially not this one. She is . . . extraordinary.*

Her face gradually relaxed. Her breathing changed with sleep and became slower.

She was pretty, when she wasn't putting dirt on her face to disguise how smooth her skin was. Her long black eyelashes matched her hair, which had come loose from the leather tie that held it back from her face. With the silky black strands falling against her cheek, anyone would be able to see how feminine she was. Her face was full and curvy, not hard or angular like a man's, and her hands were small and delicate. How had he ever been fooled into thinking she was a man, or even a boy?

He had a sudden urge to touch her cheek with his fingers.

He shook his head to stop that thought path. These were the kinds of thoughts he would have about his wife someday, and this woman was not the type of woman he imagined marrying. She was rough and had been around men, fighting with them and hearing their coarse talk. What would his mother and father say?

But he suddenly knew . . . his parents would like her. She was unselfish, and her recklessness reminded him a bit of Steffan. No wonder she confused him! And yet, she was nothing like Steffan. She was gentle and serious and determined. She was only heedless with her own life, not others'. She was courageous in defending the poor and innocent.

He shook his head again and pressed his fingers to his eyes.

Mulan gasped and sat straighter. Her eyes popped open and she looked around.

"Careful there."

"Did something happen?"

"*Nie*. Go back to sleep. I'm keeping watch."

She took a deep breath and closed her eyes, but he could tell she was not sleeping. Finally she opened her eyes and pinned him to the spot. "Why are you so guilt ridden?"

"What?"

"You are trying to take responsibility for your brother. Why do you feel guilty for what he did? Have you always tried to take the blame for his deeds?" She certainly didn't sound weak anymore. The nap must have given her this new sharpness.

"I don't. You misunderstand." He shifted away from her.

"How am I misunderstanding?"

"Perhaps I am a bit too quick to feel guilty. I . . ." He'd never told anyone what they had done, except for the priest in confession. "Something happened when Steffan and I were young boys. We . . . we disobeyed our father and a little boy died. That's why Father never sent us to train as knights." He didn't want to talk about this, but his tongue seemed to have loosened and didn't want to stop.

"We both were horrified. We never thought anything bad would happen. We never told Father the whole truth, and I suppose I do feel guilty about what happened." Was that why he wanted so much to protect people—Duke Konrad's people, Kirstyn and his other sisters, and now . . . Mulan?

Mulan's expression was soft as she leaned slightly toward him. "I'm sorry that the child died, but I'm sure you never meant to hurt anyone, and you and Steffan were only children. God forgives. That's what my priest always said. 'God forgives because of Jesus and the cross.'"

Wolfgang's heart seemed to lose some of its soreness. "Maybe if Steffan could realize this. He's always blaming the wrong people and getting angry."

"I think I understand." Mulan chewed on her lip, looking thoughtful as she stared out into the leaves of the tree. "He doesn't want to think about what he did, so he blames others, raging inside so he doesn't feel the pain. Meanwhile, you're trying to make up for what you did by being the perfect soldier, the perfect son, protecting and rescuing, to feel better about . . ."

Her eye caught his. Her words struck like arrows hitting the center of his heart. As if she saw into his very soul. Did everyone else see through him like this? Or was she some kind of prophetess? Either way, it left him hollow inside.

"I'm sorry. It's only a guess. Mostly because . . ." She sighed and pulled her knee up to her chest, her other leg—the one on the wounded side—remained stretched out on the giant branch in front of her. She rested her chin on her knee and rubbed her brow. "Because that's how I feel. Just trying to make up for my illegitimate birth, to make it up to Mother, who raised me and never resented me for the pain she felt at my father's betrayal, or for the fact that she could never have her own children."

"Is that why you became a soldier? You were making amends by ensuring she had a home?"

She shrugged one shoulder. "She would have rather I'd married the butcher."

"The butcher?"

"Algirdas." Mulan smiled, but only on one side of her mouth.

"I tried to resign myself to it, but I just couldn't." She shook her head. "Couldn't do it."

"You would have had all the meat you wanted." Why was he teasing her? Probably to distract himself from the way his gut twisted to think of her married.

She grimaced. "Mother would never berate me for not marrying him. She never berates me for anything." She sighed. "I'm a selfish daughter."

"You? The one who led the charge on the Teutonic Knights straight up a cliff? The one who ran into enemy arrows to protect your fellow soldiers?" His gut twisted again at the thought that he had not protected her and she could have been killed.

She smiled. "We were the only two who were mad—or daft— enough to position ourselves at the opening in the ring of fire and shoot at the enemy."

It was true. And though he thought of Steffan as the reckless one, he'd been reckless with his life in these battles. And so had Mulan.

They both had things they wished they could forget, but for Wolfgang, with Steffan sitting back at camp as his captive, forgetting would be impossible.

Mulan couldn't help staring at Wolfgang's face. Had she ever tried to think of a man who was both masculine and full of kindness and integrity, he would have been that man. He made her want to hear everything he might tell her about himself. And he made her want to tell him all about herself.

"My father told me stories of battles he had been in. Not very often, but when he did, he made it seem as if it were adventurous and exciting. He told of killing men and winning, but it didn't seem real or terrible. He made it sound . . . enjoyable."

"So, you enjoyed being with your father?"

"Oh no. My father was not a person to be enjoyed." She shook her head at the thought. "Summer and winter, as you know, are the seasons for war, and he was always off fighting. He was only home in the fall or the spring, and then only sometimes. Once he didn't come home for two and a half years. We knew he wasn't dead because if he were, Butautas would have come and taken our house. And when he did come home, Mother cried tears of joy at the sight of him, but he only grunted at her, got drunk on some wine he had brought home with him, and went to bed and slept for two days."

Wolfgang stared at her with his mouth agape. "What did he do on the third day?"

"The third morning he got up, saddled his horse, and left. He didn't come home until just at sundown. He ate the food that Mother had cooked and went back to bed."

"Did he not say . . . anything?"

"He said, 'Mulan has grown. You've gotten fatter. I'm going to bed.'" Mulan laughed, but softly, so the enemy wouldn't hear.

"That's not how a good man treats his wife and daughter."

He looked so serious, so concerned, she had an urge to both laugh and cry at the same time.

"How did your father treat your mother and sisters? What did he do when he had been away from home?" Her breath hitched as she waited for his answer, surprised at how hungry she was to know.

"He always went first to find my mother as soon as he

dismounted. He would kiss her and they would talk for a few moments, and then he would see my sisters, who were always asking him questions. They would throw their arms around him, and he would hug them and kiss their cheeks and say a few words to each of them. But even if he had business until suppertime, he would always eat supper with us, with Mother at his side, and they always left the table together."

Tears pricked Mulan's eyes. Longing surged from deep inside her for that kind of love and attention, for both herself and her mother. Mulan did her best to blink back the tears.

"I'm very sorry, Mulan."

Wolfgang's words and tone made the tears tickle her lashes. No. She couldn't let him see her cry. But she couldn't manage to get them under control, so she turned away and cleared her throat.

"Was your father cruel in other ways?"

She took a deep breath and let it out, driving the tears away so she could speak. "He would often promise things—he would tell me he would give me an archery lesson—but then he would go off with a man from the village to look at a horse and forget about me, or he would start drinking and fall asleep. And when I was angry, he would laugh at me. He told me anger was for fools and kings." She blew out a breath, surreptitiously slinging away the tear on her cheek.

"Everyone gets angry. Even Jesus got angry. Anger is an honest emotion, and he shouldn't have made you feel bad for it."

"He said anger was for fools because they couldn't control themselves, and for kings because they had the power to use their anger to hurt their enemies."

"Did you grieve for him at all, after he died?"

Mulan sighed. "I did cry when the priest spoke the homily

over his grave. But that may have been because Mother was crying." She heaved a sigh. "I've seen her crying over things he did or
said too many times. I would hate anyone who made my mother
cry, so why not the man who was rarely around and even more
rarely paid attention to me? I know. I know. I shouldn't hate my
own father, and I don't, not really. I do have one or two good
memories of him, after all. But I don't know why I'm telling you
this." She grimaced, peering at him from the corner of her eye.

"Sometimes it's good to talk about things."

"Then you should tell me what happened with you and Steffan
when that boy died." Again, she held her breath while waiting for
his response.

He started picking pieces of bark off the branch next to him.
"My brother and I liked to wander in the fields and forests around
Hagenheim. Usually my father would send a guard to accompany us, but many times we would slip away by ourselves. We had
befriended a boy, Heinlin, the son of one of our shepherds."

He sighed and rubbed his forehead, as if soothing an ache there.

"The boy was about my age—I was six and Steffan was eight.
But Heinlin was small and pale and wore ragged clothes. And one
day Steffan said, 'Let's chase the sheep across the stream, to see
if they will cross it.' Heinlin said we shouldn't do it. If his father
found out we'd been chasing the sheep, he would beat him. 'He
won't beat you,' Steffan said.

"I don't know where Heinlin's father was, why he wasn't
watching the sheep. But the three of us started trying to herd
the little flock of sheep over the stream. We were only able to
get two of them to follow us across the shallow water. I remember we were laughing and running with them. Before I knew it,
Steffan screamed, 'Wait! Stop!' I didn't know what he was talking

about—until one of the sheep fell over a cliff. The other sheep followed right behind him, and when we got to the edge of the rock cliff, they were both lying at the bottom, not moving.

"We were horrified. Steffan's face was ashen, but Heinlin was beside himself. He started wailing, 'Father will kill me,' over and over again. 'Father will know we were chasing them.' We tried to tell him that his father would never know what had happened and that he would never kill him. But the look on his face . . . I don't think I'll ever forget it." Wolfgang turned away so she couldn't see his eyes.

"I told Steffan on the way home that we should tell Father what we'd done, tell him that Heinlin believed his father would kill him for letting the sheep fall off the cliff. But Steffan made me promise not to tell him." Wolfgang shook his head, an almost imperceptible movement. "I wish we had told him." He took another breath and huffed it out.

"The next day Father's men found Heinlin's body. He'd been beaten to death and his father disappeared. No one in Hagenheim ever saw him again."

Her stomach sank, especially imagining the pain going through Wolfgang. He kept his head turned slightly away from her.

"What a horrible man he must have been, to do that to his own child. And it must have frightened you and Steffan so much. You were just children."

"We told Father we had been playing with Heinlin that day, but we never told him about the dead sheep or how we caused them to fall over the cliff. And not long after that, we were practicing jousting and one of the young squires was killed. And before we were born, I had a sister who was thought to have drowned. My parents had been devastated. So those three things together were why Father and Mother never let us be sent away to train to be knights.

"Steffan was never really the same after that. He was angry and defensive, especially with Father and Mother, while I just felt like I had to be good, to make sure I didn't upset them again."

His pain seemed to lodge deep in her chest. His brown eyes were close enough she could see the warm gold bits intermingled. She could stare into them forever.

Wolfgang touched her arm, then touched a finger to his lips and pointed down at the ground. Two Teutonic Knights approached the giant oak tree where she and Wolfgang were perched.

Wolfgang strained to hear what the knights were saying to each other.

". . . all summer here."

The other grunted. "Have to get it done before the rainy season."

What did he mean by "get it done"?

"The *Hochmeister* was expected to arrive today," the first one said.

Wolfgang glanced at Mulan. The two men were relieving themselves at the base of the tree, but thankfully, because of the thick leaves, they couldn't see them.

Mulan's face was scrunched, her lips pursed in a frown. They were speaking German, so she probably only understood some of what they were saying.

"Rusdorf is coming?"

"Probably already here."

"How many men?"

"Maybe fifty, since the rest are fighting in Livonia. But instead of coming here and being seen by Duke Konrad's scouts, Rusdorf will disguise himself, sneak into the castle, and get rid of Duke Konrad. He'll take over the castle from the inside."

Duke Konrad and his men would be murdered, and so would many of the helpless women and children under his protection. Wolfgang's thoughts went to Jacyna and her child, who must believe they were safe inside the castle walls.

Wolfgang stayed perfectly still. If they were seen, the knights would surely kill them. He held his breath, focusing every fragment of his attention on the men's words below them, but the next words were mumbled and he couldn't make them out. Then . . .

". . . while we are stuck here . . ."

The man said something vulgar about the local women, and the other man laughed. They started moving away and soon disappeared in the trees, reappearing in the open field of the encampment.

"What did they say?" Mulan's eyes were wide. "Something about Grand Master Rusdorf murdering Duke Konrad?"

"We have to go." Wolfgang started climbing down.

Mulan grabbed his arm and said in a harsh whisper, "What did you hear?"

"Rusdorf and some of his men will arrive today. His plan is to go straight to Zachev Castle, sneak inside, and kill the duke."

They both scrambled down the tree. She was moving slower, and the color had gone out of her cheeks again by the time she reached the ground. He'd have to make her see the necessity of staying at camp and letting him handle this. Not only did he wish to protect her, but he couldn't let her slow him down. He had to get to the castle and save the duke.

CHAPTER 14

Wolfgang and Mulan ran for camp, but she was lagging behind. Her mouth kept twisting into a grimace. Her face was so pale. Finally he slowed down, and they walked side by side.

"You're in pain. You need to remain in camp. I can take a few men with me to stop Rusdorf."

"No, I'm well. Besides, I can get in and go unnoticed much more easily than you."

He said nothing.

When they reached camp everyone turned to stare at them. The men's faces were alert and almost angry. Something was amiss.

"Where's the captain?" Wolfgang shouted.

"He went searching for the escaped prisoners." Dieter eyed Mulan and then Wolfgang.

"Steffan? Did he escape?"

Dieter's unhurried answer was, "Your brother is one of the escapees."

Wolfgang's stomach sank. But there was something else.

Everyone was staring at Mulan.

Wolfgang grabbed Dieter by the arm and asked quietly, "What is it? Why is everyone gawking?"

"Is it true that Mikolai is a woman?"

Mulan's mouth fell open, and Wolfgang's whole body tensed. "Who makes such claims?"

"Steffan said she was a woman and we were all fools for not knowing."

"Mikolai is a soldier and was honored by the duke for bravery in battle." Wolfgang's neck and face heated. What was the wisest way to handle this to save Mulan? Their fellow soldiers were gathering around, still staring at her with lowered brows and sullen expressions.

"We have no time for such nonsense. The enemy is trying to turn us against each other. We—Mikolai and I—have just discovered that Rusdorf and the Teutonic Knights plan to murder Duke Konrad. There is no time to lose—if it's not already too late."

No one moved.

"We heard them in the woods outside their camp."

"Perhaps it is an ambush," someone said.

"And you're helping your brother and the Teutonic Knights," someone else added. "You're a betrayer!"

"When has God ever used a woman in battle? That's Satan's tactic!" another man shouted.

All the men started muttering.

O God. Help us.

Wolfgang noticed a boulder a few paces away. He ran and jumped up onto it. "Mikolai has acted valiantly, and you all are the witnesses," Wolfgang shouted over them. "Did you not follow when he climbed the rock face?"

The men quieted down and looked at him.

"With Mikolai leading, did we not drive the Teutonic Knights from Zachev Castle, just when they were about to break through with their battering ram? Who among you has been braver than Mikolai?"

"Is he—she—a woman? Yes or no?"

Everyone was quiet. Then Mulan jumped up on the boulder beside him. "I am a soldier, but I'm also a woman."

Instead of shouting and calling for her head, Wolfgang was surprised at how the crowd of men became hushed.

Speaking quietly, she said, "I am a woman second and a soldier first. And now Duke Konrad and all the people in his protection are in danger. Shall we stand around doing nothing? Or shall we make a plan to stop Rusdorf, our enemy?"

Wolfgang held his breath. A few murmurs rippled through the crowd.

"It's a trick," a gruff voice said. "A woman isn't made for battle."

Then an uneasy quiet settled over them.

Finally Wolfgang said, "We cannot let this divide us, especially now. We have to stop Rusdorf before he reaches Duke Konrad."

The crowd of soldiers glanced around at each other.

Wolfgang said, "Someone must get to the castle and warn the duke before Rusdorf can carry out his plan. But if the whole company goes, he and his men will suspect something. We will lose this chance to capture Rusdorf."

Mulan said, "Several of the best archers should accompany us and wait on the hill overlooking the gatehouse, in case there's a struggle and Rusdorf's small troop of men are nearby."

Mulan spoke wisely, like a true leader, but would the men accept her instruction? And she'd said "us," as though it was a foregone conclusion that she would go to the castle to warn the duke. But he'd have to address that with her later.

Wolfgang held his breath, waiting. One soldier said, "I'll go."

Wolfgang nodded and motioned to him.

"I'll go." Dieter raised his hand. Several more men volunteered. They still didn't look glad to be in the presence of a woman soldier, but at least they were willing to put aside their vexation to save the duke.

While the men went to fetch their bows and arrows, Wolfgang leaned over and spoke softly for Mulan's ears only. "You cannot go. You are injured. I'll choose someone else to accompany me."

Mulan did not even glance at him but shook her head.

After he thought of it, could he truly risk leaving her here with only the boy Andrei to protect her?

As the crowd of soldiers accompanied them out of camp, Wolfgang walked close to her side. "Are you sure you're able? You won't faint from blood loss?"

She frowned. "I am well enough. And who else is known to the duke besides you and me? He trusts us and will listen to us."

"I do not like it. I can see by the tension on your face that the pain is worse. Your wound could be turning putrid."

Mulan shook her head. "It isn't. God is with us. Didn't your priest ever tell you so? Besides, I know God is protecting me for this mission."

"How do you know?"

"There is a prophecy concerning me."

"A prophecy?"

"A friar came to our village. He pointed me out in the crowd. I was about five or six years old. He said I would conquer an oppressor in a foreign land and a nation would call me blessed."

Wolfgang stared at her, even as they mounted their horses and began to ride away.

What manner of woman was this?

Steffan and the other prisoners hailed their fellow soldiers as they made it to the Teutonic Knights' camp. When the soldiers saw them, they cheered and commended them.

"How did you get away?" the captain asked.

"Steffan," one of them said. "He escaped first and set the rest of us free."

Several men slapped him on the back, but he didn't have time to revel in their praise. "I need to see Rusdorf. Is he here?"

"He's already left for Zachev Castle, but I think you can catch him."

Several men accompanied him as they mounted horses and rode in the direction Rusdorf had gone.

Only a few minutes passed before they overtook the small band of soldiers Rusdorf had brought with him on his mission. The grand master slowed and stopped but did not dismount. "What news have you?"

Steffan addressed him with respect. "The soldier known as Mikolai of Lithuania is an imposter. He's a woman, and his— her—fellow soldiers don't even know." Except for Wolfgang, but he decided to leave out that detail.

"What evil sorcery is this?" Rusdorf's face turned red, then dark. He didn't speak right away. He was staring at Steffan's face, but Steffan got the idea that he wasn't actually seeing him.

His jaw was as hard as stone, his eyes black. "A woman reaping the glory for defeating the Teutonic Knights?" he rasped. "Witchcraft. Demonic trickery."

No one spoke. Several men squirmed in their saddles, probably less awed by the fact that they'd been defeated by a woman than by Rusdorf's obvious fury.

"A woman and a heretic." His face twisted into a sneer. "We shall not rest until she and the rest of these heretics are vanquished. Onward, men."

Mulan mounted her horse and urged him into a gallop. Wolfgang was right beside her, staring at her as if she'd just turned purple and green. Strength flowed through her when she was speaking to the men at the camp, but now that it was just the two of them, her arms and legs trembled and her vision was spinning.

God, if You want me to conquer an enemy, strengthen my limbs and send the blood through my veins. How could she bear it if she proved Wolfgang right by fainting when he needed a soldier standing strong beside him.

Finally they neared the castle and Wolfgang slowed his horse. She followed suit, and they guided them off the road to a small house. Wolfgang spoke to the man who emerged, giving him a coin and promising him food if he watched their horses for a few hours.

When they were walking on the road to the castle, Wolfgang asked, "How do you know that prophecy wasn't the crazed ramblings of a friar who had spent too much time alone?"

Using all her energy not to appear as weak and wounded as she felt, Mulan didn't have the luxury of getting angry at him. "Several weeks after that, the word of the friar was confirmed by our priest when he left our village to go on a pilgrimage. He called me to him, put his hands on my head, and said, 'The Spirit of the

Living God says this child will be a mighty warrior someday.' My mother said he probably didn't mean an actual warrior fighting with physical weapons, but it helped inspire me to learn to use a bow and arrow."

They hastened toward the castle gatehouse with no visible weapons on them, though Wolfgang's sword was hidden under his cloak, and Mulan carried a dagger inside a sheath strapped inside the waistband of her hose.

While Wolfgang was silent, she tried to think what they would say or do when they reached the castle, but she ended up saying silent prayers to God for help and victory, her thoughts darting from her heartfelt conversation with Wolfgang to the men staring mistrustfully at her.

Wolfgang's suntanned face was serious, reminding her of when he had urged her to stay at camp. Was he worried about her? Or simply wishing for a healthier and stronger ally in this dangerous endeavor? He must truly care about her, at least a little. She knew it from the way he'd behaved when his brother shot her. But Wolfgang was the kind of man who would care about any fellow soldier.

She shoved these thoughts away as they neared the soldiers wearing Duke Konrad's colors, standing guard at the gatehouse.

"Halt. No one enters here without special permission from the duke."

Wolfgang stepped toward them. "We have information. It means life or death for the duke and everyone in the castle."

"You may not enter without permission—"

"We are Wolfgang and Mikolai. We accompanied Captain Bogdan and attended the feast the duke gave celebrating the victory over the Teutonic Knights a few days ago. Our fellow soldiers should be topping that hill over there any moment now."

Mulan and Wolfgang also showed their colors.

The two guards glanced at each other, then took a few steps back to confer. One of the men motioned them forward with his hand. "Come with me."

He made them walk in front of him while he held his sword at the ready and followed closely.

Mulan said over her shoulder, "Has a man come through the gatehouse in the last few hours with thick black hair and a black moustache and black beard?"

"No."

The man looked nervous, so she decided not to ask him any more questions. But when they entered the front doors of the castle, he called two more guards over.

"These two say they have vital information for Duke Konrad."

One of the guards flashed a broad smile. "Don't you recognize them? They were the heroes of the fight with the Teutonic Knights a few days ago." He nodded and greeted Wolfgang and Mikolai.

The guard from the gatehouse turned to Mulan. "There was a man as you described who came through. He was limping and said he needed food and shelter, that the Teutonic Knights had burned his house and killed his wife and child."

Wolfgang grasped his sword hilt. "Where is he now?"

One of the other guards said, "He went into the kitchen to get food."

They turned toward the kitchen, but Wolfgang grabbed Mulan's arm. "Wait."

The guard who had recognized them nodded. "You go warn the duke and we'll look for Rusdorf."

Another guard went with Wolfgang and Mulan while the guard from the gatehouse hastened back to his post.

They trotted down a corridor, then up some spiral steps in the tower, with gray stone on one side and long, narrow windows on the other at regular intervals. Finally they reached the middle floor, turned down another corridor, and halted in front of a door. The guard knocked. There was no sound from inside.

Wolfgang drew his sword. "Break it down."

Wolfgang and the guard counted, "One, two, three," and slammed their shoulders against the door. The wood around the lock splintered and the door swung open.

Mulan followed on the two men's heels, straining to see around their broad backs as they raced forward.

A man was holding Duke Konrad around the neck, the duke's eyes bulging. Mulan pulled out her dagger and leapt toward the man while Wolfgang and the guard were charging him with drawn swords.

The man—with black hair, mustache, and pointy goatee, just as Andrei had described Rusdorf—released his hold on the duke and hoisted an enormous sword off the wall. He spun around and attacked both Wolfgang and the guard.

Rusdorf was smaller than Wolfgang or the guard, but he swung the heavy sword and landed the first blow against the guard's blade, which snapped in two. The top fragment struck the guard in the face, and he fell to the floor.

Wolfgang engaged Rusdorf, and they were blow for blow, toe-to-toe. Mulan had drawn her dagger almost without thinking and now approached Rusdorf from the side. He swung his sword toward her, but she ducked, causing him to miss.

That bit of distraction enabled Wolfgang to strike Rusdorf hard and compel him back several steps. Wolfgang went on the offensive. The grand master was forced to hold his sword in a defensive posture. His backward steps gave Mulan an idea.

She slipped past Rusdorf, leapt behind him, and swept her leg hard against his ankles. He fell backward, still holding on to his sword. As he hit the floor, his eyes caught Mulan's and hatred shone from their dark depths.

Wolfgang slammed his foot on Rusdorf's sword, pinning it to the ground.

The guard, blood running down his cheek, stood and produced some rope. Wolfgang kicked Rusdorf's sword across the room.

Mulan helped pin Rusdorf's hands together. Wolfgang tied his wrists as the Teutonic Knight growled something in German she didn't understand. She did understand when he said, in Polish, "God shall punish you for this."

The guard and Wolfgang were also shouting for more guards. More Teutonic Knights could be hiding inside the castle.

Mulan rushed to Duke Konrad's side, as he was slumped on the floor, his head leaning against a chair. He was breathing, his eyes open, and clutching his neck with one hand.

"Your Grace, are you well? What can I do?"

"Help me up." His voice was raspy.

Mulan pulled him into a sitting position, then the duke waved her off. He used the chair to help him get to his feet.

"Rusdorf." Duke Konrad stumbled to where Wolfgang and the guard were tying the grand master's hands. "Where are the rest of your men? Surely you didn't come here alone. No doubt you planned to kill me and then send your men a signal to swarm the castle. Where are they?"

Rusdorf held his head high, his thick black hair wild and curly. With his black mustache and goatee, he looked like the devil himself.

"God has anointed me to defeat you pagans. The Lord's will be done."

Men poured into the room. Thankfully, they were wearing Duke Konrad's colors. They grabbed the prisoner and held him before their leader.

Duke Konrad eyed the man who had nearly strangled him to death. "You have failed, Rusdorf, and now you shall pay with your life. Do you have a last request?"

Rusdorf's face was now unreadable, though he still wore his arrogant half smile. As his gaze darted over the faces of the soldiers surrounding him, it seemed to linger on one.

"My only request is that I know the names of the men who thwarted me."

"The names of your conquerors?" Duke Konrad grinned in triumph. "These two brave soldiers, the bravest of my allies, are Wolfgang of Hagenheim—a German like you, but much more noble—and the small but wily Mikolai of Lithuania."

Rusdorf's eyes widened. He focused on Mulan. "You are not the Mikolai of Lithuania I know."

"I am Mikolai's daughter." She wasn't sure what made her reveal that she was a woman. She simply didn't want to tell any more falsehoods, but also, there was a perverse pleasure in letting Rusdorf know he'd been defeated by a woman, one of those "instruments of Satan" he so hated.

Rusdorf's face twisted and even seemed to darken. He pursed his lips while the whole room remained still and quiet. All eyes were on her.

Finally Rusdorf broke the silence. "A woman wearing men's garments, fighting as a soldier. Has Satan blinded you Polish pagans as he has the Lithuanians? A woman! She should be burned as a heretic for wearing the raiment of a soldier."

Duke Konrad stared at Mulan, his mouth open, but he shut it at Rusdorf's outraged tone.

"We are no pagans, Rusdorf." Duke Konrad was amazingly calm as he addressed his enemy. "True Christians respect women and hold them in high esteem. Jesus took care of His mother and treated even the lowliest women, such as the Samaritan woman at the well, with kindness. It is too bad the Teutonic Knights' minds have been warped so that they call good evil and evil good."

Mulan's heart expanded at the duke's words.

"Take him to the dungeon." Duke Konrad motioned to his guards. "I shall decide what to do with him."

The guards pulled and shoved him from the room.

It was only then that Mulan realized they were standing in the castle's chapel. A beautiful chancel graced one end of the room, along with an enormous crucifix. The floor was an intricate design in black-and-white tile, and there was a colorful stained glass window at the other end. The duke must have been praying when Rusdorf found him and tried to strangle him.

The duke turned to Wolfgang and Mulan, and they bowed as a knight might bow before his liege lord. When Mulan looked up, Duke Konrad's expression relaxed.

"My noble rescuers." He stared enigmatically at Mulan. "A woman soldier. My wife will be pleased. But how did you come to the knowledge that Rusdorf was here?"

Wolfgang began the explanation, telling what they'd overheard from their vantage point in the tree.

"We were in hope that we weren't too late," Mulan added.

Her thoughts were spinning as her mind absorbed that she had been accepted, as a woman, soldier, and rescuer, by this duke.

"Indeed, you were just in time. You two are my guardian angels, preventing evil from befalling me. I am most grateful and must think of some way to reward you."

"What will you do with Rusdorf?" Wolfgang asked.

"He is the grand master of the Teutonic Knights. I don't want to be excommunicated for killing one of the pope's favorite people. I suppose I'll have to send him to the king . . . or make his death look as if it happened in the midst of battle."

The duke smiled and then laughed, a big, booming sound. "How enraged Rusdorf must be at having been thwarted by a woman— and the daughter of Mikolai, the man he hated and accused of pagan magic!" He laughed again. "My dear, you must tell me your name, for I know it cannot be Mikolai."

"My name is Mulan."

CHAPTER 15

Once again Wolfgang was enjoying the hospitality of Duke Konrad. It was evening, and he and Mulan were given places of honor at his table in the Great Hall.

Why was it so hard to look Mulan in the eye, now that everyone knew she was a woman? He had known before, and though the knowledge had made him want to protect her, he'd still felt comfortable with her. She'd become a friend and frequent companion. He even told her his greatest secret. Now . . . she was more than a fellow soldier. With the pretense gone, it made it somehow more real.

And the way she was dressed tonight . . .

The duchess had presented her with her choice of clothing, and now Mulan sat across from him wearing a bright-blue silk cotehardie with a colorfully embroidered neckline and sleeves. Her hair, a shiny curtain of black, fell down to her shoulders. After their rest—the duke had given them beds to rest in before the evening meal—her cheeks were now full of color, her lips red. Had her lips been that red before? Her long lashes were sooty and made her eyes look bigger in the dimly lit hall. He couldn't take his eyes off her.

But something was nagging at him, like a dream he couldn't quite remember. And then it hit him.

He had bathed in front of her.

His heart collided with his throat as he strained to remember it. She'd behaved strangely, or so he'd thought at the time. She'd been so nervous and seemed eager for him to leave, hiding behind the tapestry screen. Then when he was taking his bath . . . he demanded she bring him some cheese. She stared at the floor. Little wonder.

Their eyes met across the table. Could she read his mind and see him turning red? He was behaving like a girl child. But she couldn't know what he was thinking. He forced himself to study her face.

She was not the fierce, courageous, reckless-with-her-life warrior he had come to know but instead looked shy and unsure. She glanced away.

How would the other soldiers treat her when they returned to camp? At least they had not tried to forcibly expel her earlier. He'd thought he might have to fight to protect her. If he had, the other Hagenheim knights and guards would have fought along with him. But they had only seemed a bit sullen.

Though he'd treated her badly, had even tried to hurt her after the archery contest, she never seemed to resent him for his harsh treatment. And there was just something about her that inspired confidence and respect. He imagined the other soldiers felt the same way.

She ate rather more daintily than she was wont, seeming not to notice that everyone in the room kept staring at her. Again, she glanced his way. This time she didn't avert her gaze but smiled—a ghost of a smile, but it lit up her eyes. His breath rushed out of him.

She was beautiful.

Duke Konrad's captain of the guard stood and commanded

everyone's attention. When the noisy room quieted, the captain spoke. "As you all have probably heard, the grand master of the German Order, Rusdorf, disguised himself and managed to enter the castle. He found Duke Konrad at his prayers in the chapel, and during his moments of piety, the wicked Rusdorf sneaked up behind him and, coward that he is, grabbed the duke around the throat and choked him."

Growls and murmurs sounded from the crowd gathered in the Great Hall.

"The duke would have been strangled to death, but just at that moment, two brave soldiers, who are with us tonight, came to his aid."

The cheers were loud and sincere. Of course, they'd all heard the story by now. But it was part of the ceremony of the feast to allow the duke and his captain to tell the official account.

The duke now stood, and a hush fell over the assembly.

"Friends, these two soldiers Captain Bogdan has spoken of, responsible for saving me from my adversary, are among the bravest, cleverest of soldiers. Wolfgang Gerstenberg"—the duke motioned for Wolfgang to stand—"is from an old and noble family of great integrity, and his courage is truly laudable. And the soldier known as Mikolai of Lithuania will be praised for ages to come, notable as one who fights against injustice as well as against the limitations placed upon her. She pays limitations no heed, just as she pays none to the devil's schemes. This extraordinary soldier is"—he motioned for Mulan to stand—"Mulan, a woman of great credit to all of us united in our fight against the oppression of the German Order."

The crowd of mostly men must have already heard that Mikolai was actually a woman because they roared her name without hesitation, stomping and applauding. Mulan held her head high, but Wolfgang may have been the only one to notice that she set her hand on the table, as if to steady herself. As she calmly turned to look at the men cheering for her, she could have easily been a queen observing her subjects, that ever-so-faint smile on her lips.

He was so proud of her.

But an uneasy tightening in his chest alerted him to some unwelcome emotion. He wished they were alone together in a tree, talking about their childhoods or fighting side by side. Anywhere but here where all these men were shouting for her.

His gaze roved around the room, warning them with his glares that she was his friend, not theirs. But no one was looking at him. They were all staring at her.

Mulan did her best to hide the surprise she felt at being the object of the cheers and honor of her fellow soldiers.

And though she enjoyed the acclamation, she'd rather hear Wolfgang speak his approval. Was he proud of how she'd conducted herself? Did *he* think she was brave? Or did he resent her getting extra attention just because she was a woman? After all, he'd been at least as brave and heroic as she had.

But she was foolish if she let herself think of him as anything other than a friend. For many reasons they were unsuited to . . . She couldn't allow herself to even think about the possibility of marrying him. She didn't even know how to read.

All the shouting and stomping and clapping made her heart pound. As soon as it seemed appropriate, she sank back onto the bench. She wished they had seated her beside Wolfgang instead of across from him. He had a strange look on his face, and she wanted to know what he was thinking.

A few men approached her while she ate. They were all respectful but obviously curious. Wolfgang seemed hardly able to eat, his eyes never straying from them until they moved away. His glare was nearly palpable.

The duke asked her many questions about her childhood and her family. Eventually she told them how the two men of God, the friar and the priest, had predicted her future as a warrior. He and his wife, Duchess Katarzyna, plied her with even more questions, their eyes wide.

They consumed all the food they wished, and the men were left with only wine and strong drink. Wolfgang spoke to the duke and duchess, then came around the table toward Mulan. He leaned down to speak near her ear. "We have permission to leave and go to our chambers. May I escort you?"

Should she take his arm? He was holding out his hand as if to assist her, but she saw it too late. She was already standing. In the end they simply walked side by side from the Great Hall, shouts of approbation following after them.

They were alone in the corridor and on the stairs as they began climbing to the next floor.

"I—"

"You—"

They stopped on the steps and nervously waited for the other to speak.

"What were you saying?" Wolfgang asked.

"I just was thinking, you've never seen me in a woman's gown before. I must look strange."

"Strange? No. You look beautiful, the fairest of the feast."

"You learned your smooth talk from being a duke's son, I suppose." But she smiled up at him to soften her words.

"I was taught only to speak the truth. And you look exceedingly fair. Not like any soldier I've ever seen."

She checked to see if he was smiling. He was not.

"You do seem a bit tired." He moved so he faced her. "How is your wound?"

"It has been paining me a bit, but I am well enough."

"Do you have your mother's infamous salve with you?"

"I can send for Andrei and he can bring it, especially if you need some. How is your shoulder?"

"Your salve has nearly healed it."

"'God heals; we only assist.' That's what my mother always said."

"That is a good saying, I think." Wolfgang's brows drew together as he glanced down at the floor, then back up again. "I should let you go to bed, to rest. I—"

A loud commotion of voices made them turn their heads behind them. Wolfgang started down the stairs, holding one arm out as if to protect her from the danger below.

One of Duke Konrad's guards came running up. "The duke wishes to speak to you."

"To me?"

"To you and to Mulan."

Her heart crashed against her chest. She and Wolfgang hurried down the stone steps. The duke was standing at the bottom, a dark expression boiling.

"Rusdorf escaped."

"How?" Mulan's breath left her in a rush.

"He must have had his own men inside the castle. We found two of my men dead, their clothing stolen, in the back of the dungeon."

"Then let us go search for him." Wolfgang stepped forward.

"I've got men searching. It's dark. I shall send you out tomorrow. Tonight you rest. It is enough that you saved my life."

Wolfgang seemed as if he would argue. Finally he nodded. "In the morning, at first light, I shall be ready."

Wolfgang awakened before dawn with a servant standing over him.

"What is it?"

"Duke Konrad says scouts have spotted Rusdorf's army coming downriver on ships. They could arrive within the hour."

Wolfgang leapt out of bed and dressed with haste. Would he have to meet Steffan in battle? He wouldn't have had time to get back to board the ship, probably. But it made sense that they would also attack on land. After all, Rusdorf had brought more men to join the army they already had in the area.

He met Mulan on the steps as they were both rushing down. They joined the duke's soldiers outside. The air was cool and moist, mist rising from the river, as they moved across the castle courtyard and through the front gate. The duke's entire army moved quietly behind them.

A message had been sent to their camp, and Gerke and Andrei and their horses were to meet them just outside the gate.

Captain Bogdan emerged from the mist wearing his battle gear, a gambeson and a metal helmet. Wolfgang and Mulan were dressed similarly, as were the rest of the soldiers. A few of the knights on horseback wore full suits of armor.

No one spoke as they moved closer to the riverbank. The Teutonic Knights would almost certainly outnumber them, especially if they all attacked at once. Would they finally seize the castle and kill everyone inside? They'd already ravaged so much of the countryside.

Wolfgang and the duke's forces followed the river upstream, moving quietly. Even the horses made no sound as everyone watched for the ship to emerge from the fog.

Duke Konrad, dressed in full armor and his surcoat emblazoned with his coat of arms over his breastplate, rode his horse near them. He and Mulan nodded to each other. Everyone who met her seemed to love her, and now that they all knew she was a woman, they were in awe of her. It stirred an uncomfortable feeling inside him, and he began to suspect that feeling was jealousy. And possessiveness. He'd never felt this way about a woman before—wanting her all to himself, worried she might not feel the same.

But no one knew her and cared for her like he did. Except for Andrei. Perhaps he knew her better, but he was just a boy.

Instead of mounting their horses, most of them remained on foot, as they were so near to the river. They crept along, tiny water droplets forming on his eyelashes and clinging to Mulan's hair. She wore her black tresses unfettered, a short curtain falling over her neck. Her shoulders were taut and rigid.

They were about a mile upstream from the castle now. His feet were wet and a chill ran down his neck. If they could defeat the Teutonic Knights, then they could save Duke Konrad and the Polish people. But he'd never heard of a battle fought between an army on land and an army on water. Would the enemy have the advantage since they wouldn't be able to get to them?

A ship suddenly took shape on the river just ahead, emerging from the fog and mist, silent and hulking. Wolfgang, Mulan, and their fellow soldiers halted and watched the ship as it slowly made its way down the river toward them.

Mulan's hands moved with lightning speed as she reached for an arrow and nocked it to her bowstring. Wolfgang and the others in their company did the same. Gradually the shapes of men standing on the deck of the ship came into view.

The men behind them, the trained longbowmen and cross-bowmen, scrambled to light their special pitch-coated arrows with fire. Captain Bogdan looked left and then right down the lines of soldiers. Then he shouted, "*Strzelać!* Shoot!"

Wolfgang and Mulan let their arrows fly at the same moment, and the rushing, wispy sound filled the air. The sky was thick with them, as if flocks of birds had descended from the heavens. The flaming arrows came next. They struck the ship, sending the soldiers on board scrambling to extinguish the many fires that broke out on the wooden deck, the mast, and the rolled-up sails.

Wolfgang reached for another arrow, also with a prickling sensation on the back of his neck, because if the Teutonic Knights still in the area were to attack now from the rear, they'd be caught between the two enemy companies.

Mulan was to his right, and as soon as they both released their third arrows, the man to her right fell to the ground with an agonized cry. They kept shooting as arrows flew past them from the enemy to the front, and forward from their friends behind.

After several more rounds of arrows, it became clear that the enemy was sending fewer and fewer arrows their way. Wolfgang paused for a moment to see what was happening. Mulan lowered her bow as well. The enemy soldiers, their ship burning, were shedding their armor and jumping into the water. They were swimming to the other side of the river and getting away.

Mulan looked behind her. "Where's Captain Bogdan?" She stared up at Wolfgang with a fierce expression.

They both glanced around before spotting him lying on the ground, an arrow through his neck.

Mulan felt sick when she saw Captain Bogdan and his fatal injury. But there was no time to think about it.

She grabbed the reins of his spooked horse and yanked the leather bag off the back of the saddle. She and Wolfgang had discussed with Duke Konrad and Captain Bogdan Wolfgang's idea of something that would enable them to board the ship. The duke had supplied iron implements, called grapnels, and a couple of long wooden boards. Captain Bogdan had been entrusted with as many grapnels as they could find.

Mulan leapt onto the captain's horse. Then she held up one of the iron hooks with the thick rope tied to it. "Throw the grapnels!"

Wolfgang quickly distributed the heavy four-pronged grapnels to the men who ran forward. Then he and Mulan each took one and swung it around and around over their heads. In a few more moments Mulan and Wolfgang threw their grapnels toward the ship, ropes trailing behind them.

They landed on the deck, and Mulan yanked the rope, pulling the grapnel until it stuck fast into the wood of the railing. When there were ten grapnels gripping the railing, Mulan yelled, "Pull!"

They hauled the ship through the slow-moving water. As soon as the vessel was near enough to the bank, two men threw a long plank of wood across the divide. Wolfgang and some other men ran onto the ship.

A cheer rose and swelled louder. Mulan slid off the captain's horse, feeling a bit foolish for that bit of impulse, though it had seemed necessary to get everyone's attention.

All the Teutonic Knights who were still alive on the ship surrendered. Wolfgang and his fellow soldiers led their enemies, tethered together by their wrists, as captives onto Polish soil.

Suddenly an arrow flew past Mulan's ear. She turned around to see Rusdorf himself atop a horse in the midst of a company of his mounted knights, their white surcoats and caparisons with the black cross in the middle, looking like a horde of locusts descending on them.

CHAPTER 46

Wolfgang spotted the band of Teutonic Knights descending the hill above the riverbank, Rusdorf in the midst of them. But another figure caught his eye. Steffan, he was sure of it, wielding his sword as he rode a black horse near the front of the company.

Wolfgang's heart seized. Not his brother. With all the archers turning to aim at them, he'd surely be slain. His entire family's faces appeared before his eyes. Would he have to tell them Steffan was dead?

His company's archers quickly launched a volley of arrows at the advancing knights, so thick it took down nearly half the horsemen charging toward them. Had Steffan fallen? Such a melee of tumbling men and horses, such confusion and loud cries of both man and animal ensued.

And then Mulan ran toward the new battlefront. Was it his imagination, or was Rusdorf aiming his charging steed straight at her? If he managed to reach her, she'd have to fight hand to hand with him, and she didn't have her sword.

Wolfgang left the captives with his comrades and ran toward Mulan. As he did so, Steffan burst through the tangle of horses and men. His gaze was pinned on Wolfgang. Would his own brother attack him?

As he ran, Wolfgang looked from Steffan to Mulan and back again. Whom would he reach first?

Steffan looked bent on beheading him, a sword raised over his head. Wolfgang sent up a silent prayer to God—desperate and wordless.

One of Duke Konrad's men on horseback came out of nowhere and cut him off, causing his horse to rear and scream. The soldier struck Steffan's sword and knocked him off his horse.

Wolfgang focused his attention away from his brother as Rusdorf continued to charge toward Mulan. On foot and without a sword she was defenseless as Rusdorf raised his weapon over his head and prepared to strike.

Mulan quickly nocked an arrow to her bow and aimed at Rusdorf. She might only get one shot, so she waited. As he raced toward her, his face was contorted, his eyes black to match his hair. His black mustache and goatee were like a stained glass window she had seen once of the devil tempting Jesus in the wilderness. She aimed as carefully as she could and released the arrow.

It struck and bent Rusdorf back over the rump of his horse. But when he straightened, her arrow protruded from his upper arm. She had missed her target, and now his thin lips grinned menacingly.

Mulan grabbed another arrow, trying to launch it without aiming, but Rusdorf knocked her bow out of her hands with his sword. He launched his body from the saddle toward her. She side-stepped. He smacked her shoulder with the flat side of his sword blade.

She turned her head and braced for the next blow, but when it didn't come, she found Wolfgang standing over her, slamming his blade into the grand master's.

Wolfgang's heart nearly exploded as he threw himself between them and blocked Rusdorf's blow.

A roar erupted from his throat as he beat Rusdorf back, each step making Mulan a little safer. But he feared she would never be safe while Rusdorf lived.

Rusdorf was shorter and was wounded besides, so Wolfgang continued his onslaught. If he was patient, he could decisively defeat and disarm the man. Wolfgang could end his reign of terror on Mulan as well as these innocent people whose land had attracted Rusdorf's greed.

Though he parried each strike, Rusdorf was weakening. His wounded arm must have been seizing up because he stopped using both hands to hold his sword and let his left hand dangle by his side.

Wolfgang's spirit rose as Rusdorf's face lost its arrogance. His expression went from grim determination to outright fear as he stumbled backward. Just as Wolfgang disarmed him, knocking his sword from his hand, Rusdorf fell onto his back on the grassy riverbank.

Wolfgang pressed the tip of his blade against Rusdorf's chest, over his heart. He wasn't wearing armor, so he could kill him with one thrust. They would never have to worry about him again. But it would not be the knightly thing to do. He had defeated him in a fair fight, but to kill him now . . . Tempting, but it went against everything he'd learned about nobility and chivalry.

They had fully routed the Teutonic Knights. Rusdorf and his remaining soldiers were caught and would not escape this time. A fist tightened around his heart as Wolfgang searched for Steffan. Was he injured? *God, please let him be alive.*

At least Mulan was safe. He turned to gaze at her face. So peaceful.

There could not be another woman in the world such as her.

Mulan moved out of the way of the fighting men, watching as Wolfgang beat Rusdorf back, then disarmed him and pinned him to the ground.

But Wolfgang was not even looking at Rusdorf.

"What is it?" she asked.

"Steffan. He was here, in the battle."

Two of their fellow soldiers approached. Wolfgang gave them charge of Rusdorf and rushed away.

They helped Rusdorf to his feet. Without his sword—and with the arrow protruding from his arm—he appeared small. When his gaze set on Mulan, his arrogant glare returned and never wavered. But she would not allow him the satisfaction of knowing that his black eyes made her insides quake, so she pretended not to notice him and searched for where Wolfgang went.

All around her, at her feet and beyond, bodies lay on the ground, some writhing and moaning and others silent and still. But the fighting had ended, and many prisoners were kneeling with their hands on their heads, surrendering. She and her allies had defeated Rusdorf and his Teutonic Knights.

One of the soldiers was leading Captain Bogdan's white horse toward her, a sober look on his face. "We all want you to have the captain's horse."

Men ambled toward her and soon surrounded her, staring, as if she were their captain, looking to her for what to do next. She could no longer see Wolfgang or Rusdorf because of the crowd.

Duke Konrad rode his horse at a slow walk toward where Wolfgang had captured Rusdorf. The men around Mulan parted to let him pass, sensing the meeting that was about to take place.

"Rusdorf. Once again, you are in my power." Duke Konrad dismounted, a grim look in his blue eyes. He stood staring down at his adversary. A tiny smile lifted his lips. "And so soon."

He motioned to the soldiers nearby. They tied Rusdorf's hands together behind his back, ignoring the arrow that had gone all the way through his arm and stuck out of both sides, blood soaking his sleeve.

"Don't worry," the duke went on, "we will not torture or murder you, as you might have done had we been your captives. We will tend your wound and the wounds of your men. We might even allow you some of Captain Mulan's mother's healing salve for your arm."

"Keep that witchcraft away from me," Rusdorf growled. "My men and I have need only of an honest priest and his prayers for our healing."

"As you wish." Duke Konrad appeared quite calm as he raised his brows slightly. "We have many honest Polish priests in my region who would be willing to pray for you and your men."

Rusdorf clamped his lips together in a tight line.

But what had the duke meant by calling her "Captain Mulan"? Or had she misunderstood him?

Wolfgang hastened toward where he'd last seen his brother. His fellow soldiers were taking charge of the remnants of the Teutonic Knights who could walk, tying their hands and leading them away. Finally he saw Steffan standing in a line of prisoners. His hands were tied in front of him. Blood dribbled down his face from a cut across his cheekbone. He was staring straight ahead, fury infusing his expression.

Raw emotion took hold of Wolfgang. He wanted to strike his brother and he wanted to throw his arms around him at the same time. But he turned and walked away to help with another group of prisoners.

Instead of taking Rusdorf and the other prisoners to the dungeon—since he had escaped before—Wolfgang and his soldiers took them to the Great Hall and set them on the floor in a long line against the wall. Even the wounded prisoners were laid out there and given minimal care by the servants.

Mulan and Andrei were sharing her mother's healing salve with the soldiers who were the worst off. She approached Steffan. Wolfgang lurked closer, listening.

Rather than speaking to Steffan, she bent toward him and pointed to his cheek. He gave a tiny nod, and she took a wet cloth and dabbed at it. When most of the blood was cleaned off, she examined it closer. "I shall have someone stitch it up if you like," she said softly in Polish.

He shrugged.

"But it should heal quickly without it if you'd like to try my mother's healing salve."

"What's in it?" Steffan eyed the greenish-brown concoction with raised brows.

"Oh, garlic, ox gall, and some other things. It smells foul, but it works well to keep wounds from getting putrid and to help them heal more quickly."

"Very well." Steffan tilted his head to expose his wounded cheek to her ministrations.

Wolfgang held his breath, remembering how she had applied it to his wounded shoulder before he knew she was a woman. He let it out when she moved on and Steffan let his chin fall to his chest again.

He should go talk to his brother, should try to convince him . . . of what? What good would it do? He felt the same overwhelming emotion welling up in him again. He couldn't talk to him. Later, perhaps.

Duke Konrad and his captains were in and out of the Great Hall, shouting and celebrating their victory. Always, several armed men guarded the captives, and later a feast would be held to celebrate further.

Wolfgang and Mulan were both promoted to captains rather unceremoniously.

"Wolfgang," Duke Konrad said, "your company wishes to make you a captain. For Mulan, that honor already has been bestowed."

Did this mean Wolfgang was to be only a captain instead of a knight?

But it was Mulan everyone seemed to love. And why not? How bold and fierce she had appeared atop Captain Bogdan's horse, with the grapnel raised over her head! How beautiful, how noble and courageous, a peasant girl with the obvious favor of God.

Now that the feast was underway, rather than sitting across from him, she sat at his side, smiling and talking with Duke Konrad and his wife, regaling them both with stories of the battle, at their insistence. Several times she mentioned Wolfgang, turning to involve him in the conversation, but somehow he didn't feel like conversing tonight. His spirit was stirred, but stirred to silence rather than words.

What did his future hold? Where was he to go from here? The Teutonic Knights had been so thoroughly defeated, their army had retreated and there was no one left to fight. With the battle over, would they all return home—he to Hagenheim in the German regions and she to Lithuania, on the other side of Poland from his homeland? What other choice was there? He had nothing to offer Mulan, no land, no house, no title, nothing.

Perhaps it was not his long-term goal to be a soldier for a Polish duke, but Duke Konrad was a good and fair man. And the thought of never seeing Mulan again sent a stab of pain through him.

They feasted and drank and, surprisingly, no one went over to harass the prisoners in the same room with them. One soldier, obviously drunk, tried to, but Duke Konrad had him reprimanded by one of the captains.

"There is to be no gloating over our enemies," the duke said quietly. "A priest read it to me once, something God said to the Israelites."

The way the duke and his wife smiled at Mulan . . . They had no children, as the duchess was never able to carry a child long enough, and their babies were all stillborn. Would they become attached to her? As attached as he was? For he already felt almost as close to her as he had felt toward Steffan when they'd been inseparable. But it was a different feeling. She was a woman, after all.

It wasn't the way he felt about his sisters either. Mulan made his heart do strange things when he looked into her eyes and felt the integrity and goodness there, when she was telling him how much she cared about her mother, how grateful she was for her love when her father had brought her home with him, the motherless child of her husband's foreign mistress.

Mulan had been special even as a child. Two different holy men had prophesied about her—correctly, as it turned out. That a woman should do what she had done . . . It was not something that could have been guessed. The prophecies had been God-given.

She laughed at something the duchess said. The sound was so feminine. *She* was so feminine. His heart expanded.

God, is there any hope that she might . . . fall in love . . . with me?

CHAPTER 17

Mulan awakened with a feeling of foreboding. She searched her mind and memories from the day before. They had completely defeated the Teutonic Knights and taken over a hundred prisoners, including their grand master, Rusdorf. Duke Konrad was taking no chances. He was keeping them tied up, with many more soldiers guarding them than he normally would have. Wolfgang was safe, as was Andrei, who had brought their horses to the castle. He'd also brought her more of Mother's salve, and her wounds were feeling much better.

No, there was no reason for a sense of foreboding. She must have had a bad dream she couldn't remember. That was all.

She rose to don her garments, as the sun was already coming up. But what should she wear? One of the two silk cotehardies the duchess had given her? Or the coarse linen tunic and leather hose she'd been wearing as a soldier?

Since there were no more battles to fight . . . She reached for the fine linen chemise and silk gown. She slipped them over her head. Did Wolfgang think she looked pretty in her gown last night? What would happen when they parted ways? For they could not remain as they were. He would eventually go back to his family in Germany and she would return to her mother in Lithuania.

But had the prophecies been fulfilled? Or was there more she still had to do? Would she have to remain a soldier for the rest of her and her mother's lives?

She knelt by her bed. It had been many days since she'd observed any formal prayer times. She bowed her head. "God, guide me by Your Holy Spirit and show me where to go and what to do. I love these people here as if they were my own. If there is more for me to do for them, please show me."

She felt a peace in her core, a sense of finality. A vision of sunny wheat fields ripe for harvest flooded her mind. Duke Konrad's people were safe and free to plant their fields and harvest them again without being molested and burned out of their homes.

"Thank You, God." She kept her eyes closed and held on to that feeling of peace, wishing to bask in it as long as she could. But an unsettled feeling, a strange longing, soon replaced it, and Wolfgang's face appeared before her mind's eye.

"God, what am I to do with this longing?" She waited, but no answer came to her. Gradually, the foreboding returned. "Will something bad happen to Wolfgang? To me?" Her mind was vacant. "God? Are You there?"

A knock came at the door to her bedchamber. She took a deep breath and sighed, crossed herself, then stood. "Come in."

A servant, the motherly woman she had seen the first time she had come to the castle, opened the door.

"Please excuse me, but Duke Konrad wishes to see you, whenever you are ready. I was sent to help you, but I see you are already dressed. May I help you with your hair?"

"Oh, no. It is too short to bother with."

"Not too short, but very becoming as it is." The servant smiled.

"And may I say, I feel pleased and proud to be a woman whenever I think of you." She shyly bowed her head. "We all feel that way."

Mulan opened her mouth but didn't know what to say. "God is great. He has blessed me for His purposes, to do His good will. I had very little to do with it."

"You were willing, as some women would not have been. And you didn't make yourself into a man. You fight and live as you are—a woman. But I probably shouldn't be saying—you shouldn't care what a bunch of servants think."

"I welcome your kind words, and I thank you."

The woman curtsied.

Mulan made her way down the stairs to the Great Hall. It was strange to garner so much attention. She was not so far removed from a servant herself.

Her silk cotehardie rustled as she descended. She liked this gown even more than the first one the duke had given her. The deep red color contrasted with her black hair, and it made her feel feminine and . . . beautiful.

At one end of the Great Hall, Duke Konrad sat on his throne-like chair with a few other men around him. The prisoners were gone from sight, but she recognized one of the men speaking with Duke Konrad.

Rusdorf's arm was bandaged, and his face was nearly as gray as the gray linen bandage. He stood to the side, his expression a dark mask of stony coldness. When his eyes settled on Mulan, they narrowed.

Wolfgang was standing on the other side of Duke Konrad. His eyebrows were low and his mouth was pressed in a straight line.

"We have an agreement, then?" Duke Konrad addressed Rusdorf.

"What is she doing here?" Rusdorf's gaze stayed on Mulan as she walked toward them, pretending not to be bothered by his words. "Do you allow women to involve themselves in important negotiations?"

"She is allowed to go wherever she likes, for she is one of the commanders of my army."

A harsh laugh burst from Rusdorf. "You cannot be serious."

"What objections can you have? She defeated your men more than once and was the one who overheard the information that sent her here—just in time to save me from you."

It would have been understandable if the duke had said the words angrily or gloatingly. But he looked as if he were speaking of the weather rather than his attempted murder.

Wolfgang glared at Rusdorf.

"May God's will be done. I will accept your terms."

"And you agree never to attack anyone in my region, you or any Teutonic Knights, nor to even set foot on this land again? And in exchange, I shall set you and your men free to go directly back to Malbork Castle."

"I agree."

The hair on the back of Mulan's neck prickled. If Rusdorf signed the treaty and he and his men returned to Malbork Castle and their own territory, she and the duke's people would be safe. It must be the way Rusdorf had looked at her, his sneering contempt, that made her remember her feelings of foreboding.

"I shall have my clerk draw up a peace charter with our stipulations. Tonight we shall sign it, and you and your men may be on your way."

"Very well. But I warn you, Konrad." Rusdorf's voice was so low she could barely hear him. "Women have no place in battle and certainly no place in command. They are a restless evil, leading men astray, a favorite tool of Satan from the beginning of time. And this one"—he pointed at Mulan—"is from Lithuania, that last bastion of pagan worship, a cursed people. To trust her is to invite ruin."

Duke Konrad fixed his stony glare on Rusdorf. "I will not have you speak against Mulan, a faithful Christian warrior. Her father was an ally of my father. Mulan has proven herself noble and righteous. And if you say another word against her, I shall render our treaty null and void and turn you over to your enemy Vytautas, the Grand Duke of Lithuania, you and your men. He will ransom you and will execute those whose families cannot pay. You will not leave his dungeon until every penny of the ransom is paid."

Rusdorf's jaw twitched and hardened. No one spoke. The air was thick with tension, and Mulan's stomach tightened.

After several moments, Duke Konrad laced his fingers together. "Good. We understand each other."

With a wave of the duke's hand, guards led Rusdorf away.

Wolfgang approached Mulan and touched her arm, gazing into her face.

Duke Konrad spoke. "Don't worry, my dear. That should be the last you see of that toothless lion."

"He doesn't like me very much, does he?" She tried to smile, but the way Duke Konrad had spoken to Rusdorf, and in front of Mulan . . . She shuddered to think how the grand master might already be plotting his revenge. "Do you think he will truly never attack here again?"

"The Teutonic Knights, as well as their allies, the Livonian Brothers of the Sword, have ruthlessly raided Polish lands for two centuries. But Rusdorf prides himself on being righteous. If he signs the treaty, I believe he will honor it." The duke frowned. "But we shall see tonight if he is still willing to sign it."

Wolfgang used the time before the feast—after getting cleaned up—to write a missive to his parents. He told them that he and Steffan were both safe. He decided not to worry them with the details of Steffan's minor wound, his rebellion, or the fact that he was now with the Teutonic Knights.

He told of how they defeated the enemy, and he even found himself telling all about Mulan and her exploits in battle and of the other soldiers' acceptance of her even though she was a woman. He imagined how his mother and sisters would especially enjoy hearing about her.

"You would relish meeting her, Mother, and would like her very much." He stopped himself from writing, *She is fierce and good and humble and beautiful.* His heart beat faster as he realized how that would sound.

After writing to his family, he did need to speak to his brother, but it was difficult to think of what to say. Steffan wasn't reasonable, just refused to listen. His anger controlled him, and the anger made no sense. He was angry at the people who only wanted to help him. Why could he not see that?

After passing some time in prayer, Wolfgang went downstairs. Because of their caution, he had to bring a guard with him who could vouch for him, as no one was allowed to visit the prisoners.

The stench wafted up to him before he even reached the door leading down to the dungeon, where most of the prisoners had been installed. Human excrement mingled with sweat, but he felt more determined than ever to talk to his brother.

At the checkpoints along the way, guard after guard examined Wolfgang's face and asked him questions about who he was and where he came from before approving him to continue down to Steffan's cell. Finally he arrived and the final gate was unlocked. He went inside and heard the clang of the metal gate shutting and the click of the lock behind him.

A shaft of light shone in from a small slit in a window above them, too high for the tallest prisoner to reach. Wolfgang looked around at the men in the cell. All were shackled to the wall by one ankle. No one acknowledged his presence until one prisoner stood.

"Come to gloat over your brother, have you?" Steffan leaned against the wall.

"I came to see if you were well. To see if you need anything."

Steffan's harsh laughter told him this would probably proceed as he had expected. Unfortunately.

Steffan couldn't help a wry smile when he saw his brother enter his cell. Truly, Wolfgang owed him nothing, but Wolf was a kind and good person—not like him. Steffan was cold and unfeeling. The rest of his family were all unfailingly good, every last one of them, even his sister who'd been kidnapped by their mad aunt as a small child and raised a peasant. But Steffan could see the frustration in his family's eyes when they beheld him. They wondered why he was not as they were, why he had such a tendency to go the opposite way.

But no one wondered it more than he himself did.

Wolfgang thought it was because of what happened when they were children. Perhaps it was, but what good did it do to talk about it? Besides, he didn't like being lectured by his younger brother, as if he were the wise one. And now Wolf had come to see if he needed anything. In this dung pit? In this forsaken hole?

When Wolfgang didn't speak, Steffan said, "I am well. Do you not see the fine accommodations I've been given? But do not apologize, as I understand that you cannot give everyone the luxury chamber you give your Lithuanian lady."

Of course Wolfgang was too honorable to have claimed this warrior maiden for his own. Perhaps Steffan only said it because it was the kind of thing he always said. It was expected. Furthermore, he was in no mood to humble himself to his brother. Wasn't it enough that his brother had defeated him?

Wolf opened his mouth, a look of warning in his eyes, but then he stopped himself and closed it. Once again, Wolfgang was embracing the good and resisting the bad. Always the good one.

"How is your injury?" Wolfgang pointed to his cheek.

"It will probably be healed by morning, since your ladylove gave me some of her pagan witchcraft salve."

Wolfgang lowered his chin nearly to his chest and glared at Steffan. "You may not be disrespectful to Mulan. She is honorable and she deserves respect."

Steffan made sure to look amused. "I might have expected you'd fall in love with the first woman you met once you left home."

"I might have expected you to be even more surly and ignoble once *you* left home."

Steffan laughed. "I imagine I'll be surly and ignoble wherever I go."

Wolfgang's chest rose slowly, then slowly fell as he let out the deep breath. "Is that your only wound?"

"Yes, brother. God was watching out for me, do you not think?" He said it sneeringly, even though he actually did believe it. After all, his mother and father, sisters, indeed, his whole family of good people, were no doubt praying for him.

"God *was* watching out for you. I'm grateful you were not killed."

He couldn't think of anything sarcastic to say in reply. "I see you have come through unscathed."

"I was shot in the shoulder during the evening attack when you and your friends set a ring of fire around our camp."

His stomach twisted at the thought of Wolf being injured. Lest his brother guess at his feelings, Steffan chuckled. "That was an entertaining night."

Wolfgang wiped all expression from his face. "I would have hoped you'd be ready to leave the Teutonic Knights by now."

"We are a brotherhood, Wolf. We have a higher purpose, and once we are in that brotherhood, we never leave." He had not taken the sacred oath as a Teutonic Knight yet—he hadn't been knighted—but he didn't want Wolfgang to know that.

Wolfgang was still and silent. Truthfully, Steffan was weary, not having slept much in several days, which must have been why a twinge of sorrow and remorse stabbed his gut.

He wished he had a tall cup of wine. Or three or four.

"You will probably be released on the morrow, and I just want you to know that I care what happens to you, Steffan. And I'll be praying for you to surrender your heart and actions to God."

A bitter taste made Steffan's mouth twist. How dare his brother tell him he would pray for him. He knew Wolfgang was good and he was bad, but . . . it still left a bitter taste.

"You think you're better than the Teutonic Knights? We are sanctioned by the pope himself. We are the German Order. To fight against us is to fight against the Church and your own countrymen. You're only doing this because you have no thought or ambition of your own. You can't think for yourself. You only think what Father tells you to. You always did. But someday I'll be a commander or even the grand master. You'll be married to your peasant soldier, serving in the guard of some Polish duke and living in a hovel."

His words were unjust and he knew it. But it assuaged the pain in his gut to throw them in his brother's face.

Wolfgang shook his head. His voice was raspy as he said, "I don't understand how you can be so cruel and petty, Steffan. I want to help you—we all wanted to help you—but you make it impossible." He turned to walk away.

Steffan moved forward to grab him, but the shackle around his ankle jerked him back. Pain radiated up his leg from the metal cutting into his flesh.

Wolfgang looked back at him. He paused, then called the guard, who unlocked the metal gate and let him out. Then he was gone.

Steffan pressed his back against the uneven stone wall and sank to the floor, letting the stones scrape his spine. He *was* cruel and petty. Wolfgang was right. And honestly, he didn't understand it. He couldn't explain the anger, the impulses to rebel against his parents.

As he had suspected all along—he was born bad. It just made sense that of all his parents' children, they should have one bad seed.

CHAPTER 18

The prisoners were set free along with Rusdorf the next day. Wolfgang stood on the curtain wall watching through a gap in the crenellations as the group of them slowly made their way through the gate and to the north.

If Wolfgang could stop this pain, could numb it with something . . . For the first time, he understood those men who drank until they hardly knew where they were.

Must he forget about Steffan and give him over to a reprobate mind? What choice did he have? Only God could judge the heart, but by his words and his actions, Steffan seemed lost, his mind warped.

The anger he had felt toward his brother had changed to sadness and pain the moment he left him in the dungeon the day before. He would never stop loving his brother. And to love Steffan was to feel pain. He pitied the poor woman who ever fell in love with him.

But he didn't want to harden his heart toward his brother. It was Steffan's pain that made him lash out, but Wolfgang had seen his kindness and compassion too. When they'd been young boys, it was Steffan who sometimes said, "Let's get some flowers for Mother," and had stopped to pick her some of her favorite red poppies. And once he had insisted on taking a baby bird home that had fallen out of its nest. He'd helped find worms and insects and fed it until it was big enough to fly.

Surely there was still hope for him.

Someone was walking up behind him. He turned his head and Mulan stood a couple of paces away, watching through the next gap in the stones.

"There they go." Wolfgang was glad of someone to take his mind off his thoughts. Mainly he was glad to see Mulan.

"I hope you made some peace with your brother."

He shook his head. "There isn't much peace to be had with my brother these days. But I don't want to talk about him."

"As you wish."

"Forgive me for being impolite."

"Nothing to forgive. And I'm sorry your brother is difficult. I know it's not your fault, but I can see your heart is heavy."

Mulan was looking at him with those wise, almond-shaped eyes. Her expression was ever calm—when not in battle. With how he felt about her now, could he bear it if she put her life in danger again, recklessly risking her life the way she had in recent battles?

That was even harder to think about than Steffan. He'd have to contemplate that later.

"I hate to think of him without peace and with such a wrong view of our parents." He shook his head. "He has a wrong view of everything, it seems. Only God can help him."

Mulan said nothing. She was wearing a dress again. He hadn't noticed at first, but now he noticed something else. "You have flowers—and braids—in your hair."

Blushing, she reached up to touch it. "The servants did that. I didn't ask them to."

"It is very becoming." The white flowers contrasted with her black hair. He wanted to touch her cheek. How different she was from the fierce Mulan who led men in battle. And yet this soft, feminine, quietly understanding Mulan was the same person, the same friend he welcomed the chance to talk to.

She finally turned her gaze back to him. "I wonder if I should only wear my soldier's clothing. If I stay here as a captain for Duke Konrad's guard . . . they will not want to see me in a dress."

"If you stay? Are you thinking of not taking the duke's offer?"

"I'm not certain of anything. I suppose I shall stay until I know what else I should be doing. But Butautus will not allow Mother to keep her house if I'm soldiering for Duke Konrad and not for him."

He hadn't thought of that.

"Perhaps the duke would allow me to bring my mother here."

"Of course. The duke and duchess obviously admire you very much. They would help you find a place here for your mother."

She raised her brows at him. Did she know he was trying to convince her to stay?

"Now that the peace agreement has been signed, I'm not sure Duke Konrad needs me."

"A duke always needs good guards. One never knows when a new threat might arise."

"And you? Will you be staying with Duke Konrad?"

"Perhaps." He smiled, hoping he seemed jovial and unconcerned about his future.

Mulan peered up at him. "Duke Konrad said there is a pretty area with wildflowers and a tiny stream a little way from here. He said I might like to take a picnic there since I have no duties for a few days, but I don't want to go alone. Would you like to go? With me?"

His heart tripped over itself. "I would. Yes."

Mulan tried not to think about the future, tried not to think about Wolfgang and what his thoughts or feelings were about her. But trying *not* to think about those things rather led her *to* think about them.

And now, as she rode sidesaddle through the countryside in her dress, she wondered even more what Wolfgang was thinking. After all, she'd not asked anyone else to accompany her on a picnic. It was almost as if she was trying to get him alone.

But that was silly, wasn't it? After all, they'd been alone many times when they'd gone scouting and spying together. Perhaps that was why it seemed so different now. There was no upcoming battle, no enemy to wage war against. And she was wearing a very feminine dress.

Mulan glanced at Wolfgang out of the corner of her eye. Just at that moment, he glanced at her. She averted her gaze, as if she'd done something wrong. Oh, this was getting worse and worse. She was so nervous she could feel her armpits growing damp. How foolish she was being!

"Where did Duke Konrad say this place was?" Wolfgang didn't look nervous. He wasn't as foolish as she was.

"It's on the other side of this hill, I believe. There should be a small stand of trees, and in the middle of these trees is the stream and a small clearing."

Suddenly she had an idea, something that would rid her of this vexing nervous feeling.

"Let us have a race to the trees." She grinned at him and he grinned back.

"Ready? Go!" Mulan pressed her heels into Aksoma's sides. She was not as hearty as her father's horse, Boldheart, but she did like to run fast every so often, for a short way.

But already Wolfgang was two horse lengths ahead of her. She urged Aksoma to go a bit faster. They topped the hill and had almost caught up with Wolfgang. He glanced over his shoulder at them, then started pulling farther ahead as they started down the other side.

Mulan raced toward the stand of trees, but Wolfgang reached them before her, reining his horse to a stop.

"What do I win?" Wolfgang leaned toward her in his saddle. His bottom teeth were slightly crooked, all the more endearing for their imperfection. Did he know how handsome he was? Even if he were not so well-favored, she'd still feel this warmth for him, because he was the kindest, most attentive man she'd ever met.

Nothing like Algirdas.

But Wolfgang only thought of her as a friend and fellow soldier. He did say the flowers in her hair were "becoming," but that meant nothing. He might say that to a little girl he met at the market.

"You win the opportunity to share the picnic that Cook and the kitchen servants prepared for me."

"Ah. Next time I shall specify what I wish as my prize before I race you."

"And next time I shall ride my fastest horse so that I shall win."

Wolfgang laughed. It was a joyful sound.

They both dismounted and led their horses into the trees. They soon came to the clearing and the stream. It made a trickling sound as it slid and tumbled over the rocks on its way to the river. Birds chattered nearby, adding to the peace of the place.

They took the bundles from the backs of the horses and soon had all the provisions laid out—a simple feast of bread and cheese, cold meat, nuts, and dried fruit.

They ate and listened to the birds and the stream. She couldn't help glancing often at Wolfgang in the silence, but after he caught her staring at him for the second time, she forced herself not to look at him. Instead, she watched the stream and the way the sunlight glinted and glittered on the flowing, fluctuating water.

Even when she was sure Wolfgang wasn't looking at her, she still had the strange feeling that someone was watching them, possibly from the cover of the trees that surrounded them. She peered all around but saw no one. It must be her imagination, the vigilance of a soldier who'd spent the last several days either in battle or anticipating a battle.

Wolfgang took the small metal cup from the picnic bundle. There was only one, so he dipped it in the stream and handed it to Mulan. She took and drank of the clear, cool water, then gave it back to him.

He dipped it once more in the stream and held it out to her. "More?"

"No, I thank you."

She watched as he brought it to his lips and tipped it up. His throat bobbed as he swallowed once, twice, thrice. At the same time, water dribbled from the corner of his mouth and dripped from his jawline.

What would he do if she stood up and kissed him?

She looked away, appalled at herself. Kissing him, indeed. Wolfgang was her friend. She should not be thinking such thoughts about him. Someday he'd be married. She would never want his future wife to know that she . . . Well, she didn't want to think about his future wife. A spoiled, do-nothing, pale-faced daughter of a duke. Or at the very least, she'd be a wealthy knight's daughter.

Mulan lay back on the ground and stared up at the sky, but the sun was so bright, she closed her eyes.

Truly, she didn't know Wolfgang that well. They had fought together and been in life-and-death situations. They'd saved each other's lives, certainly, but was he truly as kind as she imagined? Perhaps she was making him into a better person that he was, fooling herself because he was the first handsome young man she'd ever spent time with.

Other than Andrei, who was only twelve.

She sighed. Perhaps being in battle had ruined her sound mind.

"This place is very peaceful," Wolfgang said from nearby. He was lying only three paces away, squinting up at the sky, his head pillowed on his bent arm. He chewed on a blade of grass, drawing her gaze to his mouth.

No. She would not let herself think about . . . Battle, horses, castles, swords . . . Those were safe things to think about. Armor and helmets and wounded shoulders . . . A memory flashed before her eyes of her dabbing her mother's salve on Wolfgang's wounded shoulder . . . of Wolfgang without his shirt.

"These were your first battles, were they not?" She said the first safe thing that came to mind. "I remember you said something about what your father told you about battle, about not becoming hardened and also not feel too guilty."

"*Tak.*" He propped on his elbow and faced her.

"Were your first battles as you imagined?"

He took the blade of grass out of his mouth. "My father described it fairly accurately. What about you? Did you feel prepared? Your father must have told you stories about battle."

"Not many. Mostly it was Andrei who told me battle stories, as he usually accompanied my father into actual battles so he could carry his extra arrows and other weapons."

"Andrei seems young for that."

"Yes. But he is mature for one so young."

His eyes fixed on hers as his gaze became more intense. "Did the prophecies happen as you imagined?"

"I never imagined being carried on men's shoulders or getting shot while sitting in a tree. But yes. I suppose I do feel as if the prophecies were fulfilled. It seems so strange that God would choose me."

"God knew you were brave and fierce. And that you would give Him the glory."

Her chest filled with air at his praise. She wanted to remember it always.

"Truly." His brown hair was tousled and boyish, a short strand of it brushing against his forehead, moved by the wind. "You always had this expression when you were in battle. Your eyes were bright and shimmery, and you were like an avenging angel, bent on completing your task, no matter what." He bared his teeth as if to mimic her.

She glared. "I didn't look like that."

"You're very intense in battle. You ran toward the gap where the enemy was shooting our men while they escaped the fire. You were the only one who did that."

"The only one besides you."

"We must have been mad." Wolfgang shook his head.

"God protected us, even though you were shot in the shoulder." She could tell he was still favoring it, not carrying anything on that side, flinching if he had to lift that arm too high.

He lowered his brows. "How is your injury feeling today?"

"Better."

"I'm glad." Wolfgang lay back and flung an arm over his eyes. "You said earlier that you might not stay here with Duke Konrad. Are you longing for home and for your village?"

"No. And you? Do you miss Hagenheim?"

"I asked you first." He smiled but didn't look at her.

"I didn't know this conversation was bound by laws." Mulan hesitated to reveal too much, even though she trusted Wolfgang as much and more than anyone else. "I am not longing for my home or my village. I miss my mother, but I always wanted to leave my village, to see the world, to do things I couldn't do in my village. Honestly, the thought of going back there . . . fills me with dread."

Wolfgang turned his head toward her, emotion flitting across his face. Was it her imagination, or did he seem . . . relieved?

Wolfgang regarded Mulan. "I'm glad."

"You're glad that going back to my village fills me with dread?"

"*Tak. Nie.* I mean, I'm glad you aren't longing to go back there right away."

"Why?"

"Oh. Well." He sat up and picked at the grass. Should he tell her the truth? But then he remembered something. "Because I thought you wanted to learn to read. And I'll instruct you."

Her expression froze, then split into a smile. "I would like that very much."

"I can't teach you to read Lithuanian, I'm afraid, since I don't know that language."

"I would be thrilled to learn to read Polish, since we both know it."

"I could even teach you German."

"I would like to learn German. I only know a bit that I learned from Andrei."

She sat up, her face bright, her eyes wide. He wasn't sure he'd ever seen her so joyful. If they had been closer, he suspected she would have embraced him.

How he wished they were closer.

"How did you learn to speak Polish so well?"

"From Andrei. He is Polish, you know. My father found him, an orphan with no family. Or rather, he found my father. He followed him around, trying to be useful to him, until my father agreed to let him be his servant."

"You treat Andrei as if he was your friend instead of your servant."

"He is my friend."

He nodded.

"And how did you learn Polish? Does your family speak it?"

"*Nie*, my brothers and I learned it from our tutors, as well as from our sword-fighting and jousting instructors, some of whom were Polish."

Mulan picked a tiny wildflower and stared down at it. "And do you like being a soldier?"

He thought about it for a few moments. "Truthfully, I don't think I'd like to be a soldier all my life, always going from place to place."

"What would you like to do, if you could?"

He remembered how badly he'd wanted to protect the woman Jacyna and her baby, how he'd wished he could protect all of the people the Teutonic Knights had oppressed, and how he'd wanted to protect Mulan, even before he realized she was a woman. And yet, he longed for a home and a wife and children, a place of stability. But he couldn't exactly tell her that.

"Perhaps I could be a farmer. Can you not see me plowing fields and sowing seeds?"

She raised her brows and shrugged. "You could do anything." Her expression grew more sober. "Your family probably expects you to make your fortune by marrying a wealthy heiress. You're a duke's son, after all."

"Is that what you imagine a duke's son does?"

She shrugged again, returning her focus to her flower. "Is it not?"

Was she sad to think of him marrying a wealthy heiress? Hope surged at the possibility. But that was selfish. He was not in a position to marry her.

"Do you have an inheritance?" She peeked up at him.

"Sadly, no, as my father has many sons. I'll receive something, but nothing so grand as a home or a fortune."

She twirled her flower.

The conversation that had started out so well had veered in a sad direction. They both lay back on the ground.

Was she as tired as he was? They'd been through battles and injuries and had slept less than normal the last few days. The summer sun was warm and was making him drowsy. He closed his eyes and felt himself drifting.

CHAPTER 19

M ulan lay in the warmth of the sun. Was it possible to feel so comfortable and at ease so soon after being in mortal battle, fighting for her life and the lives of those around her? Wolfgang reclined nearby, and then he was hovering over her, his face only inches above hers. His eyes were so brown, his expression so gentle. His lips were so perfect, and she wanted to kiss them.

It was as if by her contemplation, she summoned him to lean down, closer and closer, until his lips were touching hers, and she felt the pressure of them, firm and warm.

Mulan opened her eyes to blue sky above her. She looked to her right, and Wolfgang was yawning and stretching his arms over his head.

The kiss between her and Wolfgang was a dream. Only a dream. But it was so real she could still feel the pressure of his lips on hers. Was that how a kiss felt? She covered her face with her hands as her cheeks heated.

"I think I fell asleep," he said, letting out a long breath.

"I think I did as well." Mulan sat up and rubbed her cheeks and eyes. At least he couldn't know what she had just imagined. She stood and shook her skirts to rid them of dead leaves and grass.

"Ready to go?" He squinted up at her.

"I think we should." She couldn't even look at him or the dream would come flooding over her. She gathered up their things and tied the first bundle onto her saddle.

"Are you so eager to get back?"

"Just in the happenstance that Duke Konrad needs us. I don't entirely trust that Rusdorf won't do something to violate the agreement he signed."

Wolfgang frowned. "I don't understand why Rusdorf's life was spared when so many men were killed. But God must have His reasons."

"I was thinking the same thing."

"Perhaps God is giving him a chance to repent and change. After all, Rusdorf is known for his religious fervor."

"Sometimes those are the worst deceivers of all. Mother told me the stories of the Teutonic Knights and the Livonian Brothers who attacked Lithuania and ruthlessly slaughtered poor peasants and noblemen alike, all in the name of religion. I don't see how that is the Christian way. It's man's way, and I suspect they just blamed it on God."

A smile skimmed Wolfgang's lips. "I believe my father would agree with you. He has no good opinion of the Teutonic Knights or anyone else who uses violence to force people to convert. But . . . while I agree that Rusdorf is misguided, his attempted murder of Duke Konrad was in wartime. And he even told the duke during the peace negotiations he may have misjudged him. The duke seems to have impressed Rusdorf with his Christian piety. Or perhaps he was only impressed with his gold and ivory chancel and the marble tiles of his chapel."

"Well, he certainly wasn't impressed with me—or with women

as a whole." Mulan grabbed the second bundle off the ground, but Wolfgang placed his hands on it to take it away from her.

They were standing face-to-face, and Wolfgang's fingers brushed hers. Her gaze slid to his lips, and when she looked away, her breaths were coming shallow and fast.

"I'll take this one."

She let go, and he started tying it to his saddle.

"Rusdorf does have a problem with women. I heard that he despises women and never goes near them because his mother . . . I shouldn't repeat rumors, but they say she, well, didn't embrace morality. She had many lovers, which could explain why his thinking about women is so twisted. Besides that, the Teutonic Knights take a vow of chastity. They mustn't have any relationships with women at all."

"That doesn't mean they have to despise women and say they're all instruments of the devil. That's oppressive and unjust."

"I agree. Very unjust." He finished tying the bundle and turned to her. "I'm sorry he said what he did to you. He sounded evil and vindictive, but I would never let him hurt you. I would die before I let him near you." He cleared his throat. "And Duke Konrad wouldn't let him hurt you, and neither would the other soldiers and guards."

His declaration conjured up an emotion that took her breath away. She pressed her hand to her chest and turned away from him so he wouldn't see. "Naught but a bitter man and his ravings."

"Exactly. The ravings of a man who doesn't understand love. I've heard my father say, 'The love of a good woman is God's blessing and not to be taken lightly.'"

She spun around to look at Wolfgang. "Your father said that?"

His eyes were soft as he played with his horse's reins. "I heard him say that to my older brothers, Valten and Gabe, when they were about to marry."

"Your father sounds like a good and wise man."

"He is. A loving father and a kindhearted soul. I'm sorry you . . . Never mind."

"No, I didn't have a father such as yours. But at least I had a kind and loving mother."

They mounted their horses and rode back to the castle, her thoughts tangled up in Wolfgang, dream kisses, and kind fathers who taught their sons that their wives were a blessing from the Lord.

Wolfgang stood at the top of one of the castle towers, staring out at the hills and forests in the distance on this warm, pleasant day. While he waited for Mulan to meet him for their first reading lesson, he was remembering a day from several years before, when his mother had found him in the chapel at Hagenheim Castle.

"What were you praying about, if you don't mind me asking?" Mother's voice was soft and soothing as she sat beside him on a bench against the wall.

"For Kirstyn." She'd been through so much pain, and she was still not her old self. "I feel bad for her. I was just praying for God to give her peace."

She placed a hand on his shoulder. "Thank you for praying for your sister. I am sure God will hear and answer our prayers."

"I want to help her, and it makes me angry that there is nothing I can do. I know Steffan feels the same way."

"You're a thoughtful boy. 'Nothing can hinder the LORD from

saving, whether by many or by few.' Have you ever heard that scripture?"

"I don't think so."

"You are right to want to help your sister, but sometimes the best thing we can do, the most powerful thing, is to pray. God already knows how He will help someone, and He may use us, or He may use someone else, but our prayers help make it happen."

Wolfgang had been a little frustrated with her answer at the time, but now he thought he understood. Kirstyn's husband, Aladdin, had helped her heal. They were good for each other. Besides being kind to her and praying for her, there was not much Wolfgang could do to make it happen.

"Here I am."

He turned. Mulan stood behind him.

"I want to thank you for agreeing to teach me. I hope I won't prove too daft to learn." She sat on the stool in front of the small table he'd brought up the stairs with the help of a servant. He was suddenly very glad he'd chosen to have their lesson on top of the castle tower. She was even more beautiful in the sunlight.

"I'm quite certain that will not be the case. If anything, I may prove to be a daft teacher." Wolfgang tried to remember learning how to read from his tutors, but he had been so young, and it had been so long ago, he couldn't recall exactly how it happened. So he actually did feel like a daft teacher as he stumbled through their first lesson.

"I think I learned a lot today." Mulan smiled at him as the sun lit up her eyes and the wind gently tossed her hair. "May I take these parchments with me? When I'm not carrying out my duties, I shall review them."

"Yes, of course. I borrowed them from the duke's library, but

I'm sure he would not mind." Wolfgang rolled up the loose sheets of parchment and gave them to her. She thanked him.

A sudden urge came over him to pull her into his arms. Would she respond by wrapping her arms around him? Would she feel soft and warm pressed against his chest? His chin would rest on top of her head, her silky hair against his skin.

She tilted her head, a bemused look on her face. He swallowed the lump in his throat, but she turned and left before he could recover his voice.

Mulan and Wolfgang, as Duke Konrad's captains, had duties nearly every day: patrolling, listening to reports, and occasionally standing guard. But every day they seemed to find time for studying together. After a week, Mulan worried she was not very quick-witted.

Today they were in the room the servants used sometimes to prepare food, as well as for their dining room. It was empty except for two benches, a few stools, and a wooden table. They sat next to each other, with Wolfgang at the end and she to his left.

"Do you not think I'm daft?" Mulan grimaced as she said the words. "I'm not making very good progress."

"Of course not. I'm very pleased with your progress. You've already learned some words, and Polish isn't your first language. I think you've proven that you are not daft at all but rather gifted with language, especially since you've been taught by an inexperienced tutor such as myself."

She smiled and asked him more questions, and they read a whole page together.

"Soon you'll be able to read a Polish Bible."

"You don't think I'll know German well enough to read yours?"

"Someday you will, I am certain."

"I'm almost afraid to read the Holy Writ."

"Afraid? Why?"

"What if it reveals something I've been doing wrong that I didn't know?"

"I doubt that will be the case. But even if it is, wouldn't you want to know rather than remaining in ignorance?"

"I would. But what if it says something that surprises me? What if God turns out to be . . . different than I thought?" She chewed her lip and studied Wolfgang's face for his reaction.

"Why? What do you think God is?"

"He is an all-powerful Creator God, a God who demands obedience, and He sometimes seems like a harsh judge. But I like to think that He loves us, that He's a more kind and loving Father than our human fathers." She liked to think that God was nothing like her father, Mikolai.

Wolfgang squinted at the table, the look he got when he was thinking. "The tone of the Bible changes a bit after Jesus comes. There is so much about God's grace and mercy and love for us, you will think of Him less as a demanding judge. He is a kind and gentle Father who loves us. After all, everything before Jesus was leading up to this provision, the sacrifice of the Son, as the way to be forgiven and welcomed into heaven."

His expression was so earnest while he spoke. She'd never heard a man speak so sincerely about God besides the priests and friars that had come to her small village.

"So, you like reading it?" She found herself leaning toward him.

He nodded but stared at the wall behind her, as if considering her question. "I hardly remember a time when I wasn't reading it. I do like knowing what God has said, and there are some thrilling stories in the Old Testament."

Wolfgang smiled, his brown eyes gentling as he stared into hers. With his brown hair and dark stubble on his solid jaw and square chin, he was so masculine, and yet he was nothing like her rough and manly father. Her father was rude and barely spoke, except with the other men in the village. He hurt her mother by ignoring and dismissing her. But she couldn't imagine Wolfgang doing that.

"You said most of your brothers and sisters are married. Did your parents arrange their marriages? Have they arranged yours?" Her heart leapt into her throat at the possibility.

"No, my brothers and sisters all found love on their own."

"And you?"

"Me?"

"Did you ever . . . find love?"

He shook his head and smiled as if amused. "No. My father and mother taught me that love was not something to treat lightly."

"That sounds very wise." Mulan reached for the parchment papers and tried to look as if that subject no longer interested her, pulling the papers up close to hide her face, searching her mind for a question to ask about reading.

"Why do you ask?" Wolfgang's voice was insistent.

Her heart stopped beating. "Ask what?"

"Why did you ask if I'd ever found love?"

She shrugged, keeping the paper in front of her face. "Just curious."

"Did you ever love anyone?"

"Me?" She dropped the papers to stare at him. "No."

"Just curious." He was staring quite pointedly at her face. "I don't suppose . . ." He stopped and shook his head. "We should start our lesson."

"You don't suppose what?"

"Nothing. Let us begin."

Should she insist he tell her what he had been about to say? She ended up letting him pull the papers away from her as he started his instruction for the day.

· It was probably safer that way.

CHAPTER 20

Wolfgang had been about to say, "I don't suppose you could marry, as a soldier in the duke's guard." But he thought better of it. What would she think? That he was asking her to marry him? Or that he was saying he could never marry her because she was a soldier?

He always imagined he'd wed a girl who relied on him for protection and safety. But Mulan was an equal, a fellow captain in Duke Konrad's army. That didn't particularly bother him. And yet . . . it was unusual in the extreme.

Did he want to wed Mulan? Did he love her? He certainly thought about her a lot. She was the person he wanted to talk to, the person whose face he most welcomed seeing. But as long as his future was so uncertain, he couldn't allow it. As they had discussed before, it would be unwise to take such a step lightly, to allow himself to fall in love at this time in his life.

"Wolfgang? Are you ready to hear me read?"

"Yes. You may begin."

She scrunched her face, as if afraid of embarrassing herself.

Perhaps it was unwise to pass so much time in her company. After all, he could hardly look at her without thinking how fair and pleasing she was, especially now that she wore her hair down and allowed herself to move and speak more naturally. She was incredibly comely. The womanly Mulan contrasted with the soldier Mulan somehow made her even more appealing. And the more he got to know her, the more comfortable he felt with her.

Sometimes, though, he laughed when he thought about how she used to try to deepen her voice and walk like a man.

"Are you listening?" Mulan was staring openmouthed at him.

"Keep reading."

Her shoulders slumped and she sighed. "This must be so dull and uninteresting for you. You don't have to listen."

"It's not dull. I want to hear you read. My thoughts just . . . wandered. Please. Read it again."

"What were you thinking about?"

"Nothing."

"That's not true."

"I was only thinking . . . how you used to deepen your voice when you were pretending to be a man."

She shook her head and groaned.

"Come. Read to me." He sat forward, his knee brushing hers under the table. He moved his leg back and tapped on the parchment. "Read."

She rolled her eyes but then complied.

"That's very good. You're an excellent student."

She rolled her eyes again. "I never know whether to believe you when you compliment me."

"Why do you say that? Have I not always been honest with you?"

She frowned. "Teach me some more German. How do I say, 'The weather is beautiful today. Let us go for a picnic.'"

He spent the next half hour teaching her those phrases and

a few other related words. The entire time he kept imagining her saying that to his mother. He didn't know why, because his mother could speak fluent Polish.

Mulan had been assigned to patrol with Wolfgang for the third time in only two weeks. She was beginning to suspect someone—probably either Duke Konrad or Duchess Katarzyna—of putting them together for some purpose other than a military one. But far be it from her to accuse a duke or a duchess of matchmaking.

In her heart she silently blessed them. The more time she passed with Wolfgang, the more she longed to be with him. Foolish or not.

Wolfgang smiled when he saw her in the stable.

"I'll have Boldheart saddled in a moment."

They set their horses a brisk pace, riding north past the place where they had gone on their picnic just after the battle defeating the Teutonic Knights. Later, as they settled into a slow walk, they talked of favorite foods and dishes, which led Wolfgang to talk about favorite feasts, which led to a discussion of their favorite holy days and festivals.

"I never wished for a large family before," Mulan confessed. "But you make it sound like a wonderful life, growing up with so many people."

"I am grateful for my family, that they're so loving. I do regret not being a better brother when I was a child."

"I'm sure no one holds it against you."

"I know." But he looked a bit solemn.

"Did any of your family call you Wolfie?" She felt herself

blushing at the question. But he couldn't know that she sometimes imagined calling him that, in her weaker moments, especially when she thought about that dream when he kissed her.

Those weak moments were becoming more and more frequent.

"My mother sometimes calls me Wolfie. My brothers and friends sometimes call me Wolf."

"Do you dislike it?"

He shrugged. "No. Mostly, everyone calls me Wolfgang. I used to wonder why they didn't shorten my name more often, since my brother Gabehart is nearly always called Gabe."

She felt a longing as she listened to him. It was becoming an ache inside her, to be closer. Close enough to call him Wolfie.

But she *shouldn't* long for that. And in her stronger moments, she *didn't want* to long for it, as it wasn't likely to happen. She couldn't imagine he would ever marry her.

She also longed for friends. She missed Agafia, prayed for her brother, and wished she was with her so they could talk, giggle, and Mulan could tell her all that had happened, and especially about her secret feelings about Wolfgang. And she missed her mother even more.

Thinking about Mother made tears sting her eyes. At least she managed to talk with Andrei every day. And now she talked with Wolfgang more than with anyone else.

She longed for a woman friend, someone who could relate to her in a way a man could not. She looked forward to the few words she was able to speak with Duchess Katarzyna and the servants who came to her chamber.

"You have a faraway look." Wolfgang was gazing at her. "What are you thinking?"

"I wish I knew your sisters," she blurted out. "I would have liked to have known them, since I never had any sisters. Because of the stories you told me about them."

"I hope you can meet them someday. That is . . . it would be good if you could."

He meant, of course, that she probably never would meet them, but she would like them if she did.

Pain stabbed her heart. He couldn't wed her. Of course he couldn't. But she knew that already. So why did it hurt so much to hear him acknowledge it? She hadn't realized until this moment how much she had hoped he would.

See how foolish you are? Thinking a duke's son would marry you. You are not fine or feminine enough. He needs a wife who can dance the intricate dances and say the appropriate, fancy words, and know what to do around other noblemen and women.

She knew nothing about those things.

Mulan leaned forward, nearly gasping. She had to stop this before Wolfgang asked her what was amiss. *Remember how much the other soldiers admired you for your fighting skills, how they hoisted you onto their shoulders? Remember how Duke Konrad lauded and honored you at his feasts? You are a soldier, not a wife. And you should be content with that.*

She simply would not look at Wolfgang anymore. That should help rid her of this fascination with him. After all, she'd had her chance at marrying someone of her own station, and she had not wanted it. Instead, she'd chosen to be strong and independent and to help her mother. She'd set out to make sure her mother kept her house and she'd accomplished that goal—she, a woman, had done what only sons were supposed to be able to do.

Mother would be proud of her if she could see her now, could see that she'd been promoted to a captain in Duke Konrad's guard. Mulan would dwell on that.

"You heard the reports," Wolfgang called back to her over his shoulder, "that there are stragglers from Rusdorf's army."

"The ones who are raiding the farmers' fields and livestock?" She barely glanced his way and utterly refused to look at his face. He was just another soldier, was he not? No better and no different than she was.

"One was spotted near here. I think we should search these woods. They might be making camp there."

"Very well." She shrugged as if she didn't consider his idea particularly brilliant. She turned her horse to follow his toward the section of forest to the west.

Just as they were about to enter the woods, Mulan heard hoofbeats. Two riders were coming their way.

She and Wolfgang reined in their horses and waited. Soon she recognized two of their company, Petrus and Johannes. When they were still a hundred feet away, Johannes seemed to say something to Petrus. Mulan didn't like the look on their faces, though she couldn't say exactly why.

They greeted each other, then Petrus said, "We've just come from the eastern fields where there was a report of a man stealing chickens. Then we saw his fire and where he'd been bedding down."

Petrus moved his horse between hers and Wolfgang's and talked to him about what they'd seen and heard on their patrol. Johannes moved his horse quite close to hers, so close she began to think about where her long knife was and how she could get her hand on it. But perhaps she was being overly suspicious.

"You seem to go patrolling with Wolfgang a lot." Johannes's

voice was too low for Wolfgang to hear. "Are you and he . . . ?" He raised his brows and inclined his head toward Wolfgang.

"Are we . . . ?" She glared at him, daring him to insinuate—

"Are you his love? Because if you're not . . ." He moved his horse even closer, until his knee was pressed against hers. His lips curled in a disgusting smile. "I was thinking you should meet me somewhere and we could . . ."

Mulan snatched her dagger from her belt before Johannes could react. She pressed the point against the middle of his chest. "I know you are not suggesting what it sounds like you're suggesting." Her face burning, she kept her voice low.

His eyes widened as he stared down at the knife point.

"If you ever touch me, this knife will make you rue it."

He backed up his horse, his expression turning sulky. His lips that were a few moments before curled in a lascivious smile, now puckered as if tasting something sour.

Mulan moved her knife down by her thigh, hoping not to attract the attention of Wolfgang and Petrus. But their faces betrayed the fact that they had seen at least a portion of what had passed between her and Johannes. Petrus's eyes were big and round, his mouth agape, but he soon started laughing.

Wolfgang's jaw twitched as if he was clenching his teeth. "What goes on here?" He glared at Johannes.

Johannes's horse sidestepped away from Mulan's. He didn't answer.

Wolfgang looked to Mulan.

"Johannes asked me a question and I gave him my answer." Her face still burned and her breath was beginning to quicken, as if a delayed reaction to what had happened. She made a show of putting her knife back in its sheath in her belt, taking her time.

Wolfgang's face showed his understanding as he glared at Johannes. But that man carefully avoided meeting his eye.

Petrus made an excuse for going back the way they had come, and they rode away as if a wolf were at their heels.

"Mulan, what did that man say to you? I'll go after him."

"No. It was nothing." It was something, but she didn't want Wolfgang to get involved.

"Are you all right?" Wolfgang said the words softly.

"Of course." She had to swallow hard to get past the lump in her throat. *Stop looking at me.* The compassion in his eyes made her insides tremble and tears threaten.

"If he touched you, I'll kill him."

"He didn't touch me." *He just wanted to.* Her stomach churned.

"I'll bring him back here and force him to beg your forgiveness."

"No. I don't want to see him again. Besides, if he tries to touch me, I'll cut him."

"If he ever bothers you again or if anyone else ever treats you with anything other than respect, I want you to tell me."

"Thank you, but I can take care of myself." She might not be a fit wife, but she was a soldier, and as such, she intended to defend herself from any and every danger.

Mulan and Wolfgang strode into the Great Hall where Duke Konrad spent most of his days meeting with people.

"You wished to speak with us, Your Grace?" Mulan was eager to get back to studying before she had to go on watch for a few hours. But the duke's expression made her halt midstep.

"Mulan, I have just received two messages, one from an ally

to the north whose land adjoins that claimed by the Teutonic Knights and one from Rusdorf."

The duke took a breath and blew it out. Wolfgang's shoulders stiffened, and he was clenching his jaw, just as he did in battle.

"What? What is it?" She turned and pointed at Wolfgang. "You know, don't you?"

He shook his head. "I only heard a rumor yesterday. I hoped it wasn't true."

Her face burned as fear and dread clouded her thoughts.

The duke fixed his eyes on Mulan. "Rusdorf has taken your mother from her home and brought her to Malbork Castle."

"For what purpose?" Her hand twitched to grab her bow and arrows, moving toward her back. But of course she wasn't wearing her weapons, having come from studying reading with Wolfgang. She clenched her hands into fists.

"He says he intends to try her as a heretic, accusing her of witchcraft. But he's only doing it to seek vengeance on you, perhaps even to trap you."

Mulan's heart was pounding even as her stomach sank. *Mother.* She did not deserve this. *God, please help me save her.*

"I will go and set her free."

"No, I'll go and free her." Wolfgang's expression was wild, his eyes wide and dangerous.

"From Malbork Castle? Impossible." Duke Konrad shook his head, his brows drawn together.

"She is my mother. I must save her." Everyone knew what would happen to a woman found guilty of witchcraft. She'd be burned alive. "How much time do I have? No matter, I'll leave immediately."

Mulan took two steps before Wolfgang touched her arm and halted her. "You must not go alone. I shall come with you."

"I suspect it is a trap." The duke inclined his head at her.

"I'll not let him murder my mother. I ask you, Your Grace, to allow me to go and champion my mother however I can, and then, if I live, I shall return here and serve you. But I'll not concede defeat to Rusdorf and his tyranny, not when my mother's life is in danger, and not without a fight."

"I understand, but take Wolfgang, and I shall send two more guards with you."

Mulan nodded at Wolfgang. "Very well."

"I wish I could do more, but the treaty we signed . . . If I send my army, he will see it as a sign that I'm breaking our agreement."

"I understand."

"All I can do is send a letter threatening him. If he should harm your mother in any way, he will answer to me."

They both knew that meant very little, but she thanked him anyway. Blood was flowing through her limbs, and she wanted to be on her horse and galloping toward her mother and the Teutonic Knights' Malbork Castle.

CHAPTER 24

As he followed Mulan out of the Great Hall to prepare for the journey to Malbork Castle, Wolfgang's blood boiled at what Rusdorf was doing—nothing but revenge for his wounded pride at being bested by a woman. Cruel, inhuman . . .

"Thank you for coming with me." Mulan turned around and halted on the step above him. "But I don't want anything to happen to you. This is my fight." She pressed a fingertip to her own chest.

"Perhaps God wants you to be humble enough to accept my help." Why was she being so stubborn? "I am coming with you no matter what you say."

She glared, squinting at him. Then she turned and flew up the stairs to her chamber and closed the door.

Did she not trust him, after all they'd been through? Did she have some fear of accepting help? Was it pride? Was she unable to accept that he wanted to help her, without any agenda of his own?

No time for arguing now, but the way she didn't answer him, only left him in silence . . . He had better make haste, lest she leave him behind.

He threw some clothing in a bag and sent Gerke scrambling to gather his weapons. Then he went out and found Mulan departing her chamber at the same time. They rushed down the steps together.

He imagined how he would feel if his mother were in danger and was being used as bait to deliver him into the hands of a sinister foe. The resulting emotions kept him silent.

Their horses were saddled and waiting for them—they had saddled Boldheart for her—along with an escort of two other guards, their friends Simon and Gregorius.

Andrei ran up to them. "I'm going with you!" He had his bag under his arm and he ran to the stall. "It won't take long to saddle Aksoma."

Mulan's expression was troubled but she said nothing.

Gerke followed Andrei and saddled his horse as well. Soon the six of them were ready and set off. Would they succeed in rescuing her mother from Rusdorf and the Teutonic Knights? There were many uncertainties, but he would never let Mulan take this journey or face this danger alone.

Mulan had never prayed as hard as she did that night when they stopped to make camp. Mother must be so frightened. Were they mistreating her? If only she could arrive faster, but she'd been told it would take three days. *God, send Your angel armies to surround my mother and keep her safe, and send Your power to save, that we might rescue the innocent from the unjust ruler who has imprisoned her.*

"I thought I saw someone following us," Wolfgang said as they sat around the cook fire.

"Where? I thought I saw a rider too." Simon leaned forward.

"Do you think he was following us?" Gregorius asked. "I only saw him once."

They soon concluded that they would keep an eye out for the lone rider and waylay him if he appeared again.

Mulan prayed while lying in her tent, which she no longer shared with Andrei, now that everyone knew she was a woman. Her friends surrounded her, bedded down nearby, and their presence gave her a measure of comfort. She received much more as she whispered, "God, I know You are with me. You will never let the righteous fall. You are my mother's strong tower, her deliverer, and nothing can hinder You from saving, whether by many or by few."

The Bible passages that she had asked Wolfgang to help her memorize came flooding to her mind now that she was praying. She held them like a warm embrace to her heart, closing her eyes. "God, I know You are with my mother and You will never leave her or forsake her. Because of You, God, I can sleep in peace and safety, and I'm believing that You are giving peace and safety to my mother as well. Thank You."

The next day they rode hard. Mulan focused her mind on getting there as quickly as possible. One more night and then riding another day and they should be there. But during the long hours of hard riding, fear kept attacking her. She thought of everything that could go wrong. Her mother's frightened face haunted her.

They halted at midday to rest beside a stream. As she dismounted, Mulan spotted a horse and rider two hundred feet behind them, disappearing into the dark woods they'd just passed through.

She squinted, staring hard at the spot where she thought she'd seen him vanish, but there was no sign of anyone and no movement. Did she imagine him?

On the evening of the second day of travel, Simon, Gregorius, Gerke, and Andrei went into a rather large village to see about buying food. They left Wolfgang and Mulan at a stream to build a fire and make camp.

Mulan couldn't seem to stop contemplating how unfair it was that her mother was being persecuted by an evil man who had taken vows to God.

As she took care of her horse and made sure his hooves were shod and in good condition, her thoughts went again to her mother, falsely accused, frightened and alone at Malbork Castle, possibly even sick or hurt. Mulan's chest ached and her eyes grew watery. She leaned her forehead against Boldheart's broad neck as the tears she'd been holding inside for days streamed down her cheeks.

Wolfgang's footsteps approached. She lifted her head from her horse's neck and turned away, frantically catching the tears with her fingers and wiping them on her shirt.

"Mulan?"

He was right behind her, and his low voice seemed to make the tears fall faster, faster than she could wipe them away.

"Worried about your mother?" His hand touched her shoulder, gentle but warm. "Is there anything I can do?"

He stepped in front of her, easing her shoulder toward him. She kept her head down, still wiping frantically at her wet cheeks. And yet . . . her heart weighed a hundred stone and was breaking in two.

"I can't let him hurt Mother." She choked out the words.

"Please, God." She started sobbing, and he did what she had word-lessly longed for: Wolfgang put his arms around her shoulders, pulling her forward until her damp cheek rested against his chest.

Huddled against him, she quickly suppressed the sobs and concentrated on breathing in and out. Wolfgang was holding her. Even her ugly, horrifying thoughts didn't feel quite so terrifying with his arms around her. Part of her soaked it in, even as the other part trembled with a nameless fear that this was going to lead to her hurt.

He spoke softly against her hair. "I'm so sorry this happened, but God is on the side of the righteous. He will help us save her. All will be well. Believe it."

His shirt smelled so good—like outdoors and leather and *him*. She was being foolish, but she didn't care. It felt so good to be held by Wolfgang.

Her tears had subsided, but she worried that her nose would drip. She pulled a cloth from her pocket, trying not to move too much or make him think she was trying to get away, and when she brought the cloth to her nose, he actually drew her closer. She could feel his chin resting on her head.

She never wanted to move from this spot. There was only the gentle sounds of the stream trickling over the rocks, the crunch-ing of their horses cropping the grass at their feet, and—was she imagining it?—Wolfgang's heart beating against her ear.

He cared about her, and she just might float off the ground. But in what manner did he care for her? As a soldier cares for his fellow soldier? Or as a man cares for a woman?

No, she would just enjoy this moment and not let herself think any further about it. Mother was most important now any-way. She closed her eyes as he spoke again.

"If God is for us, Rusdorf cannot win."

She took a deep breath, his scent filling her senses. Her knees went a little weak.

"We will slip into the castle unobserved and steal your mother away if we have to."

"But you have heard how many guards that place has." Mulan couldn't seem to stop herself from speaking her fears. "It's impenetrable. And very large, and we can't know where he's holding her."

"We will find a way. Perhaps your mother has already convinced him that he is evil for accusing her falsely. Perhaps he will set her free."

"You know that's not likely."

"Anything is possible with God."

She let her arms go around him—such heaven. But it was wrong to take advantage of his kindness, when he probably had no idea how much she desired more than just his friendship.

She gently pushed away from him and pressed her cloth against her eyes and nose. Wolfgang left one arm around her shoulder, still standing very close. If she lifted her head . . . would he kiss her?

Mulan squeezed her eyes shut. *Do you want to make a fool of yourself? Do you want to be rejected and embarrassed? To give Wolfgang the wrong idea about you?* He had no idea of her feelings. He certainly wasn't thinking about kissing her.

Was he?

With reluctance Wolfgang let Mulan pull away from him. If only he could have held her forever, feeling her breathe, inhaling her heady scent of fresh air, trees, and flowers—must have been some womanly scented soap the duchess gave her. And yet, if she knew how much he'd hoped she would lift her head, then close her eyes . . . If she had, he would have leaned down and kissed her.

He was nearly as bad as Johannes, contemplating taking advantage of her when she was upset and worried about her mother. Besides, a good man didn't go around kissing women and breaking their hearts. But he rather figured it was his heart, not hers, that was in danger.

He kept one arm around her while she wiped her face. She was his friend, after all. It twisted his gut to see her cry. If it would take away her sadness, he'd rip Rusdorf apart with his bare hands. But as Wolfgang had learned from his sisters, as well as from advice given by his father, women just wanted someone to be compassionate when they cried. To mend the problem was secondary.

She took a deep breath and let it out. Finally she smiled, her gaze not rising higher than his chest.

"I'm sorry for crying on you. I think I dampened your tunic." She reached out and wiped it with her cloth. There was something about the look on her face, her movements and her posture. Was she feeling this . . . whatever it was between them? Longing? Closeness? Anticipation?

"I don't mind." He didn't move, watching her cheeks blush a pretty pink, her eyes focused on his shirt. *Look up. Look up at me.* If he saw that something in her eyes, he might dare . . .

She was still wiping at his shirt. After a moment she stopped, but she still didn't lift her eyes above his chest.

"I suppose the others will be back soon." Her voice was wispy, as if she had lost her breath.

Her hand dangled now beside his. He brushed it with the back of his hand. She didn't move.

He wrapped his fingers around her hand and squeezed it, ever so gently. She didn't pull away.

Her lips parted slightly as she stared down at their joined hands. He lifted her hand slowly . . . slowly . . . and her eyes followed. He brought her hand all the way up to his lips and kissed it, reveling in her soft skin on his lips. Her eyes met his.

She stared at his mouth, her lips softly parted. A jolt shot through his middle and his heart pounded. He lifted his lips from her hand and drew it to his chest. She took a tiny step toward him. He leaned down and hesitated. She closed her eyes. He pressed his lips against hers.

There was nothing in the world except the feel of her lips on his, the sound of her breathing . . . until the sound of horses' hooves intruded.

A sharp ache stabbed his chest as he pulled away.

Her eyes fluttered open. She stared at him as if she wasn't sure what had just happened. Then she stepped away and spun around, taking hold of her horse's reins.

He groaned inwardly. Was she horrified at what he had done? He was probably fortunate she didn't grab her knife, or slap him, or both.

Or had she felt that moment of absolute rapture that had caught hold of his heart and sent it flying into the heavens?

"Mulan, I—"

She held up her hand, keeping her back to him. "The others are approaching." But then she whirled around and glared at him with narrowed eyes.

His stomach sank. What did that look on her face mean? Anger? Suspicion? Pain? He hadn't wanted to hurt her. He just wanted to show her . . . he was falling in love with her. Did she feel it too? His heart soared at the possibility that she felt it too.

But he could not just kiss her—even a gentle, brief kiss—no matter how strong the temptation had been. She didn't know what his intentions were. And neither did he, in truth.

Except he did know what his intentions were. If they could survive this impending confrontation with Rusdorf . . . Wolfgang might be just a poor soldier with nothing to bring to Mulan, but he could not imagine ever loving another woman besides her, and if she would wait for him, he would prove to her that his intentions were matrimonial.

But he should not have kissed her. She would not wish to be alone with him now. She would be suspicious and angry.

He'd just made things much harder. And yet . . . he finally knew exactly what he wanted.

CHAPTER 22

M ulan's eyes filled with tears. She had wanted Wolfgang to kiss her, but . . . what did it mean?

Wolfgang had never seemed like the type of man to trifle with a girl's heart or hurt her, and yet . . . she also would not have thought he was the type to kiss a girl when he had no means of marrying her. He had made it clear he had no fortune of his own, no home where they could live. Did he think this was a competition and he could kiss her even though she had rejected Johannes?

No. She couldn't believe Wolfgang would think like that. But she suddenly wanted to demand an explanation from him, no matter how uncomfortable that would be.

Their friends neared. How humiliating it would be if they heard Wolfgang explain why he'd kissed her! But that was not why she felt as if she were being split in two. Wanting him and yet terrified to feel so vulnerable. She was so afraid to want him!

What right did she have to be angry with him? She could have pulled away, could have stopped him, easily. He had not forced himself on her. He had even hesitated, just before he kissed her, giving her a chance to back away if she'd wished to.

She pressed a hand to her heated cheek. How could she face him now? And how could she let herself be so vulnerable, letting him kiss her?

She remembered when her father came home, having been gone for months. Hope had arisen as Mother told him how glad she was that he was home and well and safe. He barely grunted at her, did not regard her, and brushed right past her. The look on her mother's face twisted Mulan's gut even now. The pain and heartbreak. Mulan never, ever wanted to feel that.

Had she destined herself to be as hurt as her mother?

Mulan would pretend it never happened. After all, it was only a quick kiss, barely anything. She would simply have to treat him like all the other soldiers she worked with. It wouldn't be that difficult.

But as the others arrived with the food and they sat on the grassy bank next to the stream, she couldn't help sliding a glance at Wolfgang. He was glancing at her at the same moment. She looked away. *Ach! Foolish girl. Foolish heart.*

Gregorius handed her some fresh bread and fried meat.

"Can you believe we found meat?" Simon's excitement broke into her thoughts. "They said it was goat meat, but it tastes like venison."

"Probably poached from some nobleman's forest."

"I won't tell him if you won't."

They laughed. Mulan looked down at the meat and bread and the thought of eating it made her feel sick, but she forced herself to eat. A soldier needed his—her—strength.

She was sorry she'd turned away from Wolfgang earlier. She shouldn't have let him know she was upset about him kissing her. Now he'd try to talk to her, to apologize. Her stomach sank thinking about it.

They finished eating as the last of the sunlight faded from overhead. Now the only light glowed from their cook fire.

Normally they would sit and talk for a while, but they all went to their blankets and lay down in a circle around the fire. Mulan closed her eyes, immediately reliving Wolfgang's arms around her and the events that led up to his kiss. She pressed her fingers against her lips and wished she could still feel it.

She squeezed her eyes closed and prayed, her thoughts whirling and distracting her from her prayers.

Would she ever feel normal again?

Wolfgang awoke the next morning with scratchy eyes and aching limbs. He hadn't slept well, and he dreamed more than once about Mulan. Had they been joyful or romantic dreams? Oh no! Nightmares would be a more apt description. In one dream he bumped into her and sent her falling over a rocky cliff. He grabbed frantically for her with both hands, which woke him up—his hands reaching out when he opened his eyes. In his next nightmare he inadvertently let a lion out of its cage, and it leapt on Mulan. Wolfgang snatched up his sword and stabbed at the beast. When he awoke, his hands were clenched and he was stabbing the air.

He rubbed his eyes and moaned, then got to his feet. "We have to make a plan."

Wolfgang, Mulan, Simon, and Gregorius huddled together.

"We'll reach Malbork Castle before night," Simon said.

"So we don't all get captured, I say only two of us—Gregorius and I—go in first while the rest of you wait outside."

"No." Mulan shook her head. "I will not wait outside the castle. My mother is there, and I will be going in."

"You know Rusdorf wishes to destroy you."

Why was she so determined not to let him protect her? Wolfgang took a breath and deliberately softened his voice. "He only captured your mother to lure you to him."

"Which is why I must be the one to confront him."

"That's not sound reasoning."

"Sound reasoning or not, if he captured my mother to get to me, then I have to confront him to free my mother."

She was right. Was his desire to protect her interfering with his reasoning?

"Very well. If we don't come out or send word to you"—he pointed to Simon and Gregorius—"then go back to Duke Konrad and let him know. He will send help." *I hope.*

They nodded and scattered to finish getting ready for the day's ride.

Only God knew what would happen.

Mulan was very quiet. Should he tell her he was sorry for kissing her? He'd have to explain that he knew he had no right, yet, to kiss her.

He tried to find time to speak to Mulan alone, but Simon, Gregorius, Gerke, and Andrei were never far away as they quickly packed their things and tightened their saddles. Soon they were riding north again toward the main castle of the Teutonic Knights.

The day was cloudy and misty. He tried to use the time in the saddle to pray, but his thoughts kept wandering to Rusdorf, to what dangers lay ahead of them, and to Mulan.

The sky lightened after noon. They stopped for a short rest and to eat. Again, Mulan hardly spoke, but Simon and Gregorius treated her with more deference than usual, probably thinking her silence was due to her worry about her mother. And perhaps it was.

Wolfgang wanted to hold her again. He could not have been mistaken that she had wanted him to, that she had been very receptive to the comfort he'd given her. But maybe it was the kiss that had been unwelcome and untimely.

They continued on their journey. About two hours later, Simon slowed his horse and turned to them. "We're almost there."

"How much farther?"

"About half an hour at this pace."

"Have you seen anyone following us?"

Everyone shook their heads. "Not today."

Simon and Gregorius looked slightly ill at ease.

Twenty minutes later, they arrived at the village near the castle. They rode through it, then continued down the road that led through a thick forest. Finally up ahead was a clearing, and when they reached the clearing, an enormous brick wall and buildings of various heights rose before them—Malbork Castle.

It was more immense than any castle, church, or palace Wolfgang had ever seen. The red brick seemed to go on and on. Multiple buildings rose several stories and various towers extended above them. A matching red brick wall enclosed all the buildings, with a moat surrounding that.

"You had better wait here." He and Mulan would go in alone.

"Ride around to the north of the castle," Simon said. "There is only one entrance. You'll cross a drawbridge." Simon and Gregorius, along with Gerke and Andrei, stayed out of sight in the woods where they could watch them enter through the north gate.

Wolfgang turned to Mulan. "It's not too late. You can let Simon go with me while you stay here with the others."

"No."

He knew that look. She would not back down.

"Very well. Let's go."

They would seek an audience with Rusdorf, discover what was happening with her mother, then ride back. Meanwhile, Simon and Gregorius would wait two hours, and if Mulan and Wolfgang did not return, they would approach the castle with care, pretending to be travelers looking for a place to spend the night, and would find out if Rusdorf had detained them. Then they would break them free.

That was the plan.

Wolfgang rode beside Mulan, who had pulled her hair back from her face and was dressed in her soldier's garb. Her back was stiff and straight as they rode at a steady walk across the grassy area on the north side of the castle. On the western side was the Norgat River, and forests surrounded the castle to the south and east.

Straight ahead they rode toward the drawbridge. At the other end was the massive gatehouse, which was guarded by several men and a large iron portcullis.

Mulan wore her fierce battle expression. A pile of bricks didn't intimidate her.

As their horses' hooves clopped onto the wooden drawbridge, Wolfgang got a prickling feeling on the back of his neck. The guards in front of them seemed stoic and not particularly threatening—no more than the average knights standing guard in front of a castle.

He and Mulan were in the middle of the drawbridge, the dark waters of the moat beneath it, when he heard it. Horses' hooves and shouting coming from where they'd left Simon and Gregorius.

Wolfgang turned in the saddle to glance over his shoulder. A man with a crossbow sat atop a horse on the grassy area behind them, taking aim. At Mulan.

She was slightly ahead of him on the drawbridge. Wolfgang kicked his horse forward. Standing in his stirrups, he threw himself at Mulan, pulling her off her horse. But before they hit the wooden planks of the bridge, a sharp pain pierced his left side.

He landed on his right side, holding Mulan against his chest so he took the brunt of the fall.

She raised herself up, looked down at his side, and screamed.

He followed her gaze. A red stain bloomed on his tunic, growing larger by the second. And just beyond that, lying on the wooden planks, was the large metal bolt that had passed through his body.

Mulan's gaze latched on to the hole in Wolfgang's side.

One look over her shoulder showed Simon and Gregorius knocking the crossbowman to the ground and pulling his hands behind his back. She turned back to Wolfgang.

"No, no, no," she moaned, pressing her hands against the wounds in the front and back. He couldn't die. *O God, help us! Don't let him die!*

Guards surrounded them, running across the drawbridge, asking questions, shouting in German, but Mulan never took her eyes off Wolfgang's wound, blood seeping through her fingers.

"Can I help?" someone asked in Polish.

"I need bandages." Mulan's voice was raw and desperate. "Make haste!"

Someone shoved some linen cloth at her. She pressed it hard against the two wounds. Only then did she glance up at his face.

Wolfgang was ashen, his eyes scrunched in a tight grimace. He was propping himself up on his elbows.

A man dressed in the long white robe of a monk knelt beside her. "Allow me." He pressed his own hands over the wounds and nudged her aside. Another monk joined him, and they started speaking German to each other. Since they seemed knowledgeable and willing to help, she moved to kneel by Wolfie's shoulder.

He was lying flat now, his eyes closed.

"I'm so sorry." Mulan leaned close, hoping he wasn't unconscious.

His eyes flickered open. "It's not your fault."

He was obviously in great pain. Would he die? It was a more serious wound than hers had been, as the crossbow bolt was larger and had entered closer to the center of his body.

Her tears dripped onto his neck. She wiped them gently with her sleeve. "I'll take care of you, I promise. I won't let anyone hurt you." But the tears kept falling on him. "I'm so sorry."

He reached up and brushed her cheek with the back of his hand. "Don't cry."

"Oh, Wolfie." She pressed her face against his chest and made an effort to stop the sobs threatening to escape.

She took a deep breath and lifted her head. He was stroking her hair. Looking deeply into his eyes, she whispered, "You saved my life, didn't you?"

"Your hero." He started to smile but winced, his eyes closing again.

"Don't die!" she cried, then bit her lip.

"I'll try not to."

She had to be brave, had to stop begging him not to die and stop crying, stop behaving like a child.

"Who was that man who tried to kill us?" Mulan said in her most demanding voice to the monks who were applying pressure to Wolfgang's wounds. "Are we safe here?"

They looked at her, spoke to each other in German, then to her in Polish. "We don't know why the knight shot your friend, but we can assure you that you will be safe at Malbork Castle."

She must have seemed skeptical because he added, "We are men of the cross and do not attack those who come in peace to our castle. And now we need to carry him inside to better tend his wounds."

Five guards dragged the shooter across the drawbridge toward the gate, his hands bound. His eyes were wild and crazed as he went past. His clothing showed him to be the man she had glimpsed following them from Zachev Castle.

Some other men brought a litter, tanned leather stretched between two poles. They half lifted, half rolled him onto it. Wolfgang groaned, squeezing his eyes closed. Sweat beaded his face. Mulan's insides twisted at his pain.

They hoisted the litter with him on it. She followed them through the gate.

Someone set his hand on her shoulder. Mulan turned to see Andrei, along with Gerke, Simon, and Gregorius. At least with the five of them, they could put up a good fight if they needed to.

CHAPTER 23

Wolfgang rolled onto his back. Pain blurred his vision, and his eyes were reluctant to open, not wanting to dwell on where he was—Malbork Castle. But a glimpse of Mulan peering down at him made him come more fully awake.

"Drink this." She raised his head and shoulders, pushing a pillow behind him. Then she brought a cup to his lips.

He drank the liquid as he gazed at her over the rim of the cup. Drinking in her gentle features was a more pleasant distraction than what was in the cup. He wanted to tell her she looked beautiful, but the drink went down the wrong way and he coughed, pain ripping through his side.

The coughing ceased and he lay back, gritting his teeth. Every breath brought pain, but the coughing was a hundred times worse. He concentrated on keeping his breaths shallow.

Something cool touched his forehead. He opened his eyes again to Mulan stroking his face with a cloth, her jaw tight, her brows drawn together.

"I'm not dying, am I?"

"Of course not."

"Then don't look so worried." He forced himself to smile.

"I wish I had some of my mother's salve for your wounds.

But the monks promised to let me speak to her for a few minutes tonight. Perhaps she will tell me what is in her salve and I can make some myself."

To distract himself from the pain, he let his mind focus on their kiss . . . and on the gentle way she was bathing his forehead with the wet cloth.

"The monks who bandaged you up think the bolt struck a rib and broke it. That's why it hurts when you breathe."

He reached up and placed his hand on hers. He was in too pathetic a state for her to feel threatened by him. "Thank you," he rasped between breaths. "For taking care of me."

Her dark eyes were soft, beautiful, and brightened by the tears swimming in them. "And thank you, for saving my life." She leaned down and kissed his forehead.

His heart tripped over itself.

Heavy footsteps were approaching. Someone knocked on the door.

Wolfgang's winces and his shallow breathing broke Mulan's heart. When he thanked her for taking care of him, she couldn't resist leaning down and kissing his forehead.

A knock on the door had her turning away. She kept her hand on her knife, just in case, as she opened the door.

Two heavily armed Teutonic Knights stood in the doorway. "Are you Mulan, the woman soldier?"

"I am Mulan."

"Grand Master Rusdorf will speak to you. Come."

"Mulan."

A look over her shoulder showed Wolfgang had raised himself to sitting. He was making an effort to get off the bed.

"Lie still. I shall be well. Rusdorf won't attack me in his own house." And she went with the knights.

They walked down a long corridor, and then she noticed the man behind her, dressed in the habit of a monk of the Teutonic Order—a long white robe, split in the front, with a black cross on one side of the chest.

"Where are you taking me?" She addressed the monk behind her, as the Teutonic Knights seemed friendlier when they were wearing their monk's garb than when they were dressed and armed for battle.

"To the Chapter Room to meet with Grand Master Rusdorf." His voice was even and emotionless.

"Who will be there?" she demanded. She could do nothing to control her situation, and it mattered little to know who would be there, but she wanted to appear strong and fearless. Anger seemed her ally toward that goal.

"Grand Master Rusdorf and several of his officers, and your friends as well."

Fury choked her, and she allowed that fury to edge her voice. "What does he want with us?"

"I do not know."

Liar. But she had to suppress this anger. It threatened to over-whelm her. She focused her eyes on Jesus and the crucifix that hung over the doorway ahead of them, a three-foot wooden carving of Jesus suffering on the cross.

Jesus, give me strength. Don't let me be intimidated by these men who wish me harm or by their false piety and unrighteous hatred for me. But perhaps it was only Rusdorf who held that opinion.

They crossed from the Middle Castle, with its high, vaulted ceilings, grand frescos on the walls, tall, arched windows, and colorful tiles on the floor, to the equally massive High Castle. They finally came to an enormous closed door at the end of the corridor. The armed men opened it and ushered her into what must have been the Chapter Room, which was three times bigger than the church nave in her home village.

Rusdorf sat in a throne-like chair at the other end of the room, while a dozen of his "brethren," wearing the white robes of their order, flanked him on both sides. Ominous and still, they sat staring at her.

Mulan refused to look directly at them, as if they weren't important—though she was fairly certain she had offered at least one or two of them some of her mother's healing salve for their wounds when they were captured and installed in Duke Konrad's Great Hall after their last battle.

She held her head high and did not acknowledge Rusdorf as her escorts led her to the middle of the floor facing the grand master. Then the door opened behind her and more people entered. Soon Simon and Gregorius appeared beside her.

The monk behind her suddenly stepped forward, bowing to Rusdorf. Then he turned and said in a loud voice, "The Grand Master, Champion of the Cross, Paul von Rusdorf, has summoned you, and you will answer for why you have disturbed this peaceful place."

Mulan's heart raced as heat filled her face. *How dare you.*

"Thank you, Brother. Now, will you tell me the names of these . . . surprise guests?"

As if he didn't know.

"These are soldiers belonging to Duke Konrad, the Pole. Their names are Simon and Gregorius, both soldiers, and Mulan, the woman soldier of Lithuania."

Rusdorf stared impassively at her. His face was that of a forty-year-old and looking none the worse after his recent battle, defeat, and imprisonment. His black goatee appeared freshly trimmed and oiled, as did his black mustache, which was quite long, curled up on the ends.

"Mulan of Lithuania. We meet again. What brings you to our brotherhood's humble fortress?"

She had a sudden urge to laugh, but her mother needed her to use every bit of wisdom God provided. "You know exactly why I'm here."

"Do not be insolent," the monk closest to Rusdorf hissed.

She kept her eyes focused on Rusdorf. "My mother was wrongfully taken from her home by you and cruelly placed in your dungeon because of your false accusations." Perhaps it would have been better to be meek and polite, but with the anger pulsing in her head and casting a red mist over her eyes . . . She would not bow to this oppressor.

"Your mother has been accused of witchcraft, of using the devil's power to conjure the healing of fatal wounds."

"What do your own men use to heal wounds? Herbs from God's provision? My mother uses the same—herbs and fruit and roots. There is no witchcraft, no conjuring of the devil."

"That is for us, men who have made vows to God and consecrated our lives to Him, to decide. We will try her and determine that. Or I should say, God shall determine it."

"I trust God, but it's your interpretation of God's judgment I don't trust."

Rusdorf glared at her, and she was fairly certain his cheeks turned crimson.

. "You dare to malign a man approved by the pope to lead our order?" One of the larger monks leaned forward, as if about to stand.

"You have dared to malign my mother, and she is a Christian who has done nothing wrong."

Several other voices were raised while Mulan said, "'God is no respecter of persons.'" She and Wolfgang had recently read that passage.

The first monk raised his hands, and everyone quieted.

"Now then." Rusdorf steepled his fingers together, tip to tip. "My men and I will begin the trial tomorrow. All will be done in a manner that behooves us as Champions of the Cross. God is our Sovereign, and we will not shirk any duty He sets before us, even the trial of an accused witch."

She wanted to say something sarcastic about his pious assertions, but she held her tongue. Nothing she said would make a difference, except to incite these men's ire.

"And I must ask you never to wear men's clothing again while you are in this place. It is forbidden by church law and therefore by us."

"I have no objection, now that I have reached my destination and am not riding in the company of five men."

A few moments of silence passed, then he said, "How is the Duke of Hagenheim's son, Wolfgang?"

"He is badly injured, and no one has told me who shot him or why."

Rusdorf turned his head to the side, not even bothering to look at her. "One of our brother knights shot at you. He was in the battle with us in Zachev, Poland. He was not captured but escaped. He stayed on his own for many days in Poland. He was stalking you, seeing you as the enemy who had caused our defeat. He chose to shoot at you as you were entering the castle. He said he believed you were coming here to assassinate me."

"You are saying he is mad? Will he be allowed to harm us again?"

"He is not mad." He glared at her. "But he will not be allowed to harm you. No one will, as long as your behavior here is in keeping with our rules. And now you may go."

The guards stepped forward to escort her, Simon, and Gregorius from the Chapter Room.

"Oh, and . . ."

They all turned to look back at Rusdorf.

"You will be allowed to visit your mother."

Was she supposed to thank him? Mulan simply nodded.

Mulan was led, not back to her chamber in the Middle Castle or to Wolfgang's chamber, but up a long staircase in a tower. "Are you taking me to my mother?"

The guards had all gone, and the monk escorting her nodded.

Her heart leapt. But what if it was a trick? She followed up the winding stairs. They passed windows at regular intervals. She could see the lush green forest, then the river, then some more of the red brick buildings, and then the woods again. She might be locked in a battle with their leader, but Malbork Castle was undeniably impressive, the surroundings picturesque.

Finally the monk stopped at a door and unlocked it. Mulan entered behind him and found her mother sitting on a stool by a window overlooking the river.

"I shall leave you and come back soon." The monk backed out and locked the door again.

"Mulan!" Mother's face was so joyful that Mulan flung herself into her outstretched arms. "Oh, I am so proud of you, my soldier daughter!"

A lump formed in Mulan's throat. She had to swallow to speak. "Mother, I missed you so much. You are the most beautiful sight."

"And you are as well. Let me look at you."

Mulan knelt beside her. "They haven't hurt you, have they?"

"No, no. I am unharmed, and I rather like this room they've given me. I've never lived beside a river. How could I not be pleased with such a view? Have you seen it?" She motioned toward the window.

Mulan shook her head. "Only you could be pleased with being held prisoner in a tower and accused of witchcraft." And in danger of being executed in a horrific way. But she wouldn't mention that.

"I'm not pleased with being accused and held prisoner. But I am pleased to hear that you have been so courageous as to gain the attention of powerful men." She grinned like a little child. "My Mulan. I always knew you would do great things for the Lord, as was foretold."

Though she wouldn't want to admit it, Mulan's heart swelled a bit at her mother's praise. It was quite gratifying to have done something most men were never able to do—to distinguish herself in battle so that she gained the grand master of the German Order of Knights as her particular enemy. After all, the Polish and Lithuanian people had fought and struggled with the Teutonic Knights for centuries.

"You are a hero." Mother smiled. "Your name was beginning to be spoken of in Lithuania, stories of your bravery, of the fierce Lithuanian soldier who turned out to be a woman. Even Mikolai would have been amazed and proud. Sometimes I laugh when I think about it."

"Well, we are hardly in a position to laugh at this situation, I'm afraid."

"Oh, it hardly matters. Although I do want to see you live long and be happy." Mother's face lost some of its animation as her smile faded.

Mulan straightened. "I'm not planning to die."

"No, of course not."

Though they both knew it was a possibility, and her mother's death was even more likely.

"Grand Master Rusdorf does seem to have some measure of piety and uprightness. Perhaps he will not deal treacherously with us in the end."

"How can you say that? You know he falsely accused you of witchcraft just to get at me."

"He is a man, and you have tweaked his pride and defeated him. Of course he will see if he can discredit you. But ultimately, God may have more purpose in our survival than our demise. Either way, God should have the glory, and we will join Him in heaven. God has given us victory already. Is that not so?"

"Yes, but I would rather talk about something else. As in, I need to know how you make your healing salve. My friend Wolfgang has been injured seriously and is in need of it, and I have no more."

"You were injured, were you not? I heard the rumor."

"Yes, but I am well." Mulan lifted her shirt to show her mother the fresh-looking scar. "It was not serious."

"Oh my!" Mother examined it and probed it gently with her fingers.

"An arrow. It passed cleanly through the flesh."

"Yes, a good place for an injury. Nothing important was punctured, it would seem."

"But Wolfgang was not so fortunate. He took a crossbow bolt—a large metal one—through here." She pointed to a spot higher up and farther into the body. "It probably hit a rib, one of the monks said." Her voice hitched as she thought of Wolfgang's suffering and possibly not surviving the injury.

"Yes, he will need the salve. I can tell you how to make it, but it works best after it has cured for eight days or more. I had just made a large amount of it when Rusdorf's men came to take me away. They confiscated the salve and brought it here. If you could get some—"

"Oh yes. I just need to find it and steal it."

"Perhaps one of the monks will take pity on you and your friend and will fetch some for you."

"That seems unlikely."

"You might be surprised. Pray and ask for God's favor, for it surely rests upon you."

Mother was so quietly confident. Had she always been this way? Impulsively, Mulan put her arms around her mother again, laying her cheek against hers. "I love you, Mother. I want you to know how thankful I am that you were my mother, that you loved me and treated me with kindness."

"Of course, my darling." Mother squeezed her in return.

"And don't worry. I am believing that God will get us out. He will save us, just as He has saved me numerous times in battle." Her mother, along with the village priests, had taught her to trust God. "I do need to help Wolfgang. He's in a lot of pain."

"Oh." Mother was studying her face now.

"What?"

"You love this Wolfgang?"

"What makes you say that?"

"Oh, perhaps it was your voice when you said his name or the look on your face when you speak of his injuries."

"I didn't mean to love him." Mulan's voice was raspy.

"Is he a good man?"

"He is a very good man, but he cannot love me. He is from a wealthy family, the son of a duke."

"And you are a national hero." Mother smiled again.

Mulan shook her head. "That doesn't matter."

"I loved your father, but he treated me badly. I always wanted more for you. I told myself Algirdas was not like your father, didn't seem like the kind of man who would mistreat you, and would at least not leave you for months at a time. But I now realize I was wrong to push you to marry him. The way he spoke to you . . . He was not so different from your father after all. Demanding, cold and distant, without affection . . . That is not the kind of man you deserve."

"Wolfgang . . ." Mulan cleared her throat. "He's nothing like that. Nothing like Father and nothing like Algirdas. But it doesn't matter." She turned away as a stab of pain took her breath away. "He can't marry me."

Nothing would matter if she couldn't save them.

Someone was approaching the door and then scraping the key in the lock. The door opened. The monk was there to escort her back.

"Fare well, Mother."

"Don't give up hope, my daughter." She hugged Mulan tight.

"Of course." Mulan pulled away and gave her mother a smile and a wink, willing away the pain of a moment before.

She made her way down the steps with the monk. "What is your name, if I may ask?"

"I am Sir Thomas of Bremen."

"Are you a skilled healer? I know your order was once Hospitallers in the Holy Land. And if you were ever in battle, you must know the value of a good healing salve."

"I know the value of God's healing power."

Her heart sank at his answer.

"But I have examined your mother's healing salve, and she gave me the recipe for it."

Her heart lifted. "And what did you think?"

"I do not understand why it would work. It is only wine and honey and ox gall and a few other things. There is nothing magical about the ingredients. Perhaps she does use a dark spirit to give it its power—if indeed it does possess any healing power."

"I know how you can test its healing power. You can allow me to spread it on Wolfgang's injury."

He said nothing as they reached the bottom of the steps and continued walking. Was he dawdling so they could continue their conversation?

"Truly, it is God's own power, His own herbs and provision, that provide the healing. There is nothing dark about it. You can see for yourself."

"And if I allow you to apply the salve to your friend's injury, who will you tell of this?"

"If you wish me to say nothing, I will tell no one." Perhaps she shouldn't sound so eager. She held her breath, waiting for his answer.

"Perhaps I will bring you some and see it for myself. To help me judge in your mother's trial."

"Yes, of course." Mulan literally bit her tongue to keep from saying anything else, lest she cause him to change his mind.

CHAPTER 24

Wolfgang lay as still as he could, as every moment brought on sharper pain. And now he felt achy and feverish. Was he about to die? And without knowing if Mulan was able to free herself and her mother? *God, don't let me die. Please help Mulan.*

Through his feverish haze of pain and sleep, he thought he heard Mulan's voice from near the door. Then she was by his side, and a monk was with her. The monk removed the bandage from Wolfgang's side. Mulan was giving him instructions, and he smeared something cold on Wolfgang's wounds. Too much pain would make him lose consciousness, and the familiar darkness was closing in.

He tried concentrating on the small crucifix that hung on the wall next to his bed. Was this how Jesus felt before He died on the cross? Pain seeping through him as if he were an overly full sponge and the pain was a river . . . fever taking over his mind . . . hot and cold at the same time . . . always half asleep but never feeling the blessed peace of unconsciousness?

Perhaps he was hallucinating, but he saw Jesus' eyes on him as He hung there, becoming life-size. The gaze was so real, healing comfort seemed to flow into him through that look. Compassion and love poured from those eyes.

Wolfgang finally sank into perfect, restful sleep.

Mulan awakened to Wolfie's eyes staring across at her.

She sat up in the cushioned chair and rubbed her eyes. "I must have fallen asleep."

"You can go back to sleep."

"How are you feeling?"

"Am I losing my mind, or do I smell your mother's salve?"

"I procured some for you." She smiled.

"How did you manage that?"

"My monk friend, Sir Thomas, fetched us some that they brought here as evidence against my mother. He was curious to see if it would work."

"And probably charmed by you. Be careful."

"Worry not. I still retain my fighting skills."

"You are wearing women's attire."

"I must if I wish not to be tried for violating Church law." She came to stand closer and noticed he was not sweating anymore. She laid a hand on his forehead. "No more fever." She breathed out a sigh.

"I am feeling better. When did you apply the salve?"

"Yesterday. You've been asleep for twelve hours. You look much better."

"I feel better."

Just then Sir Thomas of Bremen came into the chamber. He approached Wolfgang's bed.

"What do you think?" Mulan watched the monk's face for his reaction.

"He seems improved. Perhaps it was the sleep."

"Perhaps."

She and Wolfie shared a wry smile.

"How is your pain?" Sir Thomas asked.

"It is better. In fact, I think I need to . . . have some privacy."

Mulan immediately turned and headed for the door. "I shall return later," she called over her shoulder.

Wolfgang sat, propped up with pillows. Mulan's mother's trial was supposed to start that day. Would Mulan be allowed to attend? Probably not. But at least they had been allowing her to visit her mother. And were allowing Wolfgang her salve. But probably no one knew about that except Sir Thomas.

But where was Steffan? Was he here at Malbork Castle? What would he think of how they were treating Mulan's mother? He was not completely without compassion or good sense, and what Rusdorf was doing must surely violate both, even in Steffan's mind.

Someone knocked on the door. Mulan said, "May I come in?"

"Yes, come in." His heart lifted.

She wore a pretty blue-and-yellow silk gown, much like one his sister Margaretha wore several years ago, before she married and moved away to England. But Mulan's skin and hair were much darker, she was smaller both in stature and girth, and . . . he wished he could kiss her.

Her silk skirts rustled as she walked across the room. "You're not pale anymore. How do you feel?"

"I feel like a man who was run through with a sword and trampled by a horse." He grinned. "But much better than yesterday."

"No fever?"

He wished she would put her hand to his forehead as she had done before, but her hands remained by her sides.

"I don't feel feverish anymore, and the pain is less."

"You still have a lot of healing to do, Sir Thomas said, so you must be careful not to move around too much."

Breathing was still painful, which he suspected would last for weeks, as the rib would have to mend.

"And Sir Thomas has agreed to let me know what happens today with my mother's trial." She was chewing on the inside of her lip as she glanced at the floor.

"I am praying for her." He held out his hand to her.

She took it and squeezed it. "Thank you."

He was very aware of the softness of her skin. Would she stand this close to him if he weren't injured? Would she still hold his hand if he had not gotten shot protecting her? She'd seemed angry with him when he kissed her lips that day in the woods.

Staring down at their joined hands, she brushed the back of his hand with her thumb. Perhaps now was a good time to speak of their kiss. He should hurry, before a servant or Sir Thomas came into his room.

"I am sorry if I offended you," he began, his voice raspy, "when I kissed you a few days ago."

Her thumb stopped caressing his hand and she went completely still.

"It was impulsive of me, but I want you to know I'd never take advantage of you."

She took a step back, her hand letting go of his. His stomach twisted.

"I know you are a woman of great character and integrity, and I respect you too much . . . That is, I'm hoping . . ." Why was he so tongue-tied? "If you will accept me, I would like to marry you, Mulan."

She finally brought her gaze up to his face. "I'm not sure what that means."

He must have said it wrong. This was not going the way he'd meant it to. "It means—" What could he say? That he, who had nothing, would marry her as soon as he had a house? Was she supposed to wait for him? "I know I don't have any fortune or possessions—yet—but I—"

Someone knocked on the door and immediately opened it. Sir Thomas entered. "How is Wolfgang? You look a bit pale." His face scrunched in concern. "Shall I change your bandage?"

"Can you come back in a few minutes? I need to finish speaking with Mulan. Please."

Sir Thomas looked from Wolfgang to Mulan and back again. "I see." He turned to go. "I shall return in half an hour."

Mulan's cheeks were red when Sir Thomas left the chamber. She folded her arms in front of her chest.

"Forgive me, but I would like to marry you, someday, when I have a house for us to live in. I know I am only a lowly soldier."

Her brows were lowered as she stared at him. "So you want to marry me . . . someday." She rearranged her arms across her chest, folding them tighter. "When you have a house."

He nodded, swallowing past the lump in his throat. Her expression, body, and tone of voice all said she was not impressed with what he was saying. And now that he'd said it out loud, it did not sound chivalrous or romantic. He was failing miserably at this and desperately wished he hadn't said anything.

How could he mend this? He was afraid to say anything else,

lest he make things worse. An awkward silence ensued. Was she angry? Was she only thinking?

"Well, that is what I wanted to say. I'm sorry for kissing you. That is, I'm not sorry, because I'd like to kiss you every day, but I know I have no right to kiss you at all." That also did not sound the way he'd meant it to.

She was still staring at him, but now her brows were raised and one side of her mouth curled down in a wry frown. This was getting worse and worse. He wished she would say something, anything.

"Well, I should go. Sir Thomas needs to change your bandage and put more salve on your wound." She walked backward toward the door.

"But you will come back, later? To let me know what happened with the trial?"

"Of course. I'll come back later." She darted out the door.

He groaned. How could he possibly have ruined that more completely?

When Mulan ducked out of Wolfgang's chamber and closed the door, her hands were shaking.

Wolfgang wanted to marry her. But someday, when he had a house.

Her heart throbbed. Why would he say that but not say anything about loving her? Did he not know that she wanted to be loved, not just married?

A sob escaped her and she stifled it with a hand over her

mouth. She would not let him hurt her, or at least would not let him see that he had.

She hastened down the corridor to her chamber and shut the door.

But he did wish to wed her. That was flattering, wasn't it? She had thought it would be impossible for him, a duke's son, to wed her, a peasant girl who didn't even speak German, his native language. But to be asked in such a manner . . . Was she wrong to feel insulted?

He had looked so uncomfortable and even embarrassed. Perhaps he just wasn't ready to tell her he loved her. Perhaps she could make him love her after they married.

The whole idea of begging for, or hoping for, his love made her feel sick in her stomach. And angry! Was that how Mother had felt when she married Mikolai? That she could make him love her? That had only turned into pain and heartache when Mikolai rejected and abandoned her over and over again. Mother was a good, kind, wonderful woman who deserved to be loved and cherished, not deprived of even the smallest scrap of love and affection from her husband.

If Wolfgang didn't love her, why should she marry him? She was worth more than that. She was worth a man who loved her and wouldn't ask her to marry him as if he cared more about a house than about being with her.

Her father had probably asked Mother to marry him in just such a feeble, unromantic manner as this. And she would not be trapped in that kind of marriage, no matter how handsome the man was or how much she loved him.

She could not let him know that she was in love with him. After the way he had asked her to marry him, it would be humiliating. He thought she was foolish enough to wait for him five, ten, a dozen years or more, pining for him while he did as he pleased, while he waited for Duke Konrad or someone else to provide him a house. And if he knew she had been in love with him for weeks . . .

She would rather die in battle.

CHAPTER 25

S teffan glanced around the room at his brothers in arms, all wearing their monk's garb, all pious in white with their black crosses over their hearts.

He had been afraid they thought of him as little more than a mercenary. But the fact that they had asked him to sit in on the trial proceedings for Mulan's mother gave him hope. Perhaps some-day soon he would be knighted and then could advance quickly through the ranks to become the next grand master. Then Father and Mother would have to think of him as more than the one who was different from the rest. He'd be powerful and respected, and they'd have to give him their approval.

They brought in the woman, her hands bound in front of her with a white cloth. She looked a bit confused as they led her up to stand upon the platform at one side of the chamber. Any whis-pered conversation halted and a hush fell.

"Frau Feodosia, widow of Mikolai of Lithuania." Grand Master Rusdorf spoke. "You have been brought here to answer for your crimes, or to refute the accusations against you, if you are able."

The woman said nothing as one of the other knights, Sir Thomas was his name, walked forward and translated Rusdorf's words into Lithuanian. The woman made no answer, so Rusdorf continued.

"You have been accused of colluding with the devil, or his demons, and creating a salve that has supernatural, demonic powers to cure the sick and injured, even fatal injuries, and of giving this salve to unsuspecting people all over the Continent."

"Unsuspecting? Do you mean that I am forcing it on them? Because they come to me when they have an injury."

Sir Thomas translated her words into German while she spoke.

"Silence." Rusdorf glared at her while Sir Thomas translated. "You are not allowed to speak unless invited by the court."

She bowed her head but seemed almost amused.

Rusdorf asked a brother monk to come forward. Steffan had never met him, but he was introduced as Sir Ditmar of Hildesheim. He stood in front of the assembly.

"When we apprehended this woman in her home, we confiscated all the salve in her possession—five large pottery jars and three smaller jars. She said she had just made a new batch the day before and it would not be potent for seven more days. I have brought a jar of it for you all to examine."

The jar was being passed from one man to the next where they sat along the wall. It finally came to Steffan. He opened the lid of the greenish-brown paste. It looked foul and smelled even fouler, the same salve he'd allowed Mulan to put on the cut on his cheek. He closed it and passed it to the next man.

Finally it reached Rusdorf. He stuck his nose over the top of the jar and sniffed. He scrunched his face. "What is in it?"

"We guessed that it was made of garlic, leeks, wine, honey, comfrey, and ox gall. And that is just what she claims is in it. I wrote down the recipe, which she says she has only in her memory, as she is illiterate." He passed a piece of parchment to Rusdorf.

Rusdorf read the recipe aloud, then looked up at Frau Feodosia. "Is this what is in your salve?"

After the translation, she said, "Yes, sir."

Rusdorf's face was pinched. Was he offended at her calling him only "sir"? "These are common enough ingredients. These things will not cure a wound or a sickness."

"No, sir, it does not cure sickness, only wounds on the outside of a man's—or woman's—body. Only flesh wounds."

"Are you asking me to believe that these simple things"—he looked back down at the parchment in his hand—"garlic, leeks, wine, honey, comfrey, and ox gall, will heal a wound?"

"The combination of them keeps away the putrid nature of some wounds. I have never had a man, woman, or child whose wound did not heal while using the salve. Even after the wound has become putrid, this salve will heal it."

"That is not possible. I do not believe it. There must be some sort of sorcery involved. You have been conjuring the devil and his demons to infuse your little salve with power—for your own profit and pride!"

"I do not profit from my salve. I give it away to anyone who needs it. It is God's own creation and God's own power that infuses it, if it needs that kind of power. I would never deny another human being their right to it."

Rusdorf's face was red and somehow dark at the same time. He called forward some of the knights who had been wounded in Poland and had ended up captured and held in Zachev Castle. They had been given some of Frau Feodosia's salve for their wounds.

He asked each of them, "How fast did your wound heal?" And then, "Have you ever known a wound to heal that fast before?"

"No, Reverend Father," they each said. But the last one added, "My mother used honey and comfrey on burns and garlic to keep away sickness, so perhaps it's only the healing properties in the ingredients themselves that give it power."

"My grandmother used wine and leeks for bee stings," someone else said.

"Wine and ox gall will cure anything, my old grandmother used to say."

Then they all began discussing their families' remedies for various ailments, until Rusdorf lifted a hand. "Enough! Has she bewitched you? Consecrated men of God such as yourselves? The woman is obviously a sorceress, turning men's minds against the truth with her witchcraft. Besides being from Lithuania, that bastion of pagan worship, she raised a daughter who is a heretic and dresses in men's garb and fights as a man in battle."

The men looked uncomfortable, glancing away from him, bowing their heads or staring at the floor. Indeed, Rusdorf's outburst seemed unjust and farfetched. The healer in Hagenheim had doctored many of Steffan's scrapes and cuts with just such herbs and concoctions.

Rusdorf dismissed the men and called several of the knights who were experienced in battle.

"Have you ever heard of a wound that healed as quickly as you have heard about here today?"

One by one they admitted they had not. Rusdorf dismissed them, saying, "It is sorcery, not the salve itself, that gives it this power."

Finally he addressed the woman. "Do you believe in God the Father and Jesus the Son of God?"

"I do."

"Do you believe in the Holy Spirit and Mary the holy mother of Christ?"

"I do."

"Have you received the Sacraments of Baptism, Confirmation, and the Eucharist?"

"I have."

"Do you worship other gods? Your pagan ancestors' gods?"

"No."

"Will you now renounce this pagan, demonic salve you've been making and vow never to make it again?"

Frau Feodosia hesitated. Then she stared straight at Rusdorf. "I will not."

A murmur rippled around the room.

"I do not see why I should." The woman raised her voice a bit and waited for the translator, who started coughing, but then quickly resumed his translation. "It is not pagan or demonic. My salve helps people, and when they are healed, they praise God and we give Him the glory for it. That is not wrong, and our priest approves. I will not agree to what you are asking."

Admiration welled up inside Steffan for the woman. He'd never seen anyone defy Rusdorf. She did not even appear frightened, though she must know he would have her executed.

Rusdorf did not even blink. "Why did your daughter dress as a man and go fight as a soldier? Did you instruct her to do this?"

"I did not. Her father died and she wished to help me. We had no children—only Mulan. She took her father's place in fighting for Butautus so I could remain in our home."

"And this is the reason she became a soldier? You did not try to stop her? Did you not know that it is forbidden for a woman to wear men's clothing?"

"She was doing God's will." The woman lifted her chin a notch higher.

"How dare you accuse God!"

"A friar and a priest prophesied about her, when she was a child, that she would save a nation. It was God's will."

A slight noise, like a gasp, shot through the room.

"Explain this outrageous assertion." Veins popped out, big and purple, becoming visible at Rusdorf's temple and the side of his neck.

The entire room seemed to be holding its collective breath as the Teutonic Knight-Monks all leaned forward to listen to her.

Steffan shouldn't even be here. Something about the woman's expression made him squirm. He wasn't a monk, as he had not taken his vows yet. And honestly, he had been lying awake at night, between all the rituals and prayers, between matins and lauds, thinking . . . Did he truly wish to take a vow of celibacy? To vow never to know a woman? He wanted to be a knight, to be powerful and important, but that was the part of the vows that gave him pause.

Rusdorf's voice seethed as he said, "Are you telling us that prophecies were made about your daughter, Mulan? Who was this friar? I want his name. And the priest."

A chill came over Steffan. What if the woman was right? What if Rusdorf had become obsessed with destroying Mulan and it was not God's will? Steffan might not be as righteous as the rest of his family, but he knew God was to be treated with reverence and fear. He had heard the stories of miracles from people who would never tell a falsehood, how his brother-in-law Sir Gerek had been led by God to find Steffan's sister, though she had been seized and taken several days' ride from Hagenheim and no one knew where. How his father had killed a demon-possessed man, whose demons visibly left his body as he died. How God had brought his brother Gabe just in time to save his future wife, Sophie, and how the man who had been hired to kill her had not been able to do it and had fled from her while she was tied to a tree. There had been numerous other stories of how God had wreaked His vengeance on the enemies of Steffan's family. Vengeance, indeed, belonged to the Lord.

And Rusdorf should take care he did not fall into the Lord's wrath.

But what did Steffan know? Perhaps this woman was not so innocent as she seemed. Who was he to judge? Rusdorf had risen to the rank of grand master, so he must have the favor of God on him. Steffan must just listen and keep quiet.

With bated breath Mulan listened to her mother's account of the day's trial proceedings. Her heart pounded and she felt sick.

"What did Rusdorf say? Mother? What happened?"

"He said he would call me back there tomorrow and give me another chance to renounce my evil conjurings and vow never to make my salve again. But I will not, of course." Mother crossed her arms, pressing her lips together.

Mulan wrung her hands, then rubbed her cheek. "Perhaps you *should* promise never to make the salve again."

"Why would I do that?"

"Because you will lose your life if you don't. If you live you can give the recipe to other people and they can continue to make it, to help people. Rusdorf read the recipe aloud, but you know he will never allow the monks to concoct and use it."

"But he said I would have to vow never to give the recipe to anyone."

Mulan paced up and down her mother's small tower chamber. She went to the window and gazed out, propping her elbow against the wall. "What choice do you have, Mother? Rusdorf will never stop . . ." She put her hand over her eyes.

"I can ask for trial by combat, for a champion. Whoever fights for me will win." Mother looked so calm and composed.

Perhaps Mother was right. There seemed to be no other option. "Are you sure you won't . . . ?"

"No." She shook her head. "I shall invoke my right to trial by combat."

"Either Simon or Gregorius could be your champion and fight for you, but Rusdorf already sent them back to Duke Konrad. And though Wolfgang is better, he is still very much injured. He can barely walk. So I will do it."

"You? But isn't trial by combat a joust? Then hand-to-hand combat with a sword? You are too small for jousting, and you said yourself you were not very good at sword fighting. No, someone else will do it."

But there was no one else. A Teutonic Knight would never fight for an accused sorceress. Besides that, they'd be fighting one of their own brothers in arms. And, of course, Rusdorf would assume Mulan would be her mother's champion, and he would gleefully expect her to be slain—his hope and aim all along. But God would not allow that to happen. Would He?

Trial by combat, by definition, allowed God to judge and choose the outcome. It was thought that He would grant victory to the side that deserved it.

God, please grant me victory and Mother her vindication.

Steffan watched as they led Mulan's mother into the Chapter Room for the trial. The back of his neck prickled. He had begun to suspect the reason why they had asked him, who had not even taken his vows yet, to sit in on the trial.

Again, Frau Feodosia appeared calm and—dare he even think it?—as innocent and guileless as anyone he had ever seen. When Rusdorf demanded she renounce the right to make or share her special healing salve, she again refused.

"Do you have anything else to say for yourself? You do know that the penalty for witchcraft is death?"

"I do know, and I wish to claim the right to trial by combat. I make entreaty for a champion to fight on my behalf."

Rusdorf's lips curled, obviously pleased. "And that champion would be your own child, Mulan, I presume?"

This was the first time Frau Feodosia's confident look faltered. She almost seemed confused. "If no one else will champion my cause, then yes, God will use Mulan to gain victory and vindication for me against my oppressors."

Rusdorf's nostrils flared and a pinched look marred his face, but only for a moment, as she ended her statement.

"You have two days to find a champion. The combat trial will be at noon."

Frau Feodosia's only response was a slight widening of her eyes. Two days was not very much time.

Mulan might be a fierce warrior and skilled archer, but she was no match for an experienced jouster and sword fighter, and the Teutonic Knights were both. And Wolfgang was seriously injured. Steffan had heard that he was improving but was still far from healed. The arrow that struck him had been large and had possibly punctured an internal organ, and definitely broke a rib. He'd not be able to joust again for weeks.

Steffan imagined what Wolfgang would feel when he heard Mulan would be forced to be her mother's champion. His stomach tightened in sympathy.

Although he didn't know why he should feel pity for Wolfgang, after the way they had parted. Though he and his brother had walked the same path most of their lives, his path and his brother's had diverged, and they likely would never come together again.

CHAPTER 26

Wolfgang looked around for his sword as he listened to what Gerke was saying.

"Mulan is preparing to fight one of the Teutonic Knights tomorrow in the trial by combat. I watched her practice, and she cannot even hold the lance tip in the right position for more than ten paces while her horse charges down the list. And aiming? She cannot aim at all. She will miss the rider entirely and probably run her lance into the ground and unhorse herself. And even if that doesn't happen, she's so small and light, she'll be easily thrown from the saddle."

"There must be someone else who can fight. Send for Sir Thomas." Wolfgang leaned forward and swung his legs over the side of the bed.

"Where are you going?" Gerke looked alarmed. "I'll go get Sir Thomas, but you must not get up."

Gerke rushed from the room before Wolfgang could even get his feet to the floor. He groaned, sharp pains shooting through his body with every movement.

A few minutes later, Gerke came back with Sir Thomas.

"I don't think you should be getting up." The white-robed monk hastened over, lifted Wolfgang's legs, and placed them back on the bed.

"I can walk. I walked the length of this chamber this morning." But he was as weak as a kitten and he knew it.

"I offered myself as Mulan's mother's champion this morning," Sir Thomas said with perfect calm. "Grand Master Rusdorf was not pleased. He told me that I'd been bewitched and was under the influence of the devil, and then he forbade me from taking Mulan's place. It seems that this is what he had hoped for all along—to have Mulan face one of his men and be . . . defeated."

He said "defeated," but what he meant was "killed."

Wolfgang could not let that happen. He had to come up with a way, especially since she still seemed somewhat angry with him, or at least distant. She had not been to visit him since he'd so clumsily asked her to marry him.

"I have been searching for someone who will take Mulan's place in the lists," Sir Thomas went on, "but I suspect Rusdorf will forbid any Teutonic Knight who offers to do so. I will continue searching, but I admit I do not know anyone in this part of the world besides my knight-brethren."

Wolfgang sat up straighter. "I will do it."

"You?" Both Sir Thomas and Gerke made the exclamation.

"You cannot," Gerke protested.

"It is impossible." Sir Thomas came closer. "Your wounds are not healed. The skin has not even knitted together yet, not to mention the internal wounds. Have you even the strength to hold a lance?"

"I may be injured, but it is only my side. And every day I am better. My arm has not forgotten how to hold a lance or how to swing a sword. I should be the one to do it."

"No." Sir Thomas shook his head while Gerke mumbled frantically in his native German.

"Are you certain Mulan will lose if she attempts to fight?"

"If it were an archery contest, I would bless her and say, 'Go to it.' But in a joust . . ." Sir Thomas heaved a sigh. "She will certainly be killed."

"Then I must. Gerke, go and fetch my supplies. I want my armor polished and ready by morning."

"Sir, please . . ." Gerke's desperate, pleading expression quickly turned to resignation as Wolfgang speared him with a stern look. "Yes, sir."

"And, Gerke?"

"Yes, sir?"

"Ask Mulan and Andrei to come to me. I need to speak with them. It's very urgent."

Wolfgang's head swam as he stood, leaning back against the side of his bed, as he waited for Mulan and Andrei to come to his chamber. Gerke said she had agreed to see him after evening prayers, and he wanted to appear well and strong.

Finally footsteps approached. Gerke opened the door and he, Andrei, and Mulan entered.

His heart stuttered as his eyes met Mulan's. She was wearing her woman's garb, and her hair was damp. Her expression softened when she saw him, then hardened again, back to her battle face, putting up the wall that she used to protect herself. But why would she feel the need to protect herself from him?

"Thank you for coming." He stood up straight, pushing off from the bed. "I volunteer to be Mulan's mother's champion in the combat trial."

"No." Mulan's jaw was set. She took two steps toward him and stopped. "You are injured. I will be her champion."

"You are not trained to joust and sword fight. I am."

"I also was not skewered by a crossbow bolt." She lowered her head and peered up at him through her lashes. "It is good of you to want to take my place, but it's impossible. You must rest."

"I want to do it. I believe I must."

Andrei and Gerke were watching them silently, never opening their mouths.

"You must?" She widened her eyes and braced her hands on her hips.

"I don't want you to be hurt, and this is playing into Rusdorf's plan to destroy you. I cannot let him do that."

"Why not?"

"Why can you not just accept my help?" But getting frustrated would only cause him to say things that would make her angry.

"Because you will be killed. You're injured. You cannot, and it's my fight. I will not let you do it."

He stepped toward her. "I love you."

Mulan blinked once, then rapidly. Her chin quivered and she pressed her lips together.

He walked the rest of the way to her and whispered, "Please, let me do this."

She shook her head and took three steps back. When she finally spoke, her eyes were swimming in tears. "You cannot even sit on a horse in your condition." She blinked and the tears disappeared. A scowl replaced them.

"I'll be well enough tomorrow. I'm getting better every day."

"You cannot get well that quickly and you know it."

"Can you hold a lance weighing twenty-five stones and aim it at your opponent, all while sitting atop a galloping horse? You'll get yourself killed, and I cannot let you do that."

"And I cannot let you die in my place." She was glaring at him.

This, again, was not how he had planned this meeting. He wanted to reason with her, to make her see that she should let him do this. And while he was right about her not being able to hold and aim a heavy lance, she was also right about him. He was in no condition to joust and fight, but it was easier to believe that he'd be better tomorrow than it was to believe that she wouldn't get killed. He rubbed a hand over his cheek.

"Mulan," Andrei spoke up. They all looked at him. "Perhaps you should let Wolfgang do it. After all, he's trained and you're not."

Slack-jawed, Mulan stared at her attendant and friend. "I appreciate that you are willing to sacrifice Wolfgang's life for mine, but I am not willing."

"I won't die," Wolfgang protested, his heart twisting inside him. She must love him, mustn't she? Or perhaps . . . she just didn't want a man's death on her conscience. And if he failed, her mother would die as well.

"You have an open wound, a broken rib—"

"I can put on many layers to protect the wound, and a broken rib won't slow me down. I can do it."

She bit her lip, then shook her head.

"It's the best hope of saving your mother from Rusdorf."

"What about God? Isn't God's will and intervention the whole point of trial by combat?" She stared first at him, then at Andrei and Gerke. "God will fight for me. I only have to be there."

Everything inside him still screamed to take her place, although he didn't want to argue that God would not give her victory. "If God will fight for you, wouldn't He also fight for me?"

Mulan pointed to her chest. "It is my responsibility, my fight, my mother. It is me Rusdorf hates."

"Which is exactly why you shouldn't let him draw you into his schemes."

"No." She pointed her finger now at Wolfgang. "No, I will not let you do this. I will not be responsible for your death."

What hurt the most? The fact that she wouldn't let him help her, or that she had slammed a door on him that he thought she'd finally opened? He could see it in her eyes: she had shut him out.

He tried one last time. "Let me do this. Trust me, and trust God."

Was her lip trembling? She bit it and folded her arms over her chest.

Abruptly, she turned around and stomped to the door, her silk skirts swishing. She yanked it open and was gone.

Gerke, Andrei, and Wolfgang all glanced at each other.

"I didn't want to do this," Wolfgang said, "but I have no other choice. Men, will you help me?"

"Whatever you wish," Gerke said.

"I will, if it will save Mulan," Andrei said.

"Good. This is the plan." Wolfgang proceeded to give them their precise instructions for the next day.

Steffan was lying on his bed, staring up at the ceiling and waiting for the bell that would call everyone to midnight prayers. His one small candle gave off a feeble light that sent shadows dancing on the walls.

A knock came at his door. Steffan opened it and Rusdorf stood there.

"Grand Master Rusdorf. Please come in." He stepped back.

"Steffan. I have an assignment for you."

"Of course. As you wish." But his gut twisted at what he feared his superior was about to say.

"I know you are skilled in all that a knight should be skilled in—you are one of the best jousters I've ever seen. You brother Valten, Lord Hamlin, was the greatest tournament champion of our time."

Steffan tried not to moan.

"And you proved yourself a very good soldier during our recent battles with Duke Konrad in Poland. I probably should have knighted you so you could take your vows . . ."

Was Steffan about to receive what he'd always wanted? But the prospect did not fill him with joy as he'd always imagined it would.

The candle cast long shadows over the grand master's face, encircling his eyes with darkness and elongating his goatee and swooping mustache. He stared at the wall, as if forgetting where he was.

"I have always wished to be a Teutonic Knight," Steffan prompted.

"And you shall be, my son. But there are some who question your loyalty, with your brother fighting on the side of our enemies. They think perhaps your getting captured by your brother and the heretic woman was only a ruse."

"I assure you it was not, and my loyalty is to the German Order of Knights and to God only."

"You feel no loyalty to your family, then?" One of Rusdorf's eyebrows went up to a point in the middle. His eyes were hawkish as they focused on Steffan's face.

Steffan remembered how he had parted from his father, though if he was truthful, the contention and anger came mostly from Steffan. "No."

Rusdorf's head dipped in a slow nod.

"What is it you wish me to do?" Steffan shifted his feet. Why couldn't Rusdorf simply say what he wanted to say? He did not like this mystery and suspense.

"I wish you to uphold the cause of Christ." Rusdorf turned his body fully toward Steffan and leaned forward. "I wish to eradicate witchcraft and paganism from the world, once and for all. If I see anything heretical in our society, I wish to stamp it out. The Lord's zeal is on me!" His face was so animated, even in the half light, Steffan found himself taking a step back.

Steffan inhaled deeply to infuse a bit more patience in himself. *Get to the point.*

Rusdorf seemed to catch himself and relaxed his shoulders. "What I wish is for you to be God's champion. I wish you to face the champion of the woman accused of witchcraft. I am choosing you to joust in the trial by combat."

Just as he'd suspected, but Steffan's stomach sank anyway.

"Are you willing to face the woman soldier, Mulan, in battle?"

He did not like the idea of fighting a woman—he'd already shot and injured her once and felt less than noble about that. But if he said no, he might never be a knight. "I am."

Rusdorf grinned.

"There is a rumor that Wolfgang, not Mulan, will be Frau Feodosia's champion."

"So I have heard." Rusdorf's eyes narrowed. "Are you willing to face your brother in combat? You must examine again where your loyalties lie."

Again, if he said no, he would never be able to join the Teutonic Knights. He'd never wanted to be anything but a knight. Without that, he had no purpose. And what was life without a goal or purpose of some kind? He wouldn't know what to do next.

Surely Mulan and their attendants would never allow Wolfgang, with his recent serious injury, to fight. The rumor was surely untrue. But if Wolfgang did fight, Steffan could easily knock him off his horse and defeat him. And, hopefully, Rusdorf wouldn't insist they had to fight to the death.

"I am."

Rusdorf nodded, a quick, curt movement. "You may wear the crest of the Teutonic Knights into combat tomorrow. And afterward, you shall be knighted and we shall celebrate and honor you, after you take your vows, with a feast. You shall have a great career, lofty responsibilities, and all of your brother knights shall look up to you."

"Thank you, sir." Steffan bowed his head. He should have felt pleased and proud, but the emotion inside him was something completely different. Still . . . he would do what he had to do. If the entire order of the Teutonic Knights was behind him, which included the Church, how could he be wrong? For once, he should feel like the good son, not the one bad one.

So why did it seem as if a boulder had settled on his chest?

A strange calm settled over Mulan as she readied herself for the trial by combat. It all felt a bit unreal.

Andrei helped her strap on her armor—real hammered-steel armor, which she had never worn before and which had been loaned to her by one of the smaller Teutonic Knights. But Andrei was taking so long, she finally spoke up.

"You know I'm doing the right thing, don't you?"

Wolfgang's face haunted her, and his words, *"Trust me, and trust God."*

"You must do what you think is best." Andrei kept working, not meeting her eye. "My prayers are for you, and for those who love you . . . Wolfgang and *Ponia* Feodosia."

Her stomach twisted as she thought of her mother, facing her own execution. And Andrei . . . He was only a child. What would happen to him if both she and her mother perished today? But Wolfgang would take care of him. As would God.

"We are all in God's hands, Andrei, never more than now. And in God's hands is a good place to be."

Andrei nodded, still not looking at her. "But perhaps you should let Wolfgang take your place. You have never jousted before, after all, and he's very experienced."

"How can you say that? This isn't Wolfgang's responsibility."

"But he wants to help you, to do it for you."

Tears instantly stung her eyes. Why didn't Andrei understand? "I can't."

"But why?"

"I . . ." Was it because she loved Wolfgang too much to let him get killed for her? That was part of it, but it was more than that. Even though he'd proven himself, part of her still didn't trust him. Was she imagining that all men, even Wolfgang, would hurt her, like her father did? She'd risked her own life so many times in battle. She'd always taken responsibility and never asked anyone for help. She had to do it herself. Was that wrong? Never to let anyone help her?

"I just can't, Andrei."

But Andrei was giving her a look that said, "That's not good enough."

"Whatever the reason, I can't let Wolfgang put himself in harm's way for my mother."

"He said he loves you."

Her heart fluttered. She'd pushed that memory aside, unsure how to fit that into what she knew was true. Why did Andrei have to bring it up now?

"Do you not believe him?" Andrei's eyes were clear, blue, and innocent.

"Today is about saving Mother, not about me and not about Wolfgang."

"You don't believe him, do you?"

"He can't marry me, Andrei. How could he? He's the son of the Duke of Hagenheim. Look at me! I'm not a suitable woman. It's not possible, and I don't want to talk about it. You're too young to understand."

"I understand that he cares about you. And just remember, he does what he does because he loves you."

Her face heated. To be lectured by a twelve-year-old about Wolfgang . . .

A knock came at the door.

"I'll see who it is." Andrei hurried to the door, jerked it open, and said over his shoulder, "Forgive me, Mulan."

He was out the door in a trice and shut it behind him, the key scraping inside the lock.

"Andrei!" Her heart leapt into her throat. She ran to the door and attacked the handle, but it wouldn't open.

"Andrei! Andrei, no!" She pounded on the door with her

fists. "Open this door!" But nothing happened. No sounds came from other side.

The blood drained from her face, making her skin tingle. Her friend had tricked her.

This was Wolfgang's doing. She turned and looked all around her little chamber. No window, and the room did not adjoin any others.

She was trapped.

CHAPTER 27

W olfgang made sure his helmet visor was closed as he waited atop his horse just outside the lists behind Malbork Castle. The large jousting field was divided down the middle by a short wooden wall to keep the jousters' horses from colliding.

A tall, wooden platform where Rusdorf and his officers would watch the combat loomed at one end. Many of the Teutonic Knights stood around the perimeter watching. But most attention grabbing was Frau Feodosia standing at the bottom of the platform with her hands bound to a pole behind her back. Firewood was stacked all around her, piled up to her waist.

Rusdorf's plans were clear, if and when her champion failed to defeat Rusdorf's champion.

The trial by combat was to start at noon, and the sun hung straight overhead. The assembly was silent as Rusdorf raised his voice. "Who will champion this woman, accused of witchcraft, in this sacred trial by combat? Come forth."

Wolfgang rode forward into the middle of the field of battle. He wore no colors and no crest on his helmet. His horse also wore no trapper or other decorations, and he carried no flag. His armor was plain and indistinguishable. He turned his horse all the way around and faced Rusdorf.

Wolfgang's vision was somewhat obstructed by the helmet, as the eye holes only allowed him to see straight ahead, but his eyes met Rusdorf's, who obviously knew that he was not Mulan. The grand master's face reddened, his expression rock hard. But there was nothing he could do. It was a sacred trial that he himself had ordained.

"Do you agree to champion this accused sorceress?" Rusdorf shouted.

Wolfgang bowed at the waist to show his agreement.

Rusdorf then glared down at Mulan's mother. "And do you accept this combatant as your champion?"

"I accept."

But Rusdorf suddenly didn't seem as upset when he turned and looked to the other end of the lists. "Let the knight come forth who has accepted the sacred duty of fighting against the accused."

A knight rode forward dressed in armor. His visor was also closed. But Wolfgang recognized that horse, and he recognized that suit of armor. Rusdorf had played one final evil trick on them—he had designated Wolfgang's brother to be his opponent.

Wolfgang's blood went cold. He certainly was not at his best. His body still pained him just to sit up straight, and riding his horse caused even more pain as his wound was jostled by the movement. He was still a bit weak from blood loss. But Sir Thomas had kindly given him a bracing potion of powerful herbs to help him ignore the pain, give him more strength, and keep away the dizziness.

Wolfgang had no more desire to injure his brother than he desired to be injured. They had jousted against each other many times in practice, but this was not practice. An innocent woman's life was at stake, not to mention that she was the mother of the woman Wolfgang loved.

Steffan rode straight up to him and turned his horse toward Rusdorf. He carried a flag with the Prussian cross and crest of the Teutonic Knights, and wore a white surcoat with the familiar black cross over his armor.

"Do you fight against the accused's champion, to determine justice in the name of the Lord almighty?"

Steffan raised his visor. "I do." He quickly lowered it without turning his gaze toward Wolfgang. But he must know who it was he was about to face.

The herald called to them to take their places. Wolfgang rode his horse to one end of the long jousting field. Gerke brought him his lance, and Andrei handed him his shield.

Wolfgang was ready.

Mulan periodically beat on the door. She paced the floor, at turns growing so angry she thought her head would explode, and then becoming so horrified at what was happening in the lists with Wolfgang and her mother. Had the combat begun yet? Was Wolfgang lying dead? And her mother . . .

She ran to the door and beat on it again with her fist. The fleshy side of her hand below her little finger was bruised all the way down into her wrist, but she continued knocking, now using her knuckles. But her efforts must continue to be fruitless, as anyone who might hear her was outside watching the trial by combat.

She leaned her head against the door, too overcome with dread to even cry.

Were those footsteps she heard outside the door? She beat both hands on the door. "Help me! Open the door! Is someone there?"

A metallic scraping came from the lock. Her heart pounded and the door opened.

Sir Thomas stood in the doorway. He stepped back as she grabbed his arm. "Is it over? What is happening?"

"The combat is just beginning."

Mulan ran down the corridor, trying to pray in her head, but no words would come except, *O God, please. Please, O God.*

She raced out of the castle and down the slight hill toward the lists. When she reached it, Wolfgang was sitting atop his horse, his lance ready, as he faced a knight at the other end. She ran through the gate toward Andrei, who stood near to the field of combat. Gerke stood with him.

"Is this . . . ?"

"The first tilt."

Then she noticed her mother, standing with her hands and feet bound together. She didn't look terrified, hurt, or even angry. She was watching the joust as if she were just another spectator.

In contrast, Mulan's heart was racing, and she imagined climbing up that platform and choking the life out of Rusdorf.

She crossed herself. "Father, forgive me," she whispered. Murder, and even contemplating it, was a sin.

"Please let Wolfgang win."

She was so angry with him. *I only want him to win so Mother can be saved.* She quickly added, *But please don't let him be killed.*

The herald had not given the signal yet for them to charge each other, so she grabbed Gerke's arm. "Who is that other knight?"

"I . . . I think it's Steffan."

"Does Wolfgang know?"

"Probably."

Mulan's gut twisted. Though they did not have the best relationship, Wolfgang loved his brother. *O God, please, in Your infinite mercy . . .*

The herald gave the signal and the two riders' horses sprang forward.

Wolfgang urged his horse forward. Thankfully his horse knew exactly what to do. He charged down the lists, following close to the low wall. Wolfgang lowered the lance, carefully aiming at the center of his opponent's breastplate. But the lance had never felt so heavy. He just had to keep it level, not let it drop, and not die. *God, if I win, it will be because of You and Your miraculous strength. And don't let Steffan die.*

Their lances slammed into the other's armor. At least Wolfgang had made a hit. Steffan's lance struck Wolfgang in the shoulder, knocking him backward, but the cantle on the back of his saddle kept him from falling off.

When he reached the end of the lists, he turned his horse around and saw that neither of them had broken their lances.

"Are you all right?" Gerke stood beside him with another lance.

Was he all right? His whole body burned and ached, but as long as he was sitting in the saddle and could hold a lance . . . "I'm all right."

He thought he caught a glimpse of Mulan off to the side. He had to turn his head to look at her. When he did, she turned her back to him and covered her face. No doubt she was still furious with him for locking her in her room and taking her place.

He took the new lance, even though his old one seemed fine,

to let Gerke examine the old one for cracks. Steffan was doing the same at the other end.

The blow from Steffan's lance had vibrated through his body, not to mention how far back he had bent, pulling at his injury. The pain was sharp, but he could ignore it. He had to.

Wolfgang went back to his starting position in the lists. His head was getting dizzy, his vision spinning. He closed his eyes and opened them again. He could see Mulan's mother, dressed all in white, standing in the place where she'd be executed if he failed. *God, be merciful.*

The herald gave the signal and Wolfgang spurred his horse forward. They seemed to be moving in slow motion. Steffan was coming at him, lowering his lance.

This was it. He wasn't sure he could take another direct hit. Either God would save him, or He wouldn't.

Wolfgang struggled to keep his lance steady. He worked to aim it, but his arm was losing strength. Just as Steffan reached him, his brother threw his lance to the ground while Wolfgang's lance tip crashed into Steffan's breastplate.

A sudden, stabbing pain jolted Wolfgang's body. His vision quickly went dark, and he felt himself falling.

No, no, no. If he fell off his horse he'd either have to fight Steffan hand to hand, or he would be declared the loser, especially if he couldn't rise.

He hit the ground. He'd knocked himself out of the saddle just by striking Steffan, since Steffan had not even landed a blow.

Wolfgang still held his lance, which had shattered all the way up to the vamplate protecting his hand. His head was still spinning, but at least the black had retreated to the edges of his vision. Summoning every drop of his strength, and using what was left of his lance, he pushed himself up off the ground and to his feet.

Where was Steffan? Was he coming up behind him? Wolfgang turned around, staggering. Steffan's riderless horse was on the other side of the wall so Wolfgang stumbled to one end and walked around it. There lay Steffan on the ground, not moving.

O God. He can't be dead.

The dizziness grew worse, but he concentrated on putting one foot in front of the other.

"Steffan!" Wolfgang called out.

Steffan did not move.

As soon as Wolfgang reached him, he bent and flipped up his visor. Steffan's eyes were closed, his face pale, his lips ashen. Blood oozed from a cut over his eye.

Wolfgang waved his gauntleted hand and three attendants swarmed around him. They knelt beside the fallen combatant and were talking to him, but Steffan was not answering.

They worked at his helmet, trying to take it off. Finally they raised his head and shoulders, then pulled off the helmet.

Wolfgang caught a glimpse of his face, which was perfectly still. *No, God, please. Steffan is not a bad person. He just needs You.*

How could he bear it if he had killed his brother? The guilt that had dogged his steps since he was a child would completely overwhelm him.

Someone put his ear near to Steffan's mouth. "He breathes!"

A Hospitaller's pallet had been brought out. They picked him up and placed him on it. With four of them hefting it off the ground, they carried him off the field.

Wolfgang raised his visor and looked over at Rusdorf. He was scowling as darkly as Wolfgang had ever seen him. Everyone was staring at him now. The trial by combat was over. Surely no one could dispute the outcome.

Rusdorf's assistant quieted the crowd by motioning with his hands. Still, Rusdorf said nothing. People began to murmur and glance around. Finally he spoke. "The outcome of this trial by combat is that Frau Feodosia is innocent of witchcraft."

The spectators were now milling around the lists. Two guards were freeing Mulan's mother from her bonds. As soon as she was loose, Mulan threw her arms around her.

Thank You, God, for sparing Mulan's mother. Now he just had to wait and see if his brother would recover.

Gerke brought a stool and forced Wolfgang to sit—forced him, as the slight pull on his arm made him sink onto it. Then Gerke and Andrei went to work taking off his helmet.

The cool air on his face and neck revived him a bit, and he opened his eyes. Mulan was standing just behind Gerke, squinting at him.

Sir Thomas appeared beside her. "Steffan opened his eyes and spoke before losing consciousness again, but I think he will survive."

The breath went out of him at this good news.

Gerke and Andrei were working on getting the rest of his armor off. Wolfgang was in pain, but he had not killed Steffan or himself, so he would not complain. And the fact that Mulan was not glaring at him also helped.

The pauldrons came off of his shoulders, then the rerebrace, the vambrace, and the couter from both arms, as well as his gauntlets. Everyone seemed to be talking at once, discussing the joust and snatches of conversations they'd heard from Rusdorf's men. But his gaze followed Mulan the entire time.

She would only glance at him as she talked with her mother

and Sir Thomas and Andrei. When they removed the breastplate, they all gasped, including Mulan. He looked down and bright-red blood was oozing down his side from his wound.

Sir Thomas drew closer and knelt beside Wolfgang. Someone had fetched some bandages and now held them out. Sir Thomas pressed the bandages against the wound. The herbal drink Sir Thomas had given him earlier must have worn off because his vision was spinning worse than ever, and he wasn't sure he had the strength to stay upright on the stool. He closed his eyes and concentrated on breathing, sweat running down his face.

But he was alive. Steffan was alive. And Mulan's mother was alive.

All was well, thanks to God.

CHAPTER 28

M ulan gasped at the bright-red blood flowing from Wolfgang's body. He himself seemed to swoon, but when Sir Thomas asked him, "Can you walk?" Wolfgang said, *"Ja."*

The boys had taken off his leg armor, and now they helped him to stand.

She could still feel the heat in her head from her fury over being locked in her chamber. Andrei had betrayed her and helped Wolfgang. But he was in pain, and he had hurt his own brother to save her mother. She wasn't sure if she wanted to yell at him or kiss him.

But she could hardly do either, with so many people around. So she quietly helped and watched . . . and waited for her mother to finish conversing with several monks standing in line for their turn to congratulate her on winning her trial by combat.

Mother was smiling and even giving them her blessing, promising to leave some of her salve for them. Mulan's gaze slid from her mother to Wolfgang and back again. She decided to stay with her mother as Wolfgang had a man on either side of him, helping him keep his balance. He hobbled off the field with his head down.

Mother broke away from the monks, and Mulan took her arm.

"All has turned out as it should," Mother said with a knowing smile.

"I should have been as at peace about it as you were." Mulan's nerves were still jumping underneath her skin, reminding her of the extreme anxiety she'd experienced watching Wolfgang charge at full tilt toward danger or even death, as well as seeing her mother only moments away from being burned at the stake.

If she could have trusted God as her mother did, she could have saved herself the torment of fear and a sleepless night.

Her mother was chattering away about the monks she had just met. "They were very interested in my methods of healing, and especially the recipe for my healing salve. We had a good discussion about herbs and honey and the uses of wine."

Mulan nodded and said, "Mm . . . uh-huh," every so often, but her thoughts focused on Wolfgang. Was he hurt worse than he seemed? What could she say to him? After he locked her in her room . . . She could not just overlook that. She was still furious with him! But he had saved her mother. She loved him. She hated him.

"Mulan, you are not listening."

Mother was staring at her in the middle of her bedchamber.

"I'm sorry, Mother. What did you say?"

"I am tired and wish to lie down for a while. You may go and find out how Wolfgang is faring, the dear man." She smiled and patted Mulan's cheek.

"Are you sure? Do you need anything?"

"No, no. I am tired from the crowd. I'm not used to so much attention."

"Very well. I love you, Mother." She kissed her wrinkled cheek and hastened from the room.

She hurried down the stairs, her heart beating faster at the thought of seeing Wolfgang again. She pressed her hand against her chest and slowed her descent.

She followed the corridors, thinking at one point that she had become lost in the circuitous route from her mother's tower room to Wolfgang's room in the Middle Castle. But soon she reached his door and knocked.

Sir Thomas opened the door only enough to stick his head in the opening. "Forgive me, Mulan, but Wolfgang is not dressed. We are tending his wound. He may be able to see you a little later."

"But he is not hurt badly . . . is he?" She spoke softly, hoping Wolfgang couldn't hear her.

"No, my dear. He has just reopened his injury, but we are applying your mother's salve. I am sure your prayers will speed his recovery."

Sir Thomas closed the door on her just as she got a glimpse of Wolfgang's grimacing face.

She wrung her hands. *I should pray.* She began the Lord's Prayer and paced the floor in front of Wolfgang's chamber, making sure to keep her footsteps soft and quiet.

Finally, after praying for so long she couldn't think of anything else to say, the door creaked open.

Mulan halted as Gerke, Andrei, and Sir Thomas emerged. "You may go in and see him now." Sir Thomas smiled.

She examined Andrei's and Gerke's faces as well. No tears or sorrow. So she slipped into Wolfgang's room and shut the door behind her.

He was leaning back against the pillows. When he saw her, he sat up and swung his legs off the side of the bed.

He wore a loose linen shirt that laced up at the neck but lay open, exposing a bit of his chest. His eyes were pinned on hers.

"Now, Mulan." His voice was strained. "I know you are angry, but all turned out well, did it not? Your mother is safe. And I would not . . ."

Slowly she advanced toward him, remembering all the dire things she'd plotted to do and say to him while she was locked in her room, pounding on the door and screaming for someone to open it.

". . . would not have done it if I could have thought of another way . . . Mulan?" He leaned back as she reached him.

She pointed her finger at his chest. "You had Andrei lock me in my room." She kept her voice calm. "No one has ever locked me in a room before."

"I'm sorry, Mulan. I couldn't think of any other way."

He leaned forward, his eyes imploring hers. "I only did it because I love you. I love you, and I had to protect you."

She reached out and cupped his cheek. Then she leaned in and pressed her lips to his.

Wolfgang's lips were gentle and lingering as he kissed her back. Then she brought her other hand up and held his face between her hands. She kissed him again, and Wolfgang's arms wrapped around her.

Her anger was tapping her on the shoulder, but she shrugged it away. Her heart pounded, her breathing shallowed, and kissing him was the only thing she wanted to think about.

Mulan was kissing him. Wolfgang's stomach turned inside out, and he slid his arms around her shoulders and pulled her closer. He returned her kiss, hardly believing she was kissing him instead of berating him.

The initial kiss turned into two kisses, then three. Her kissing became nearly as fierce as the way she fought a battle. But he kissed her with equal fervor, hoping to convince her of his devotion.

She pulled away enough to gaze into his eyes. "You locked me in a room."

"Forgive me. I promise never—"

She kissed him again, still fierce.

"—never to do it again," he managed to say between kisses.

Finally she pulled back until she was nearly at arm's length. "I'm still angry with you."

"I'm a little angry with you too."

Her eyes narrowed.

"It hurt that you didn't let me take your place. Will you always be that stubborn?"

Her shoulders tensed. "You are as stubborn as I am. You made Andrei lock me in a room."

"Perhaps I should not have, but Andrei did it willingly. To save you."

She glared at him but did not pull completely out of his arms.

"I will always feel the need to protect you. Will you always fight me when I want to help you? Is this to be a pattern? Because I will never stop wanting to keep you safe."

She spoke in a breathy whisper. "I don't know. I . . . I was too afraid."

"Afraid? Of what?"

"Afraid you didn't really care about me, afraid you would get killed, afraid I was a fool for thinking you really wanted to help me. I don't know. I know it doesn't make sense, but I was . . . protecting myself."

"From what?"

"From you hurting me, from you rejecting me. Something inside me told me not to trust you, that I had to be the one to protect Mother and myself."

She was right. It didn't make sense. But perhaps it did. "Your father hurt you and rejected you and your mother. But I'm not like your father."

"You said you loved me." Her cheeks reddened to match her lips as her gaze flitted away from him, as if she couldn't meet his eyes.

"I do love you." He set his hands on her waist and managed to pull her a bit closer.

"And you want to marry me."

"I will marry you today if you are willing."

"You are the son of a duke, and I am a poor girl who has no education and doesn't even know your native language. I don't know how to be among nobility or how to dance or even how to be feminine enough. How could you want to marry me?"

"I can marry anyone I wish. And you don't need to be anything other than what you are at this moment for me and my family to love you. Besides that, do you think I want a woman for her education or for who her family is? For your dancing skills? And you conversed quite well with Duke Konrad and Duchess Katarzyna."

Her lowered brows lifted and the crease between her eyes slowly relaxed and disappeared.

"I love you, Mulan. And I will get a house. It may not be palatial, but I will get a house where we can live."

"But when you locked me in my chamber," she said, tears pooling in her eyes, "I beat on the door for half an hour at least before Sir Thomas came and let me out."

Her palms were pressed against his chest. She pushed away from him. He gently grasped her wrists and held her hands out so he could see them.

Purple bruises marred the sides, below her little fingers. The knuckles were also bruised, and two or three bore signs of blood and broken skin. A giant fist squeezed his heart.

"*Liebling,*" he whispered. He brought her hands up to his lips and kissed them, first brushing the bruises on the side of each hand with his lips, then turning them over and kissing the knuckles.

If this was a dream, that Mulan was yielded and still and letting him kiss her, he didn't want to ever wake up.

CHAPTER 29

A slight moan bubbled up from Mulan's throat, but she stifled it. If this was how it would be to fight with Wolfgang and how he apologized . . . Her anger was quickly dissipating. His lips were so gentle, and the tender way he held her hands made her stomach turn flips.

He continued to kiss her knuckles slowly, one at a time.

"Wolfie," she breathed.

Her eyes lit on a smear of drying blood on his jawline, reminding her of all that he'd been through to save her mother. She leaned forward and kissed his temple.

"I love when you call me Wolfie." His voice was deep and raspy, and she could feel his breath in her hair.

"Wolfie." She kissed his cheek. Then she kissed his lips.

A knock sounded on the door behind her, making her pull away. She took another step away from him, her cheeks burning. The look of anguish on Wolfgang's face, as if it were physically painful to end their kiss, sent a jolt of lightning through her middle.

Wolfgang caressed her cheek. Finally he called, "Come in."

Sir Thomas entered. Mulan pressed a hand over her mouth. Could Sir Thomas see Wolfgang's kisses there? Because she could still feel them.

"I am sorry to . . . interrupt, but Rusdorf wishes to speak to you both. May I tell him he is invited to your chamber?"

Wolfgang didn't answer right away. "We probably do not have much choice. We'd prefer to have you here when he comes."

"I shall tell him." The monk-soldier turned and left.

Wolfgang pulled Mulan closer. She turned to face him.

"You're so beautiful," he whispered.

"Wearing this?" She glanced down at her ugly brown quilted and padded gambeson.

"It doesn't matter what you wear. I will always see you as beautiful."

An image of Algirdas's face flashed across her vision as he gazed down at the stains on her dress. But Wolfie was not like Algirdas. Or her father.

His gaze focused on her lips again when she heard heavy footsteps coming down the corridor. She quickly pulled away from him, this time letting go of his hand. She was standing with her arms crossed when Rusdorf entered through the open door.

"Greetings." Rusdorf nodded to Wolfgang. He only glanced at Mulan, then his focus returned to Wolfgang.

"Greetings," Wolfgang said.

Mulan said nothing. Why should she greet the man who wanted to kill her mother and wasn't even acknowledging her? But at least he was speaking Polish so she could understand.

Rusdorf's lips twisted and his throat bobbed. "The reports that came to me of Frau Feodosia's salve and its miraculous powers must have been exaggerated or misunderstood. But God in His mercy has graciously given her another chance to live a righteous life. She is free to return to her home."

"What will happen to my brother?" Wolfgang's voice and

demeanor were both stern. He was not trying to assuage Rusdorf's guilt, and he certainly wasn't praising his current behavior to gain his favor.

Mulan had never loved him more.

"Your brother's injuries are not serious. But he did not acquit himself according to the rules of the joust. He deliberately threw down his lance. Therefore I cannot honor my promise to knight him and hear his vows or accept him into our holy order of knights."

"I wish to speak to him."

Rusdorf was silent for a few moments. "I care not if you speak with him. You are not a prisoner and may do as you wish. In the meantime . . ." He turned his gaze on Mulan. "She must dress as a woman while she's enjoying the hospitality of Malbork Castle."

"I have no problem with wearing women's attire. But I will be dressed in my riding clothes to make the journey back to Zachev Castle."

"Very well. I give my consent to you wearing your men's clothing on the day you depart. And I ask that you never return here. A woman pretending to be a man is not what I wish these righteous brothers to be exposed to. When Wolfgang is sufficiently recovered from his injur—"

"When he is recovered from his injuries," Mulan said forcefully, "we shall leave and never return, I assure you, but not because you are righteous and I am unrighteous." Her breathing was coming fast and heat rose into her head. How dare this arrogant man try to make her feel less righteous than he?

Rusdorf stared at her with his cold, beady eyes, a spot of red on both cheeks. He made eye contact with Wolfgang, bowed quickly, and left the room.

Mulan leaned toward Wolfgang. He kept his head down, but he slipped an arm around her and pulled her closer.

"What are you thinking about?" Mulan tried to see his expression, but since he was sitting and she was standing, his head was slightly lower than hers.

"I was thinking about Steffan. What will happen to him now? He always only wanted to be a knight."

"I am sorry. I know how much you love your brother."

His brown-eyed gaze slid to hers, and the corners of his mouth curled into a lopsided smile.

"What else are you thinking about?" she asked in response to that smile.

"That it's probably good that Rusdorf left the door open. We might forget ourselves." He was staring at her lips.

She moved away from him a bit. "That is true."

She probably should not have kissed him the way she had. She had opened a door to temptation, certainly. It seemed wise to talk of something else.

"How are your injuries? Are you in much pain?"

"Not when you're with me."

"Much blood loss?"

"Not very much." He reached out and fingered a tendril of her hair that had come loose from its tie.

"We should talk about what our plans are. I haven't spoken to Mother, but I was hoping she might go back to Duke Konrad's with us. She has no close family in Lithuania. They've all died, and I am in Poland now."

"I think that would be a very good thing." He lifted her hand and kissed it.

"When do you think you'll be well enough to travel? We can

set a slower pace on the way back to Zachev Castle, especially if we have Mother with us."

"I can leave tomorrow, if needed."

"I think you need at least two full days and nights of rest. We can depart on the third day from today."

He trailed the backs of his fingers down her cheek. "When did you first fall in love with me?"

Her heart fluttered, but she had to stay firm. She stepped out of his embrace, standing just out of his reach. "I cannot tell you that. Your head will swell twice its size, and no one will be able to recognize you."

"Do you think so little of me?" But he was smiling, a spark glittering in his eyes.

"I think that you're tired and need your rest."

He narrowed his eyes at her. "But you love me, *tak*?"

"*Tak*."

He tried to pull her closer, but she extricated herself from his arms and stepped back. "I will go so you can speak to your brother alone." She hurried away.

Even when she was in her own chamber, her heartbeat did not slow to normal. Never had she felt so exhilarated, happy, and terrified all at the same time. She pressed her hands to her head, a hundred thoughts tangling within.

Wolfgang was lying in his bed. It had been hours since Mulan left his room, but he was still thinking about her.

Someone knocked on the door and Steffan entered his room without waiting.

His brother had a cut under his eye that had not been bandaged and a bright-white bandage just over his eye. His upper arms and shoulders strained against his shirt as he crossed his arms over his chest. He didn't speak.

Wolfgang sat up and faced him. "Thank you for not killing me."

Steffan leaned his head back, then forward. "I could have."

"I know."

They stared at each other.

"I hope you're not hurt too badly," Wolfgang said.

"If the splinter from your lance had struck a bit lower . . ." He gestured to his eye. "But I still have both eyes." Another pause. "You don't look like you were hurt much."

"Just got knocked off my horse by my older brother. I've survived that before, and worse." Wolfgang smiled. "What will you do now?"

Steffan shrugged and stared down at the floor. "Don't know. I've always wanted to ride about the countryside seeking damsels in distress I could rescue—for the right amount of reward, of course." He smiled again.

"I can actually imagine you doing that. But I would also like you to come to Poland with us. I'm sure Duke Konrad would add you to his guard."

Steffan frowned. "I'm not ready for something like that. Don't know if I'll ever be."

Wolfgang nodded.

"Your Mulan seems . . . good for you. I suppose you'll marry her soon."

"I plan to."

Steffan nodded.

"Will you stay and see us off in two days?"

Steffan opened his mouth, hesitated, then said, "Perhaps. The truth is . . ." He swiped a hand down the side of his face, then rubbed his brow while staring at the wall. "I think you were right. I was bothered—a lot—by what happened to that little boy all those years ago." He cleared his throat, hanging his head. "I talked to the priest here. It was the first time I'd told anyone else about it. I just—" Steffan cleared his throat again. "I felt like it was my fault he died, but it made me very angry—and I know that doesn't make sense. I don't understand it myself."

"It does make sense. I felt so guilty. I ignored the guilt as long as I could, but it wouldn't go away. I've tried to be good, to make up for what happened. The problem is . . . I can't always be good."

Steffan gave a slow nod. He crossed his arms and stared down at the floor. "I know I need to stop being angry. I don't really know how."

"We were only children, Steffan. God forgives us for being careless and not knowing what to do. We'll never be able to be good enough to make up for what happened. I guess we have to accept that God's grace is sufficient." He wished he'd realized this sooner. But if it hadn't been for Mulan, he might not realize it now. "And Heinlin, being only a small child when he died, is in heaven with God and is no longer being abused by his cruel father."

"I'm just glad . . ." Steffan's voice thickened and he cleared his throat again. "Glad I didn't kill you in the joust."

"As am I." Wolfgang smiled, a little relieved Steffan wasn't arguing with him, even though he was changing the topic.

Steffan looked him in the eye, more humble than Wolfgang had ever seen him.

"I thought I wanted to be a knight, but once I got here and

saw the monastic life . . ." He shook his head. "I always wanted to be a knight, but I never wanted to be a monk."

Wolfgang laughed.

"I will say, though, these men are good men, most of them, and they are truly dedicated to God. I admire that. But I . . . I'm not a monk."

"I find it hard to imagine you as a monk."

"To get up out of bed three times a night to go kneel and pray . . . I like my sleep too much for that."

"And marriage? You could never get married."

"Never be with a woman at all." Steffan shook his head. "Better not to make a vow than to break it."

"You are growing quite wise, my brother."

"*Ach*, I know you are laughing at me, but I have learned . . . I don't want to be a Teutonic Knight. I don't want to be a soldier at all. I want to do something, I just don't know what it is yet." He rubbed the back of his neck. "I wonder if I'll ever know."

"You'll know, someday. Ask God and He will lead you." Who would have thought his brother would become rather humble while staying here with the Teutonic Knights? "You should write to Mother and Father, go talk to them."

Steffan's mouth twisted, raising his brows. "I will. Eventually. Father and I did not part in the best of ways."

Wolfgang wanted to tell him that was his fault, not Father's, but Steffan might not be ready to hear that. He had come much further than Wolfgang would have imagined, though, and for that miracle, he was thankful.

CHAPTER 30

Mulan glanced around. Where was Wolfgang? They should be leaving. The sun was already up.

Three days had passed, giving Wolfgang time to rest and heal. Mulan was helping Andrei tie their supplies onto their horses' backs. Aksoma and Boldheart were already saddled, as were Wolfgang's and Gerke's horses. They had also readied the horse the Teutonic Knights lent them for her mother, who would be traveling with them to Duke Konrad's castle instead of going home to Lithuania.

Steffan came riding from the other stable, walking his white horse straight up to Mulan. "If you and Wolfgang will allow me, I would like to accompany you to make sure you have a safe journey."

She stared at his face but found no trace of amusement. She'd had a hard time trusting him after his lack of remorse for shooting her. But he was Wolfie's brother, he seemed sincere enough now, and she had forgiven him and felt no grudge against him. "Thank you."

Wolfgang and Rusdorf walked toward them from the opposite direction. Steffan stared hard at them, scrunching his brows together. Mulan's thoughts went to the location of her bow and an arrow, just in case she needed them. Then she noticed another man walking slightly behind Rusdorf, flanked on both sides by a guard.

Lifting his head high, Rusdorf almost made himself look as tall as the men around him. Almost.

The ends of his long black mustache fluttered in the slight breeze as he said in a loud voice, "In the interest of peaceful relations between Duke Konrad of Zachev, his ally Duke Wilhelm of Hagenheim, and the Order of the Teutonic Knights, I wish to present this Knight of the Order of Teutonic Knights as the one who wrongfully shot Wolfgang Gerstenberg as he entered Malbork Castle."

The guards nudged the man forward, his hands tied in front of him, hair flopped over his eyes. He didn't lift his head.

"He is Sir Joseph of Berlin. He was ignorant of the peace agreement I signed with Duke Konrad and was attempting to kill those whom he perceived as enemies of Christ. But he understands that killing outside of war is wrong, and therefore you are safe to enter or depart any fortress belonging to the Teutonic Knights, now and in the future."

Rusdorf did not have to be terribly wise to realize he did not need to make an enemy of the Duke of Hagenheim.

Finally the man who had tried to shoot her, but shot Wolfgang instead, lifted his head. Something about his expression as his gaze captured hers sent a shiver down her spine. His eyes seemed wild and crazed, like those of a wolf she'd once seen inside a cage at the market.

"I shall personally ensure that he never harms you again." Rusdorf's lips curled slightly.

Mulan was grateful when they turned the man around and walked him back toward the castle.

Wolfgang acknowledged Rusdorf's words with a nod. If God was willing, he and Mulan would never have to come near another Teutonic Knights' castle again.

He couldn't help watching Steffan as Rusdorf and Sir Joseph turned and went back toward the castle.

"And now it is your time." Steffan stood at his shoulder, grinning. "Are you ready, little brother?"

"I'm ready." Wolfgang's heart beat hard against his chest as he was reminded of the morning's plan. He reached into his saddlebag and pulled out the two rolled-up sheets of parchment. He took a deep breath and searched for Mulan. She stood nearby, talking to her horse and patting his neck. Andrei was beside her, but he was looking at Wolfgang and smiling.

"Mulan of Lithuania, captain of the guard at Zachev Castle."

Mulan turned around, a slight frown on her lips, her eyelids narrowing, as everyone in the grassy courtyard gave him their attention.

"I have two letters in my hands." He held them up, each bearing his family's seal. "With a word from you, I will either tear them up or send them out by courier, one to your home village in Lithuania and the other to Hagenheim, Germany."

She folded her arms in front of her chest and stared, unblinking.

"But I beg you with all my heart," he said, placing both his hands, even though they held the letters, over his heart, "to allow me to send out these missives asking the priests in our hometowns to cry the banns over us. I beseech you, Mulan, daughter of Mikolai, to marry me and love me as much as I love you. For I love you and pledge here and now to always cherish you." He held his breath as he stared back at her.

She unfolded her arms and took a step toward him. He stepped toward her, and she smiled.

"What is your answer?" he asked as they were still several paces away from each other.

"I say, yes, you may send the letters."

"You will marry me?"

"I will marry you."

His two couriers advanced toward him and took the missives from his hands, then backed away. He just stood there looking at her, waiting, as about twenty or thirty of the Teutonic Knights, Mulan's mother, Steffan, Andrei, and Gerke stood still and quiet, watching them.

Mulan suddenly ran to him, threw her arms around him, and kissed him.

Finally. He got it right.

Mulan ran to him and kissed him, eager to show that Wolfgang's love would not be given in vain. She would accept it and return it, with all her heart.

He held her tight in his arms, kissing her back. When she pulled away, he looked into her eyes and whispered, "Thank you."

She had to bury her face in his shoulder to keep anyone from seeing the tears as she nearly sobbed . . . that he should thank her for accepting his proposal of marriage.

Wolfie had looked so brave and vulnerable at the same time, asking her to marry him, declaring his love for her—*her*—forever, this almost unbearably handsome, courageous soldier, son of the wealthy and powerful Duke of Hagenheim, with his kind brown eyes and oh-so-worthy heart. Oh, how she loved him.

But she had to control herself. Many people were around, and they would have to get on their horses and ride out of the Malbork Castle compound, away from the place where so much had happened in a short amount of time.

She touched Wolfgang's cheek and pulled out of his arms as men were beginning to wish them well in their life together. She kept her arm pressed against his and her head down, letting Wolfgang thank them for their words of blessing as she surreptitiously wiped her eyes with her fingers.

Finally everyone was walking away. She tipped her head up to look into Wolfgang's eyes.

"You haven't said you love me yet," he said quietly.

"I do love you. I love you with all my heart."

"And I love you." He leaned down and kissed her lips, then her cheek. "I guess we should go."

Their little traveling party mounted their horses and were finally off, riding toward Zachev Castle. And even though she and Wolfgang lagged behind the others and kept staring at each other, no one teased them for it, not even Steffan.

EPILOGUE

Wolfgang and Mulan were married four weeks later in the chapel at Zachev Castle. Mulan's heart was still full to overflowing at the wedding feast. Her mother sat nearby, along with Wolfgang, his brother Steffan, Duke Konrad, and Duchess Katarzyna.

Wolfgang's family had made the journey and sat with them as well: Duke Wilhelm, Lady Rose, Valten and his wife, Lady Gisela, his sister Rapunzel and her husband, Sir Gerek, and his younger sister Adela and brother Toby. He had such a loving family, and she adored them already. Never would she have believed that she could feel so comfortable talking with two dukes, two duchesses, and an earl. But they never made her feel as if she was less important than they were. Rather, they seemed to love her, and not just because Wolfgang loved her.

Farther down the table, Simon and Gregorius and several other soldiers with whom she and Wolfgang had fought sat eating and talking and laughing. And at Wolfgang and Mulan's request, Andrei and Gerke also sat at the highest table, smiling and laughing.

Wolfgang suddenly caught her hand under the table and squeezed it. "What are you thinking of?"

She gazed up into his brown eyes. "How happy I am to be with the people I love on the most joyful day of my life. And how I might have been married to a village butcher right now instead of you."

His face fell and his mouth opened.

She wrapped her arms around his arm, still looking up at him. "Except that God saved me from that terrible fate and gave me the best man in the world."

His eyes closed as he leaned down and kissed her. "You truly are the most remarkable woman in the world, Mulan. Especially if you think I'm the best man in the world."

"That's the only reason I'm remarkable?" She smiled, enjoying flirting with her husband.

He narrowed his eyes at her jest. "By no means. You are good and kind. You are fair of face and form. You are brave, bold, clever, and highly skilled with a longbow. You fight like an enraged badger—"

She burst out laughing, drawing several people's attention.

"What is so funny?" Steffan asked.

Just then a servant tilted a flask of wine toward his goblet to fill it the rest of the way to the top. Steffan placed his hand over it and shook his head. The servant moved on to pour more wine in someone else's cup.

Steffan looked toward Duke Konrad and held up his goblet. "I think it is time to offer some well wishes to our newly married couple."

Duke Konrad frowned at Steffan's impertinence, but in keeping with the spirit of the occasion, he seemed to brush off the offense and stood. Raising his own goblet, he waited until the crowd quieted and gave him their attention.

"To these two great and mighty warriors, Wolfgang and Mulan, let us raise a shout of admiration!"

The room burst into a fevered roar, shouting, clapping,

banging, and stomping. Mulan felt her cheeks warm. She peeked at Wolfgang, who smiled modestly.

The crowd finally quieted, and Duke Konrad spoke again. "And to their union we offer our prayers of blessing, joy, peace, fruitfulness, and prosperity."

Everyone cheered.

"And because of the great service they have done for me and my people, and the great regard the duchess and I have come to feel for them, I am prepared tonight to bestow a wedding gift on Wolfgang of Hagenheim and his new wife, Mulan."

Mulan and Wolfgang exchanged a look.

"I have a castle and a tract of land called Tieflasu to the west along the border with the German regions of the Holy Roman Empire. I need a strong force to protect that area, and I wish to grant it to Wolfgang and Mulan."

Mulan's gasp was drowned out by a loud cheer.

She could hardly breathe as she and Wolfgang gazed at each other, then at Duke Konrad.

"May they live long and continue to defend the Polish people and Polish lands from invaders and usurpers."

A few minutes later, after the duke had sat back down, Wolfgang faced him. "We are very grateful to you for this honor and privilege. It is a great and generous gift." It was the kind of gift a father gave to a son.

The duke rested his hand on Wolfgang's shoulder. "You are deserving, you and Mulan, for all you have done. I shall rest easier knowing you are there protecting it. There are no better soldiers, nor nobler people, than you and Mulan."

When he turned back to Mulan she said, "Now you can be the protector you always wanted to be."

His eyes shone with joy. He pulled her close, and she knew his heart was too full to speak.

Soon the music began, and Wolfgang and Mulan danced with several of the other guests. When they finally sat down, Steffan leaned toward them. "I am telling you, Wolfgang, you have the right idea. Fall in with a foreign duke and get him to bestow some land on you. I think I will try it myself."

Wolfgang nodded. "I pray you find a wife as well, and that she will help you find joy."

"Indeed. I shall rescue a princess in distress, and her father shall reward me handsomely."

Mulan frowned. What would become of Steffan? He had made some changes for the better, but he still had a lot of maturing to do. She'd have to remember to pray for him—and his future wife.

"Would you not consider joining Duke Konrad's guard?" Wolfgang asked Steffan. "He needs experienced and well-trained fighters, now more than ever."

Steffan frowned on one side of his mouth. "I think I'd rather see more of the world. There seems to be a shortage of princesses and wealthy heiresses in need of saving around here." He grinned, and Mulan shook her head at him.

Another guest tapped Steffan on the shoulder, and he turned around and seemed to forget Wolfgang and Mulan.

"Your brother turned down more wine," Mulan said quietly next to Wolfgang's ear. At least that was good. "But it doesn't sound as if he has a solid plan for his future."

"Perhaps he still has a way to go before he finds true direction." Wolfgang was gazing into her eyes as he stroked her arm. "I have you on my mind now. I do not think we would create a stir if we left quietly."

Mulan smiled up at him. "I would like to try it, then."

Wolfgang turned to speak to the duke and duchess. The duchess smiled and nodded to Mulan, while the duke winked at Wolfgang.

Wolfgang held out his hand to Mulan to help her up from the bench, and they walked with linked arms, slipping out of the Great Hall into the corridor to the stairs.

She pulled on his arm. He halted and turned to her. She kissed him.

He asked, "Do you think your mother will come with us to our new home? It's a long way from Lithuania."

"I believe she will. She has said many times that the joy of her life will be to hold my children."

He gave her another kiss as they continued up the stairs.

"Will you be happy in our new home? We will be not as far from Hagenheim, but still a long way."

"Only three days' ride. And if you are there, I shall be happy and content."

"Then I shall be too. I hope I don't disappoint you with my lack of skill at running a household."

"You couldn't disappoint me. I'm sure the servants know what to do."

"What if I miss wearing a soldier's garb and practicing for battle?"

"If you do, I shall steal away with you, and we shall have an archery competition."

She widened her eyes. "As long as you promise not to make me sword fight."

"I promise." He grinned before kissing her again and hurrying her up the stairs.

ACKNOWLEDGMENTS AND
HISTORICAL NOTE

Many thanks to Adriana Gwyn for her German translation and research help. I could not find very much at all on the one historical figure I wished to use in this story, Paul von Rusdorf, the grand master of the Teutonic Knights, also known as the Order of Brothers of the German House of Saint Mary in Jerusalem, also known as the German Order of Knights, in the year my story takes place. So I went to my friend and German language scholar, Adriana Gwyn, for help, which she very kindly gave. Even in German we only found a small amount written about him. I took quite a bit of creative license, having so little to draw from, but I did stay true to his appearance—a head full of black hair, black mustache, pointed nose, and black goatee. His portrait went perfectly with how I imagined him.

So thanks, Adriana, for going above and beyond in translating those articles and Skyping with me! You are a blessing!

And what fun to set a small part of the story in the very real Malbork Castle in Poland, also known as Marienburg Castle. I love castles the way a fan loves her favorite rock star and the way Velvet Brown loves horses, and this is definitely a castle that puts a flutter in my chest. I hope someday I can visit this one in person.

Another historical note is about Frau Feodosia's healing salve.

I got the ingredients from an actual medieval medical recipe, found in a medieval handbook on medicine and medical procedures that modern researchers have recently duplicated. They've found that it actually works better on certain bacterial infections than some of our modern antibiotics. I think that proves that medieval people were much smarter and more advanced than most twenty-first-century people think they were.

I want to thank my beta reader daughter, Faith Dickerson, for always reading my stories, even before my editor, and giving me her valuable feedback. Thanks, Faith!

And I want to thank my agent, Natasha Kern, who is such a blessing, watching out for me in all the ways you might wish an agent to. Thanks, Natasha!

And thanks to my amazing editors, Kimberly Carlton and Julee Schwarzburg, who did a great job helping me make this story the best it could be, strengthening the weak points and making the strengths even stronger.

Thanks to the whole Thomas Nelson team, who do such a great job with all the tasks that happen behind the scenes—marketing, sales, PR, etc. All your hard work is greatly appreciated.

I also wish to thank all the brave women who have served in our military, including my friends: Mary Freeman, Tatyana Freeman, Tina Russo Radcliffe, Patti Sands, Toni Shiloh, Evelyn Pierson, Adrienne Gill Bowling, Susan Korecki, Margie Burchfield, Anne Marie Costello, Jennifer Hibdon, Linda L. Frey, and Christina Egler Borden. Thank you for being willing to risk your lives for your fellow countrymen. God bless you.

Thanks as always to my amazing readers, who support me in so many ways. I love and cherish you, pray for you, and appreciate you, more than you know!

DISCUSSION QUESTIONS

1. Why was Mulan contemplating marrying Algirdas the butcher? Why did Mulan decide not to marry Algirdas?
2. What made Mulan's mother agree to let her become a soldier?
3. Wolfgang was upset that Steffan wished to become a Teutonic Knight. Why? What were Steffan's reasons for wanting to join the Teutonic Knights?
4. Why did Wolfgang dislike Mulan and resent her after the first day they met?
5. What was it about Mulan/Mikolai that raised Wofgang's suspicions that something wasn't quite right about the boy?
6. Andrei was angry when Wolfgang beat Mulan and injured her slightly in the sword fight. What excuses did Mulan make for Wolfgang's harsh behavior?
7. What did Mulan do that won him over and changed his negative opinion of her?
8. How did Wolfgang discover Mulan was not a boy, but a woman? What was his reaction?
9. How did their fellow soldiers react to the fact that Mikolai was a woman? Did she win them over? How?

10. Why did Rusdorf object to Mulan's mother making and using her healing salve? Sometimes when people get upset at us, it has very little to do with us, but everything to do with their issues, which stem from their past. What do you think were some of Rusdorf's underlying issues?

11. Was Wolfgang wrong to lock Mulan in her room in order to take her place in the joust? Why or why not?

12. What were the issues Mulan had to overcome to be able to receive Wolfgang's love?

13. What did you think of Mulan's mother's attitude toward being held captive and wrongly accused and tried for witchcraft? What could we take away from this that might help our own issues with fear or anxiety?

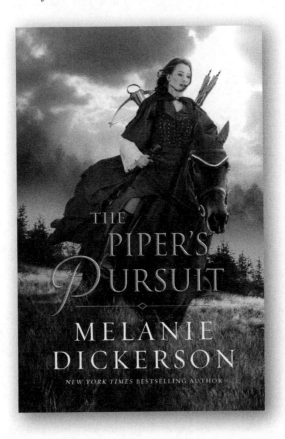

From *New York Times* bestselling author
Melanie Dickerson comes an inspired
retelling of the beloved folk tale Aladdin.

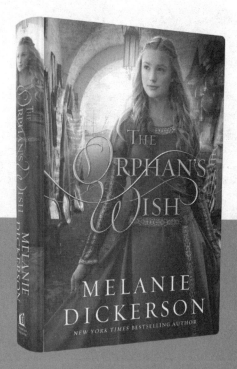

"When it comes to happily-ever-afters, Melanie
Dickerson is the undisputed queen of fairy-tale
romance, and all I can say is—long live the queen!"

—Julie Lessman, award-winning author

She lost everything to the scheme of an evil servant. But she might just gain what she's always wanted . . . if she makes it in time.

Available in print, e-book, and audio!

The Silent Songbird

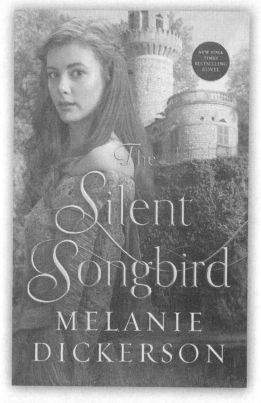

"This book will have you jumping out of your seat with anticipation at times. Moderate to fast-paced, you will not want this book to end. Recommended for all, especially lovers of historical romance."

—*RT Book Reviews*, 4 stars

AVAILABLE IN PRINT, E-BOOK, AND AUDIO!

THOMAS NELSON
Since 1798